RISE OF THE DRAGONS

(KINGS AND SORCERERS—BOOK 1)

MORGAN RICE

Books by Morgan Rice

For Sindre Johansen Sola

*A true hero, whose strength, courage and perseverance
is extraordinary*

"Men at some time are masters of their fates:
The fault, dear Brutus, is not in our stars,
But in ourselves, that we are underlings."

--William Shakespeare
Julius Caesar

CHAPTER ONE

Kyra stood atop the grassy knoll, the frozen ground hard beneath her boots, snow falling around her, and tried to ignore the biting cold as she raised her bow and focused on her target. She narrowed her eyes, shutting out the rest of the world—a gale of wind, the sound of a distant crow—and forced herself to see only the skinny birch tree, far-off, stark-white, standing out amidst the landscape of purple pine trees. At forty yards, this was just the sort of shot her brothers couldn't make, that even her father's men couldn't make—and that made her all the more determined—she being the youngest of the bunch, and the only girl amongst them.

Kyra had never fit in. A part of her wanted to, of course, wanted to do what was expected of her and spend time with the other girls, as was her place, attending to domestic affairs; but deep down, it was not who she was. She was her father's daughter, had a warrior's spirit, like he, and she would not be contained to the stone walls of their stronghold, would not succumb to a life beside a hearth. She was a better shot than these men—indeed, she could already outshoot her father's finest archers—and she would do whatever she had to to prove to them all—most of all, her father—that she deserved to be taken seriously. Her father loved her, she knew, but he refused to see her for who she was.

Kyra did her best training far from the fort, out here on the plains of Volis, alone—which suited her well, since she, the only girl in a fort of warriors, had learned to be alone. She had taken to retreating here every day, her favorite spot, high atop the plateau overlooking the fort's rambling stone walls, where she could find good trees, skinny trees hard to hit. The thwack of her arrows had become an ever-present sound echoing over the village; not a tree up here had been spared from her arrows, their trunks scarred, some trees already leaning.

Most of her father's archers, Kyra knew, took aim at the mice that covered the plains; when she had first started, she had tried that herself, and had found she could kill them quite easily. But that had sickened her. She was fearless, but sensitive, too, and killing a living

8

thing with no purpose displeased her. She had vowed then that she would never take aim at a living thing again—unless it were dangerous, or attacking her, like the Wolfbats that emerged at night and flew too close to her father's fort. She had no qualms about dropping them, especially after her younger brother, Aidan, suffered a Wolfbat bite that left him ill for half a moon. Besides, they were the fastest moving creatures out there, and she knew that if she could hit one, especially at night, then she could hit anything. She had once spent an entire night by a full moon firing away from her father's tower, and had run out eagerly at sunrise, thrilled to see scores of Wolfbats littering the ground, her arrows still in them, villagers crowding around and looking with amazed faces.

Kyra forced herself to focus. She played through the shot in her mind's eye, seeing herself raising her bow, pulling it back quickly to her chin and releasing without hesitation. The real shooting, she knew, happened before the shot. She had witnessed too many archers her age, on their fourteenth year, draw their strings and waver—and she knew then that their shots were lost. She took a deep breath, raised her bow, and in one decisive motion, pulled back and released. She did not even need to look to know she had hit the tree.

A moment later she heard its thwack—but she had already turned away, already looking for another target, one further off.

Kyra heard a whining at her feet and she looked down at Leo, her wolf, walking beside her as he always did, rubbing against her leg. A full-grown wolf, nearly up to her waist, Leo was as protective of Kyra as Kyra was of him, the two of them an inseparable sight in her father's fort. Kyra could not go anywhere without Leo hurrying to catch up. And all that time he clung to her side—unless a squirrel or rabbit crossed his path, in which case he could disappear for hours.

"I didn't forget you, boy," Kyra said, reaching into her pocket and handing Leo the leftover bone from the day's feast. Leo snatched it, trotting happily beside her.

As Kyra walked, her breath emerging in mist before her, she draped her bow over her shoulder and breathed into her hands, raw and cold. She crossed the wide, flat plateau and looked out. From this vantage point she could see the entire countryside, the rolling hills of Volis, usually green but now blanketed in snow, the province of her father's stronghold, nestled in the northeastern corner of the kingdom of Escalon. From up here Kyra had a bird's-eye view of all the goings-on in her father's fort, the comings and goings of the village folk and warriors, another reason she liked it up here. She liked to study the ancient, stone contours of her father's fort, the shapes of its battlements and towers stretching impressively through the hills, seeming to sprawl forever. Volis was the tallest structure in the countryside, some of its buildings rising four stories and framed by impressive layers of battlements. It was completed by a circular tower on its far side, a chapel for the folk, but for her, a place to climb and look out at the countryside and be alone. The stone complex was ringed by a moat, spanned by a wide main road and an arched stone bridge; this, in turn, was ringed by layers of impressive outer embankments, hills, ditches, walls—a place befitting one of the King's most important warriors—her father.

Though Volis, the final stronghold before The Flames, was several days' ride from Andros, Escalon's capital, it was still home to many of the former King's famed warriors. It had also become a beacon, a place that had become home to the hundreds of villagers and farmers that lived in or near its walls, under its protection.

Kyra looked down at the dozens of small clay cottages nestled in the hills on the outskirts of the fort, smoke rising from chimneys, farmers hurrying to and fro as they prepared for winter, and for the night's festival. The fact that villagers felt safe enough to live outside the main walls, Kyra knew, was a sign of great respect for her father's might, and a sight unseen elsewhere in Escalon. After all, they were a mere horn sounding away from protection, from the instant rallying of all her father's men.

Kyra looked down at the drawbridge, always packed with throngs of people—farmers, cobblers, butchers, blacksmiths, along with, of course, warriors—all rushing from fort to countryside and back again. For within the fort's walls was not only a place to live and train, but also an endless array of cobblestone courtyards which had become a gathering place for merchants. Every day their stalls were lined up, people selling their wares, bartering, showing off the day's hunt or catch, or some exotic cloth or spice or candy traded from across the sea. The courtyards of the fort were always filled with some exotic smell, be it of a strange tea, or a cooking stew; she could get lost in them for hours. And just beyond the walls, in the distance, her heart quickened to see the circular training ground for her father's men, Fighter's Gate, and the low stone wall surrounding it, and she watched

10

with excitement as his men charged in neat lines with their horses, trying to lance targets—shields hanging from trees. She ached to train with them.

Kyra suddenly heard a voice cry out, one as familiar to her as her own, coming from the direction of the gatehouse, and she turned, immediately on alert. There was a commotion in the crowd, and she watched as through the bustle, spilling out of the throng and out onto the main road, there emerged her younger brother, Aidan, led by her two older brothers, Brandon and Braxton. Kyra tensed, on guard. She could tell from the sound of distress in her baby brother's voice that their older brothers were up to no good.

Kyra's eyes narrowed as she watched her older brothers, feeling a familiar anger rise up within her and unconsciously tightening her grip on her bow. There came Aidan, marched between them, each taller by a foot, each grabbing his arm and dragging him unwillingly away from the fort and into the countryside. Aidan, a small, thin, sensitive boy, barely ten, looked extra vulnerable sandwiched between his two brothers, overgrown brutes of seventeen and eighteen. They all had similar features and coloring, with their strong jaws, proud chins, dark brown eyes, and wavy brown hair—though Brandon and Braxton wore theirs cropped short, while Aidan's still fell, unruly, past his eyes. They all looked alike—and none like her, with her light blonde hair and light gray eyes. Dressed in her woven tights, woolen tunic, and cloak, Kyra was tall and thin, too pale, she was told, with a broad forehead and a small nose, blessed with striking features that had led more than one man to look twice. Especially now that she was turning fifteen, she noticed the looks increasing.

It made her uncomfortable. She did not like calling attention to herself, and she did not view herself as beautiful. She cared nothing for looks—only for training, for valor, for honor. She would rather have resembled her father, as her brothers did, the man she admired and loved more than anyone in the world, than have her dainty features. She always checked the mirror for something of himself in her eyes, yet no matter how hard she looked, she could not find it.

"I said, get *off* of me!" Aidan shouted, his voice carrying all the way up here.

At her baby brother's call of distress, a boy who Kyra loved more than anyone in the world, she stood ramrod straight, like a lion watching its cub. Leo, too, stiffened, the hair rising on his back. With

11

their mother long gone, Kyra felt obliged to watch over Aidan, to make up for the mother he never had.

Brandon and Braxton dragged him roughly down the road, away from the fort, on the lone country road toward the distant wood, and she saw them trying to get him to wield a spear, one too big for him. Aidan had become a too-easy target for them to pick on; Brandon and Braxton were bullies. They were strong and somewhat brave, but they had more bravado than real skills, and they always seemed to get into trouble they could not quite get out of themselves. It was maddening.

Kyra realized what was happening: Brandon and Braxton were dragging Aidan with them on one of their hunts. She spotted the sacks of wine in their hands and knew they'd been drinking, and she fumed. It was not enough that they were going to kill some senseless animal, but now they were dragging their younger brother along with them, despite his protests.

Kyra's instincts kicked in and she leapt into action, running downhill to confront them, Leo running by her side.

"You're old enough now," Brandon said to Aidan.

"It's past time you became a man," Braxton said.

Bounding down the grass hills she knew by heart, it did not take Kyra long to catch up to them. She ran out onto the road and stopped before them, blocking their path, breathing hard, Leo beside her, and her brothers all stopped short, looking back, stunned.

Aidan's face, she could see, fell in relief.

"Are you lost?" Braxton mocked.

"You're blocking our way," Brandon said. "Go back to your arrows and your sticks."

The two of them laughed derisively, but she frowned, undeterred, as Leo, beside her, snarled.

"Get that beast away from us," Braxton said, trying to sound brave but fear apparent in his voice as he tightened his grip on his spear.

"And where do you think you're taking Aidan?" she asked, dead serious, looking back at them without flinching.

They paused, their faces slowly hardening.

"We're taking him wherever we please," Brandon said.

"He's going on a hunt to learn to become a *man*," Braxton said, emphasizing that last word as a dig to her.

But she would not give in.

"He's too young," she replied firmly.

Brandon scowled.

"Says who?" he asked.

"Says me."

"And are you his mother?" Braxton asked.

Kyra flushed, filled with anger, wishing their mother was here now more than ever.

"As much as you are his father," she replied.

They all stood there in the tense silence, and Kyra looked to Aidan, who looked back with scared eyes.

"Aidan," she asked him, "is this something you wish to do?"

Aidan looked down at the ground, ashamed. He stood there, silent, avoiding her glance, and Kyra knew he was afraid to speak out, to provoke the disapproval of his older brothers.

"Well, there you have it," Brandon said. "He doesn't object."

Kyra stood there, burning with frustration, wanting Aidan to speak up but unable to force him.

"It is unwise for you to bring him on your hunt," she said. "A storm brews. It will be dark soon. The wood is filled with danger. If you want to teach him to hunt, take him when he's older, on another day."

They scowled back, annoyed.

"And what do you know of hunting?" Braxton asked. "What have you hunted beside those trees of yours?"

"Any of them bite you lately?" Brandon added.

They both laughed, and Kyra burned, debating what to do. Without Aidan speaking up, there wasn't much she could do.

"You worry too much, sister," Brandon finally said. "Nothing will happen to Aidan on our watch. We want to toughen him up a bit—not kill him. Do you really imagine you're the only one who cares for him?"

"Besides, Father is watching," Braxton said. "Do you want to disappoint him?"

Kyra immediately looked up over their shoulders, and high up, in the tower, she spotted her father standing at the arched, open-aired window, watching. She felt supreme disappointment in him for not stopping this.

They tried to brush past, but Kyra stood there, doggedly blocking their way. They looked as if they might shove her, but Leo stepped between them, snarling, and they thought better of it.

"Aidan, it's not too late," she said to him. "You don't have to do this. Do you wish to return to the fort with me?"

She examined him and could see his eyes tearing, but she could also see his torment. A long silence passed, with nothing to break it up but the howling wind and the quickening snow.

Finally, he squirmed.

"I want to hunt," he muttered half-heartedly.

Her brothers suddenly brushed past her, bumping her shoulder, dragging Aidan, and as they hurried down the road, Kyra turned and watched, a sickening feeling in her stomach.

She turned back to the fort and looked up at the tower, but her father was already gone.

Kyra watched as her three brothers faded from view, into the brewing storm, toward the Wood of Thorns, and she felt a pit in her stomach. She thought of snatching Aidan and bringing him back—but she did not want to shame him.

She knew she should let it go—but she could not. Something within her would not allow her to. She sensed danger, especially on the eve of the Winter Moon. She did not trust her elder brothers; they would not harm Aidan, she knew, but they were reckless, and too rough. Worst of all, they were overconfident in their skills. It was a bad combination.

Kyra could stand it no longer. If her father wouldn't act, then she would. She was old enough now—she did not need to answer to anyone but herself.

Kyra burst into a jog, running down the lone country path, Leo by her side, and heading right for the Wood of Thorns.

CHAPTER TWO

Kyra entered the gloomy Wood of Thorns, just west of the fort, a forest so thick one could barely see through it. As she walked through it slowly with Leo, snow and ice crunching beneath their feet, she looked up. She was dwarfed by the thorn trees that seemed to stretch forever. They were ancient black trees with gnarled branches resembling thorns, and thick, black leaves. This place, she felt, was cursed; nothing good ever came out of it. Her father's men returned from it injured from hunts, and more than once a troll, having broken through The Flames, had taken refuge here and used it as a staging ground to attack a villager.

As Kyra entered, immediately she felt a chill. It was darker in here, cooler, the air wetter, the smell of the thorn trees heavy in the air, smelling like decaying earth, and the massive trees blotting out what remained of daylight. Kyra, on guard, was furious at her older brothers. It was dangerous to venture here without the company of several warriors—especially at dusk. Every noise startled her. There came a distant cry of an animal, and she flinched, turning and looking for it. But the wood was dense, and she could not find it.

Leo, though, snarled beside her and suddenly bounded off after it.

"Leo!" she called out.

But he was already gone.

She sighed, annoyed; it was always his way when an animal crossed. He would return, though, she knew—eventually.

Kyra continued on, alone now, the wood growing darker, struggling to follow her brothers' trail—when she heard distant laughter. She snapped to attention, turning to the noise and weaving past thick trees until she spotted her brothers up ahead.

Kyra lingered back, keeping a good distance, not wanting to be spotted. She knew that if Aidan saw her, he would be embarrassed and would send her away. She would watch from the shadows, she decided, just making sure they did not get into trouble. It was better for Aidan not to be shamed, to feel like he was a man.

A twig snapped beneath her feet and Kyra ducked, worried the sound would give her away—but her drunk older brothers were oblivious, already a good thirty yards ahead of her, walking quickly, the noise drowned out by their own laughter. She could see from Aidan's body language that he was tense, almost as if he were about to cry. He clutched his spear tightly, as if trying to prove himself a man, but it was an awkward grip on a spear too big, and he struggled under the weight of it.

"Get up here!" Braxton called out, turning to Aidan, who trailed a few feet behind.

"What are you so afraid of?" Brandon said to him.

"I'm not afraid—" Aidan insisted.

"Quiet!" Brandon suddenly said, stopping, holding out a palm against Aidan's chest, his expression serious for the first time. Braxton stopped, too, all of them tense.

Kyra took shelter behind a tree as she watched her brothers. They stood at the edge of a clearing, looking straight ahead as if they had spotted something.

She crept forward, on alert, trying to get a better look, and as she weaved between two large trees, she stopped, stunned, as she caught a glimpse of what they were seeing. There, standing alone in the clearing, rooting out acorns, was a boar. It was no ordinary boar; it was a monstrous, Black-Horned Boar, the largest boar she had ever seen, with long, curled white tusks and three long, sharpened, black horns, one protruding from its nose and two from its head. Nearly the size of a bear, it was a rare creature, famed for its viciousness and its lightning-quick speed. It was an animal widely feared, and one that no hunter wanted to meet.

It was trouble.

Kyra, hair rising on her arms, wished Leo were here—yet was also grateful he was not, knowing he would bound off after it and unsure if he would win the confrontation. Kyra stepped forward, slowly removing her bow from her shoulder while instinctively reaching down to grab an arrow. She tried to calculate how far the boar was from the boys, and how far away she was—and she knew this was not good. There were too many trees in the way for her to get a clean shot—and with an animal this size, there was no room for error. She doubted one arrow could even fell it.

Kyra noticed the flash of fear on her brothers' faces, then saw Brandon and Braxton quickly cover up their fright with a look of bravado—one she felt sure was fueled by drink. They both raised their spears and took several steps forward. Braxton saw Aidan rooted in place, and he turned, grabbed the small boy's shoulder, and made him step forward, too.

"There's a chance to make a man of you," Braxton said. "Kill this boar and they'll sing of you for generations."

"Bring back its head and you'll be famed for life," Brandon said.

"I'm...scared," Aidan said.

Brandon and Braxton scoffed, then laughed derisively.

"Scared?" Brandon said. "And what would Father say if he heard you say that?"

The boar, alerted, lifted its head, revealing glowing yellow eyes, and stared at them, its face bunching up in an angry snarl. It opened its mouth, revealing fangs, and drooled, while at the same time emitting a vicious growl that erupted from somewhere deep in its belly. Kyra, even from her distance, felt a pang of fear—and she could only imagine the fear Aidan was feeling.

Kyra rushed forward, throwing caution to the wind, determined to catch up before it was too late. When she was just a few feet behind her brothers, she called out:

"Leave it alone!"

Her harsh voice cut through the silence, and her brothers all wheeled, clearly startled.

"You've had your fun," she added. "Let it be."

While Aidan looked relieved, Brandon and Braxton each scowled back at her.

"And what do you know?" Brandon shot back. "Stop interfering with real men."

The boar's snarl deepened as it crept toward them, and Kyra, both afraid and furious, stepped forward.

"If you are foolish enough to antagonize this beast, then go ahead," she said. "But you will send Aidan back here to me."

Brandon frowned.

"Aidan will do just fine here," Brandon countered. "He's about to learn how to fight. Aren't you, Aidan?"

Aidan stood silent, stunned with fear.

Kyra was about to take another step forward and snatch Aidan's arm when there came a rustling in the clearing. She saw the boar edge its way closer, one foot at a time, threateningly.

"It won't attack if it's not provoked," Kyra urged her brothers. "Let it go."

But her brothers ignored her, both turning and facing it and raising spears. They walked forward, into the clearing, as if to prove how brave they were.

"I'll aim for its head," Brandon said.

"And I, its throat," Braxton agreed.

The boar snarled louder, opened its mouth wider, drooling, and took another threatening step.

"Get back here!" Kyra yelled out, desperate.

But Brandon and Braxton stepped forward, raised their spears, and suddenly threw them.

Kyra watched in suspense as the spears flew through the air, bracing herself for the worst. She saw, to her dismay, Brandon's spear graze its ear, enough to draw blood—and to provoke it—while Braxton's spear sailed past, missing its head by several feet.

For the first time, Brandon and Braxton looked afraid. They stood there, open-mouthed, a dumb look on their faces, the glow from their drink quickly replaced by fear.

The boar, infuriated, lowered its head, snarled a horrific sound, and suddenly charged.

Kyra watched in horror as it bore down on her brothers. It was the fastest thing she'd ever seen for its size, bounding through the grass as if it were a deer.

As it approached, Brandon and Braxton ran for their lives, darting away in opposite directions.

That left Aidan standing there, rooted in place, all alone, frozen in fear. His mouth agape, he loosened his grip and his spear fell from his hand, sideways to the ground. Kyra knew it wouldn't make much difference; Aidan could not have defended himself if he tried. A grown man could not have. And the boar, as if sensing it, set its sights on Aidan, aiming right for him.

18

Kyra, heart slamming, burst into action, knowing she would only have one chance at this. Without thinking, she bounded forward, dodging between the trees, already holding her bow before her, knowing she had one shot and that it had to be perfect. It would be a hard shot, even if the boar weren't moving, in her state of panic—yet it would have to be a perfect shot if they were to survive this.

"AIDAN, GET DOWN!" she shouted.

At first, he did not move. Aidan blocked her way, preventing a clean shot, and as Kyra raised her bow and ran forward, she realized that if Aidan did not move, her one shot would be lost. Stumbling through the wood, her feet slipping in the snow and damp earth, for a moment she felt all would be lost.

"AIDAN!" she shouted again, desperate.

By some miracle, he listened this time, diving down to the earth at the last second and leaving the shot open for Kyra.

As the boar charged for Aidan, time suddenly slowed for Kyra. She felt herself entering an altered zone, something rising up within her which she had never experienced and which she did not fully understand. The world narrowed and came into focus. She could hear the sound of her own heart beating, of her breathing, of the rustling of leaves, of a crow cawing high above. She felt more in tune with the universe than she ever had, as if she had entered some realm where she and the universe were one.

Kyra felt her palms begin to tingle with a warm, prickly energy she did not understand, as if something foreign were invading her body. It was as if, for a fleeting instant, she had become somebody bigger than herself, somebody much more powerful.

Kyra entered into a state of non-thinking, and she allowed herself to be driven by pure instinct, and by this new energy flowing through her. She planted her feet, raised the bow, placed an arrow, and let it fly.

She knew the second she released it that it was a special shot. She did not need to watch the arrow sail to know it was going exactly where she wanted it to: in the beast's right eye. She shot with such force that it lodged itself nearly a foot before stopping.

The beast suddenly grunted as its legs buckled out from under it, and it fell face-first in the snow. It slid across what remained of the clearing, writhing, still alive, until it reached Aidan. It finally came to a stop but a foot away from him, so close that, when it finally stopped, they were nearly touching.

It twitched on the ground, and Kyra, already with another arrow on her bow, stepped forward, stood over the boar, and put another arrow through the back of its skull. It finally stopped moving.

Kyra stood in the clearing, in the silence, her heart pounding, the tingling in her palms slowly receding, the energy fading, and she wondered what had just happened. Had she really taken that shot?

She immediately remembered Aidan, and as she spun and grabbed him he looked up to her as he might have to his mother, eyes filled with fear, but unharmed. She felt a flash of relief as she realized he was okay.

Kyra turned and saw her two older brothers, each still lying in the clearing, staring up at her with shock—and awe. But there was something else in their looks, something which unsettled her: suspicion. As if she were different from them. An outsider. It was a look Kyra had seen before, rarely, but enough times to make her wonder at it herself. She turned and looked down at the dead beast, monstrous, huge, stiff at her feet, and she wondered how she, a fifteen-year-old girl, could have done this. It went beyond skills, she knew. Beyond a lucky shot.

There had always been something about her that was different from the others. She stood there, numb, wanting to move but unable. Because what had shaken her today was not this beast, she knew, but rather the way her brothers had looked at her. And she could not help wondering, for the millionth time, the question she had been afraid to confront her entire life:

Who was she?

CHAPTER THREE

Kyra walked behind her brothers as they all hiked the road back to the fort, watching them struggle under the weight of the boar, Aidan beside her and Leo at her heels, having returned from chasing his game. Brandon and Braxton labored as they carried the dead beast between them, tied to their two spears and draped across their shoulders. Their grim mood had changed drastically since they had emerged from the wood and back into open sky, especially now with their father's fort in sight. With each passing step, Brandon and Braxton became more confident, nearly back to their arrogant selves, now at the point of laughing, heckling each other as they boasted of *their* kill.

"It was *my* spear that grazed it," Brandon said to Braxton.

"But," countered Braxton, "it was my spear that incited it to veer for Kyra's arrow."

Kyra listened, her face reddening at their lies; her pig-headed brothers were already convincing themselves of their own story, and now they seemed to actually believe it. She already anticipated their boasting back in their father's hall, telling everyone of *their* kill.

It was maddening. Yet she felt it was beneath her to correct them. She believed firmly in the wheels of justice, and she knew that, eventually, the truth always came out.

"You're liars," Aidan said, walking beside her, clearly still shaken from the event. "You know Kyra killed the boar."

Brandon glanced over his shoulder derisively, as if Aidan were an insect.

"What would *you* know?" he asked Aidan. "You were too busy pissing your pants."

They both laughed, as if hardening their story with each passing step.

"And you weren't running scared?" Kyra asked, sticking up for Aidan, unable to stand it a second longer.

With that, they both fell silent. Kyra could have really let them have it—but she did not need to raise her voice. She walked happily, feeling good about herself, knowing within herself that she had saved her brother's life; that was all the satisfaction she needed.

Kyra felt a small hand on her shoulder, and she looked over to see Aidan, smiling, consoling her, clearly grateful to be alive and in one piece. Kyra wondered if her older brothers also appreciated what she had done for them; after all, if she hadn't appeared when she had they would have been killed, too.

Kyra watched the boar bounce before her with each step, and she grimaced; she wished her brothers had let it remain in the clearing, where it belonged. It was a cursed animal, not of Volis, and it didn't belong here. It was a bad omen, especially coming from the Wood of Thorns, and especially on the eve of the Winter Moon. She recalled an old adage she had read: *do not boast after being spared from death*. Her brothers, she felt, were tempting the fates, bringing darkness back into their home. She could not help but feel it would herald bad things to come.

They crested a hill and as they did, the stronghold spread out before them, along with a sweeping view of the landscape. Despite the gust of wind and increasing snow, Kyra felt a great sense of relief at being home. Smoke rose from the chimneys that dotted the countryside and her father's fort emitted a soft, cozy glow, all lit with fires, fending off the coming twilight. The road widened, better maintained as they neared the bridge, and they all increased their pace and walked briskly down the final stretch. The road was bustling with people, eager for the festival despite the weather and falling night.

Kyra was hardly surprised. The festival of the Winter Moon was one of the most important holidays of the year, and all were busy preparing for the feast to come. A great throng of people pressed over the drawbridge, rushing to get their wares from vendors, to join the fort's feast—while an equal number of people rushed out of the gate, hurrying to get back to their homes to celebrate with their families. Oxen pulled carts and carried wares in both directions, while masons banged and chipped away at yet another new wall being built to ring the fort, the sound of their hammers steady in the air, punctuating the din of livestock and dogs. Kyra wondered how they always worked in this weather, how they kept their hands from going numb.

As they entered the bridge, merging with the masses, Kyra looked up ahead and her stomach tightened as she saw, standing near the gate, several of the Lord's Men, soldiers for the local Lord Governor appointed by Pandesia, wearing their distinctive scarlet chain mail armor. She felt a flash of indignation at the sight, sharing the same resentment as all of her people. The presence of the Lord's Men was oppressive at any time—but on the Winter Moon it was especially so, when they could surely only be here to demand whatever gleanings they could from her people. They were scavengers, in her mind, bullies and scavengers for the despicable aristocrats that had lodged themselves in power ever since the Pandesian invasion.

The weakness of their former King was to blame, having surrendered them all—but that did them little good now. Now, to their disgrace, they had to defer to these men. It filled Kyra with fury. It made her father and his great warriors—and all of her people— nothing better than elevated serfs; she desperately wanted them all to rise up, to fight for their freedom, to fight the war their former King had been afraid to. Yet she also knew that, if they were to rise up now, they would face the wrath of the Pandesian army. Perhaps they could have held them back if they had never let them in; but now that they were entrenched, they had few options.

They reached the bridge, merging with the mob, and as they passed, people stopped, stared, and pointed at the boar. Kyra took a small satisfaction in seeing that her brothers were sweating under the burden of it, huffing and puffing. As they went, heads turned and people gaped, commoners and warriors alike, all impressed by the massive beast. She also spotted a few superstitious looks, some of the people wondering, as she, if this were a bad omen.

All eyes, though, looked to her brothers with pride.

"A fine catch for the festival!" a farmer called out, leading his ox as he merged onto the street with them.

Brandon and Braxton beamed proudly.

"It shall feed half your father's court!" called out a butcher.

"How did you manage it?" asked a saddler.

The two brothers exchanged a look, and Brandon finally grinned back at the man.

"A fine throw and a lack of fear," he replied boldly.

"If you don't venture to the wood," Braxton added, "you don't know what you'll find."

A few men cheered and clapped them on the back. Kyra, despite herself, held her tongue. She did not need these people's approval; she knew what she had done.

"They did not kill the boar!" Aidan called out, indignant.

"You shut up," Brandon turned and hissed. "Any more of that and I will tell them all that you pissed your pants when it charged."

"But I did not!" Aidan protested.

"And they will believe you?" Braxton added.

Brandon and Braxton laughed, and Aidan looked to Kyra, as if wanting to know what to do.

She shook her head.

"Don't waste your effort," she said to him. "The truth always prevails."

The throngs thickened as they crossed over the bridge, soon shoulder to shoulder with the masses as they passed over the moat. Kyra could feel the excitement in the air as twilight fell, torches lit up and down the bridge, the snowfall quickening. She looked up before her and her heart quickened, as always, to see the huge, arched stone gate to the fort, guarded by a dozen of her father's men. At its top were the spikes of an iron portcullis, now raised, its sharpened points and thick bars strong enough to keep out any foe, ready to be closed at the mere sound of a horn. The gate rose thirty feet high, and at its top was a broad platform, spreading across the entire fort, wide stone battlements manned with lookouts, always keeping a vigilant eye. Volis was a fine stronghold, Kyra had always thought, taking pride in it. What gave her even more pride were the men inside it, her father's men, many of Escalon's finest warriors, slowly regrouping in Volis after being dispersed since the surrender of their King, drawn like a magnet to her father. More than once she had urged her father to declare himself the new King, as all his people wanted him to—but he would always merely shake his head and say that was not his way.

As they neared the gate, a dozen of her father's men charged out on their horses, the masses parting for them as they rode out for the training ground, a wide, circular embankment in the fields outside the fort ringed by a low, stone wall. Kyra turned and watched them go, her heart quickening. The training grounds were her favorite place. She would go there and watch them spar for hours, studying every move they made, the way they rode their horses, the way they drew their swords, hurled spears, swung flails. These men rode out to train despite the coming dark and falling snow, even on the eve of a holiday feast, because they *wanted* to train, to better themselves, because they would all rather be on a battlefield than feasting indoors—like her. These, she felt, were her true people.

Another group of her father's men came out, these on foot, and as Kyra approached the gate with her brothers, these men stepped aside, with the masses, making room for Brandon and Braxton as they approached with the boar. They whistled in admiration and gathered around, large, muscle-bound men, standing a foot taller than even her brothers who were not small, most of them wearing beards peppered with gray, all hardened men in their thirties and forties who had seen too many battles, who had served the old King and had suffered the indignity of his surrender. Men who would have never surrendered on their own. These were men who had seen it all and who were not impressed by much—but they did seem taken with the boar.

"Kill that on your own, did you?" one of them asked Brandon, coming close and examining it.

The crowd thickened and Brandon and Braxton finally stopped, taking in the praise and admiration of these great men, trying not to show how hard they were breathing.

"We did!" Braxton called out proudly.

"A Black-Horned," exclaimed another warrior, coming up close, running his hand along the back of it. "Haven't seen one since I was a boy. Helped kill one myself, once—but I was with a party of men—and two of them lost fingers."

"Well, we lost nothing," Braxton called out boldly. "Just a spear head."

Kyra burned as the men all laughed, clearly admiring the kill, while another warrior, their leader, Anvin, stepped forward and examined the kill closely. The men parted for him, giving him a wide berth of respect.

Her father's commander, Anvin was Kyra's favorite of all the men, answering only to her father, presiding over these fine warriors. Anvin had been like a second father to her, and she had known him as long as she could remember. He loved her dearly, she knew, and he looked out for her; more importantly to her, he always took time for her, showing her the techniques of sparring and weaponry when others would not. He had even let her train with the men on more than one occasion, and she had relished each and every one. He was the toughest of them all, yet he also had the kindest heart—for those he liked. But for those he didn't, Kyra feared for them.

Anvin had little tolerance for lies, though; he was the sort of man who always had to get to the absolute truth of everything, however gray it was. He had a meticulous eye, and as he stepped forward and examined the boar closely, Kyra watched him stop and examine its two arrow wounds. He had an eye for detail, and if anyone would recognize the truth, it would be him.

Anvin examined the two wounds, inspecting the small arrowheads still lodged inside, the fragments of wood where her brothers had broken off her arrows. They had snapped it close to the tip, so no one would see what had really felled it. But Anvin was not just anyone.

Kyra watched Anvin study the wounds, saw his eyes narrow, and she knew he had summed up the truth in a glance. He reached down, removed his glove, reached into the eye, and extracted one of the arrowheads. He held it up, bloody, then slowly turned to her brothers with a skeptical look.

"A spear point, was it?" he asked, disapproving.

A tense silence fell over the group as Brandon and Braxton looked nervous for the first time. They shifted in place.

Anvin turned to Kyra.

"Or an arrowhead?" he added, and Kyra could see the wheels turning in his head, see him coming to his own conclusions.

Anvin walked over to Kyra, drew an arrow from her quiver, and held it up beside the arrowhead. It was a perfect match, for all to see. He gave Kyra a proud, meaningful look, and Kyra felt all eyes turn to her.

"Your shot, was it?" he asked her. It was more a statement than a question.

She nodded back.

"It was," she replied flatly, loving Anvin for giving her recognition, and finally feeling vindicated.

"And the shot that felled it," he concluded. It was an observation, not a question, his voice hard, final, as he studied the boar.

26

"I see no other wounds besides these two," he added, running his hand along it—then stopping at the ear. He examined it, then turned and looked at Brandon and Braxton disdainfully. "Unless you call this grazing of a spearhead here a wound."

He held up the boar's ear, and Brandon and Braxton reddened while the group of warriors laughed.

Another of her father's famed warriors stepped forward—Vidar, close friend to Anvin, a thin, short man in his thirties with a gaunt face and a scar across his nose. With his small frame, he did not look the part, but Kyra knew better: Vidar was as hard as stone, famed for his hand-to-hand combat. He was one of the hardest men Kyra had ever met, known to wrestle down two men twice his size. Too many men, because of his diminutive size, had made the mistake of provoking him—only to learn their lesson the hard way. He, too, had taken Kyra under his wing, always protective of her.

"Looks like they missed," Vidar concluded, "and the girl saved them. Who taught you two to throw?"

Brandon and Braxton looked increasingly nervous, clearly caught in a lie, and neither said a word.

"It's a grievous thing to lie about a kill," Anvin said darkly, turning to her brothers. "Out with it now. Your father would want you to tell the truth."

Brandon and Braxton stood there, shifting, clearly uncomfortable, looking at each other as if debating what to say. For the first time she could remember, Kyra saw them tongue-tied.

Just as they were about to open their mouths, suddenly a foreign voice cut through the crowd.

"Doesn't matter who killed it," came the voice. "It's ours now."

Kyra turned with all the others, startled at the rough, unfamiliar voice—and her stomach dropped as she saw a group of the Lord's Men, distinctive in their scarlet armor, step forward through the crowd, the villagers parting for them. They approached the boar, eyeing it greedily, and Kyra saw that they wanted this trophy kill—not because they needed it, but as a way to humiliate her people, to snatch away from them this point of pride. Beside her, Leo snarled, and she laid a reassuring hand on his neck, holding him back.

"In the name of your Lord Governor," said the Lord's Man, a portly soldier with a low brow, thick eyebrows, a large belly, and a face bunched up in stupidity, "we claim this boar. He thanks you in advance for your present on this holiday festival."

He gestured to his men and they stepped toward the boar, as if to grab it.

As they did, Anvin suddenly stepped forward, Vidar by his side, and blocked their way.

An astonished silence fell over the crowd—no one ever confronted the Lord's Men; it was an unwritten rule. No one wanted to incite the wrath of Pandesia.

"No one's offered you a present, as far as I can tell," he said, his voice steel, "or your Lord Governor."

The crowd thickened, hundreds of villagers gathering to watch the tense standoff, sensing a confrontation. At the same time, others backed away, creating space around the two men, as the tension in the air grew more intense.

Kyra felt her heart pounding. She unconsciously tightened her grip on her bow, knowing this was escalating. As much as she wanted a fight, wanted her freedom, she also knew that her people could not afford to incite the wrath of the Lord Governor; even if by some miracle they defeated them, the Pandesian Empire stood behind them. They could summon divisions of men as vast as the sea.

Yet, at the same time, Kyra was so proud of Anvin for standing up to them. Finally, somebody had.

The soldier glowered, staring Anvin down.

"Do you dare defy your Lord Governor?" he asked.

Anvin held his ground.

"That boar is ours—no one's giving it to you," Anvin said.

"It *was* yours," the soldier corrected, "and now it belongs to us." He turned to his men. "Take the boar," he commanded.

The Lord's Men approached and as they did, a dozen of her father's men stepped forward, backing up Anvin and Vidar, blocking the Lord's Men's way, hands on their weapons.

The tension grew so thick, Kyra squeezed her bow until her knuckles turned white, and as she stood there she felt awful, felt as if somehow she were responsible for all this, given that she had killed the boar. She sensed something very bad was about to happen, and she cursed her brothers for bringing this bad omen into their village, especially on Winter Moon. Strange things always happened on the

28

holidays, mystical times when the dead were said to be able to cross from one world to the other. Why had her brothers had to provoke the spirits in this way?

As the men faced off, her father's men preparing to draw their swords, all of them so close to bloodshed, a voice of authority suddenly cut through the air, booming through the silence.

"The kill is the girl's!" came the voice.

It was a loud voice, filled with confidence, a voice that commanded attention, a voice that Kyra admired and respected more than any in the world: her father's. Commander Duncan.

All eyes turned as her father approached, the crowd parting ways for him, giving him a wide berth of respect. There he stood, a mountain of a man, twice as tall as the others, with shoulders twice as wide, an untamed brown beard and longish brown hair both streaked with gray, wearing furs over his shoulders and bearing two long swords on his belt and a spear across his back. His armor, the black of Volis, had a dragon carved into its breastplate, the sign of their house. His weapons bore nicks and scrapes from one too many battle and he projected experience. He was a man to be feared, a man to be admired, a man who all new to be just and fair. A man loved and, above all, respected.

"It is Kyra's kill," he repeated, glancing disapprovingly at her brothers as he did, then turning and looking at Kyra, ignoring the Lord's Men. "It is for her to decide its fate."

Kyra was shocked at her father's words. She had never expected this, never expected him to put such responsibility in her hands, to leave to her such a weighty decision. For it was not merely a decision about the boar, they both knew, but about the very fate of her people.

Tense soldiers lined up on either side, all with hands on swords, and as she looked out at all the faces, all turning to her, all awaiting her response, she knew that her next choice, her next words, would be the most important she had ever spoken.

CHAPTER FOUR

Merk hiked slowly down the forest path, weaving his way through Whitewood, and he reflected on his life. His forty years had been hard ones; he had never before taken the time to hike through a wood, to admire the beauty around him. He looked down at the white leaves crunching beneath his feet, punctuated by the sound of his staff as he tapped the soft forest floor; he looked up as he walked, taking in the beauty of the Aesop trees, with their shining white leaves and glowing red branches, glistening in the morning sun. Leaves fell, showering down on him like snow, and for the first time in his life, he felt a real sense of peace.

Of average height and build, with dark black hair, a perpetually unshaven face, a wide jaw, long, drawn-out cheekbones, and large black eyes with black circles under them, Merk always looked as if he hadn't slept in days. And that was always how he felt. But now. Now, finally, he felt rested. Here, in Ur, in the northwest corner of Escalon, there came no snow. The temperate breezes off the ocean, but a day's ride west, assured them of warmer weather and allowed leaves of every color to flourish. It also allowed Merk to sojourn wearing but a cloak, with no need to cower from the freezing winds, as they did in much of Escalon. He was still getting used to the idea of wearing a cloak instead of armor, of wielding a staff instead of a sword, of tapping the leaves with his staff instead of piercing his foes with a dagger. It was all new to him. He was trying to see what it felt like to become this new person he yearned to be. It was peaceful—but awkward. As if he were pretending to be someone he was not.

For Merk was no traveler, no monk—nor was he a peaceful man. He was still, in his blood, a warrior. And not just any warrior; he was a man who fought by his own rules, and who had never lost a battle. He was a man who was unafraid to take his battles from the jousting lanes to the back alleys of the taverns he loved to frequent. He was what some people liked to call a mercenary. An assassin. A hired sword. There were many names for him, some even less flattering, but Merk didn't care for labels, or about what other people thought. All he cared about was that he was one of the best.

Merk, as if to fit his role, had gone by many names himself, changing them at his whim. He didn't like the name his father had given him—in fact, he didn't like his father, either—and he wasn't about to go through life with a name someone else slapped on him. Merk was the most frequent name change, and he liked it, for now. He did not care what anyone called him. He cared only about two things in life: finding the perfect spot for the point of his dagger, and that his employers pay him in freshly minted gold—and a lot of it.

Merk had discovered at a young age that he had a natural gift, that he was superior to all others at what he did. His brothers, like his father and all his famed ancestors, were proud and noble knights, donning the best armor, wielding the best steel, prancing about on their horses, waving their banners with their flowery hair and winning competitions while ladies threw flowers at their feet. They could not have been more proud of themselves.

Merk, though, hated the pomp, the limelight. Those knights had all seemed clumsy at killing, vastly inefficient, and Merk had no respect for them. Nor did he need the recognition, the insignias or banners or coats of arms that knights craved. That was for people who lacked what mattered most: the skill to take a man's life, quickly, quietly, and efficiently. In his mind, there was nothing else to talk about.

When he was young and his friends, too small to defend themselves, had been picked on, they had come to him, already known to be exceptional with a sword, and he had taken their payment to defend them. Their bullies never tormented them again, as Merk went that extra step. Word had spread quickly of his prowess, and as Merk accepted more and more payments, his abilities in killing progressed.

Merk could have become a knight, a celebrated warrior like his brothers. But he chose instead to work in the shadows. Winning was what interested him, lethal efficiency, and he had discovered quickly that knights, for all their beautiful weapons and bulky armor, could not kill half as fast or effectively as he, a lone man with a leather shirt and a sharp dagger.

As he hiked, poking the leaves with his staff, he recalled one night at a tavern with his brothers, when swords had been drawn with rival

31

knights. His brothers had been surrounded, outnumbered, and while all the fancy knights stood on ceremony, Merk did not hesitate. He had darted across the alley with his dagger and sliced all their throats before the men could draw a sword.

His brothers should have thanked them for their lives—instead, they all distanced themselves from him. They feared him, and they looked down on him. That was the gratitude he received, and the betrayal hurt Merk more than he could say. It deepened his rift with them, with all nobility, with all chivalry. It was all hypocrisy in his eyes, self-serving; they could walk away with their shiny armor and look down on him, but if it hadn't been for him and his dagger they would all be lying dead in that back alley today.

Merk hiked and hiked, sighing, trying to release the past. As he reflected, he realized he did not really understand the source of his talent. Perhaps it was because he was so quick and nimble; perhaps it was because he was fast with his hands and wrists; perhaps it was because he had a special talent for finding men's vital points; perhaps it was because he never hesitated to go that extra step, to take that final thrust that other men feared; perhaps it was because he never had to strike twice; or perhaps it was because he could improvise, could kill with any tool at his disposal—a quill, a hammer, an old log. He was craftier than others, more adaptable and quicker on his feet— a deadly combination.

Growing up, all those proud knights had distanced themselves from him, had even mocked him beneath their breath (for no one would mock him to his face). But now, as they were all older, as their powers waned and as his fame spread, he was the one enlisted by kings, while they were all forgotten. Because what his brothers never understood was that *chivalry* did not make kings kings. It was the ugly, brutal violence, fear, the elimination of your enemies, one at a time, the gruesome killing that no one else wanted to do, that made kings. And it was he they turned to when they wanted the *real* work of being a king done.

With each poke of his staff, Merk remembered each of his victims. He had killed the King's worst foes—not by poison—for that, they brought in the petty assassins, the apothecaries, the seductresses. The worst ones they often wanted killed with a statement, and for that, they needed him. Something gruesome, something public: a dagger in the eye; a body left strewn in a public square, dangling from a window, for all to see the next sunrise, for all to be left in wonder as to who had dared oppose the King.

When the old King Tarnis had surrendered the kingdom, had opened the gates for Pandesia, Merk had felt deflated, purposeless for the first time in his life. Without a King to serve he had felt adrift. Something long brewing within him had surfaced, and for some reason he did not understand, he began to wonder about life. All his life he had been obsessed with death, with killing, with taking life away. It had become easy—too easy. But now, something within him was changing; it was as if he could hardly feel the stable ground beneath his feet. He had always known, firsthand, how fragile life was, how easily it could be taken away, but now he started to wonder about preserving it. Life was so fragile, was preserving it not a greater challenge than taking it?

And despite himself, he started to wonder: what was this thing he was stripping away from others?

Merk did not know what had started all this self-reflection, but it made him deeply uncomfortable. Something had surfaced within him, a great nausea, and he had become sick of killing—he had developed as great a distaste for it as he had once enjoyed it. He wished there was one thing he could point to that triggered all of this— the killing of a particular person, perhaps—but there was not. It had just crept up on him, without cause. And that was most disturbing of all.

Unlike other mercenaries, Merk had only taken on causes he believed in. It was only later in life, when he had become too good at what he did, when the payments had become too large, the people who requested him too important, that he had begun to blur the lines, to accept payment for killing those who weren't necessarily at fault— not necessarily at all. And that was what was bothering him.

Merk developed an equally strong passion for undoing all that he had done, for proving to others that he could change. He wanted to wipe out his past, to take back all that he had done, to make penitence. He had taken a solemn vow within himself never to kill again; never to lift a finger against anyone; to spend the rest of his days asking God for forgiveness; to devote himself to helping others; to become a better person. And it was all of this that had led him to this forest path he walked right now with each click of his staff.

Merk saw the forest trail rise up ahead then dip, aglow with white leaves, and he checked the horizon again for the Tower of Ur. There was still no sign of it. He knew eventually this path must lead him there, this pilgrimage that had been calling to him for months now. He had been captivated, ever since he was a boy, by tales of the Watchers, the secretive order of monks/knights, part men and part something else, whose job was to reside in the two towers—the Tower of Ur in the northwest and the Tower of Kos in the southeast—and to watch over the Kingdom's most precious relic: the Sword of Fire. It was the Sword of Fire, legend had it, that kept The Flames alive. No one knew for sure which tower it was in, a closely kept secret known by none but the most ancient Watchers. If it were ever to be moved, or stolen, The Flames would be lost forever—and Escalon would be vulnerable to attack.

It was said that watching over the towers was a high calling, a sacred duty and honorable duty—if the Watchers accepted you. Merk had always dreamed of the Watchers as a boy, had gone to bed at night wondering what it would be like to join their ranks. He wanted to lose himself in solitude, in service, in self-reflection, and he knew there was no better way than to become a Watcher. Merk felt ready. He had discarded his chain mail for leather, his sword for a staff, and for the first time in his life, he had gone a solid moon without killing or hurting a soul. He was starting to feel good.

As Merk crested a small hill, he looked out, hopeful, as he had been for days, that this peak might reveal the Tower of Ur somewhere on the horizon. But there was nothing to be found—nothing but more woods, reaching as far as the eye could see. Yet he knew he was getting close—after so many days of hiking, the tower could not be that far off.

Merk continued down the slope of the path, the wood growing thicker, until, at the bottom, he came to a huge, felled tree blocking the path. He stopped and looked at it, admiring its size, debating how to get around it.

"I'd say that's about far enough," came a sinister voice.

Merk recognized the dark intention in the voice immediately, something he had become expert in, and he did not even need to turn to know what was coming next. He heard leaves crunching all around him, and out of the wood there emerged faces to match the voice:

cutthroats, each more desperate looking than the next. They were the faces of men who killed for no reason. The faces of common thieves and killers who preyed on the weak with random, senseless violence. In Merk's eyes, they were the lowest of the low.

Merk saw he was surrounded and knew he had walked into a trap. He glanced around quickly without letting them know it, his old instincts kicking in, and he counted eight of them. They all held daggers, all dressed in rags, with dirty faces, hands, and fingernails, all unshaven, all with a desperate look that showed they hadn't eaten in too many days. And that they were bored.

Merk tensed as the lead thief got closer, but not because he feared him; Merk could kill him—could kill them all—without blinking an eye, if he chose. What made him tense was the possibility of being forced into violence. He was determined to keep his vow, whatever the cost.

"And what do we have here?" one of them asked, coming close, circling Merk.

"Looks like a monk," said another, his voice mocking. "But those boots don't match."

"Maybe he's a monk who thinks he's a soldier," one laughed.

They all broke into laughter, and one of them, an oaf of a man in his forties with a missing front tooth, leaned in with his bad breath and poked Merk in the shoulder. The old Merk would have killed any man who had come half as close.

But the new Merk was determined to be a better man, to rise above violence—even if it seemed to seek him out. He closed his eyes and took a deep breath, forcing himself to remain calm.

Do not resort to violence, he told himself again and again.

"What's this monk doing?" one of them asked. "Praying?"

They all burst into laughter again.

"Your god won't save you now, boy!" another exclaimed.

Merk opened his eyes and stared back at the cretin.

"I do not wish to harm you," he said calmly.

Laughter rose up, louder than before, and Merk realized that staying calm, not reacting with violence, was the hardest thing he had ever done.

"Lucky for us, then!" one replied.

They laughed again, then all fell silent as their leader stepped forward and got in Merk's face.

"But perhaps," he said, his voice serious, so close that Merk could smell his bad breath, "we wish to harm you."

A man came up behind Merk, wrapped a thick arm around his throat, and began squeezing. Merk gasped as he felt himself being choked, the grip tight enough to put him in pain but not to cut off all air. His immediate reflex was to reach back and kill the man. It would be easy; he knew the perfect pressure point in the forearm to make him release his grip. But he forced himself not to.

Let them pass, he told himself. *The road to humility must begin somewhere.*

Merk faced their leader.

"Take of mine what you wish," Merk said, gasping. "Take it and be on your way."

"And what if we take it and stay right here?" the leader replied.

"No one's asking you what we can and can't take, boy," another said.

One of them stepped up and ransacked Merk's waist, rummaging greedy hands through his few personal belongings left in the world. Merk forced himself to stay calm as the hands rifled through everything he owned. Finally, they extracted his well-worn silver dagger, his favorite weapon, and still Merk, as painful as it was, did not react.

Let it go, he told himself.

"What's this?" one asked. "A dagger?"

He glared at Merk.

"What's a fancy monk like you carrying a dagger?" one asked.

"What are you doing, boy, carving trees?" another asked.

They all laughed, and Merk gritted his teeth, wondering how much more he could take.

The man who took the dagger stopped, looked down at Merk's wrist, and yanked back his sleeve. Merk braced himself, realizing they'd found it.

"What's this?" the thief asked, grabbing his wrist and holding it up, examining it.

"It looks like a fox," one said.

"What's a monk doing with a tattoo of a fox?" another asked.

36

Another stepped forward, a tall, thin man with red hair, and grabbed his wrist and examined it closely. He let it go and looked up at Merk with cautious eyes.

"That's no fox, you idiot," he said to his men. "It's a wolf. It's the mark of a King's man—a mercenary."

Merk felt his face flush as he realized they were staring at his tattoo. He did not want to be discovered.

The thieves all remained silent, staring at it, and for the first time, Merk sensed hesitation in their faces.

"That's the order of the killers," one said, then looked at him. "How did you get that mark, boy?"

"Probably gave it to himself," one answered. "Makes the road safer."

The leader nodded to his man, who released his grip on Merk's throat, and Merk breathed deep, relieved. But the leader then reached up and held a knife to Merk's throat and Merk wondered if he would die here, today, in this place. He wondered if it would be punishment for all the killing he had done. He wondered if he was ready to die.

"Answer him," their leader growled. "You give that to yourself, boy? They say you need to kill a hundred men to get that mark."

Merk breathed, and in the long silence that followed, debated what to say. Finally, he sighed.

"A *thousand*," he said.

The leader blinked back, confused.

"What?" he asked.

"A thousand men," Merk explained. "That's what gets you that tattoo. And it was given to me by King Tarnis himself."

They all stared back, shocked, and a long silence fell over the wood, so quiet that Merk could hear the insects chirping. He wondered what would happen next.

One of them broke into hysterical laughter—and all the others followed. They laughed and guffawed as Merk stood there, clearly thinking it was the funniest thing they'd ever heard.

"That's a good one, boy," one said. "You're as good a liar as you are a monk."

The leader pushed the dagger against his throat, hard enough to begin to draw blood.

"I said, answer me," the leader repeated. "A *real* answer. You want to die right now, boy?"

Merk stood there, feeling the pain, and he thought about the question—he truly thought about it. Did he want to die? It was a good question, and an even deeper question than the thief supposed. As he thought about it, really thought about, he realized that a part of him did want to die. He was tired of life, bone tired.

But as he dwelled on it, Merk ultimately realized he was not ready to die. Not now. Not today. Not when he was ready to start anew. Not when he was just beginning to enjoy life. He wanted a chance to change. He wanted a chance to serve in the Tower. To become a Watcher.

"No, actually I don't," Merk replied.

He finally looked his captor right in the eye, a resolve growing within him.

"And because of that," he continued, "I'm going to give you one chance to release me, before I kill you all."

They all looked at him in silent shock, before the leader scowled and began to break into action.

Merk felt the blade begin to slice his throat, and something within him took over. It was the professional part of him, the one he had trained his entire life, the part of him that could take no more. It meant breaking his vow—but he no longer cared.

The old Merk came rushing back so fast, it was as if it had never left—and in the blink of an eye, he found himself back in killer mode.

Merk focused and saw all of his opponents' movements, every twitch, every pressure point, every vulnerability. The desire to kill them overwhelmed him, like an old friend, and Merk allowed it to take over.

In one lightning-fast motion, Merk grabbed the leader's wrist, dug his finger into a pressure point, snapped it back until it cracked, then snatched the dagger as it fell and in one quick move, sliced the man's throat from ear to ear.

Their leader stared back at him with an astonished look before slumping down to the ground, dead.

Merk turned and faced the others, and they all stared back, stunned, mouths agape.

Now it was Merk's turn to smile, as he looked back at all of them, relishing what was about to happen next.

"Sometimes, boys," he said, "you just pick the wrong man to mess with."

CHAPTER FIVE

Kyra stood in the center of the crowded bridge, feeling all eyes on her, all awaiting her decision for the fate of the boar. Her cheeks flushed; she did not like to be the center of attention. She loved her father for acknowledging her, though, and she felt a great sense of pride, especially for his putting the decision in her hands.

Yet at the same time, she also felt a great responsibility. She knew that whatever choice she made would decide the fate of her people. As much as she loathed the Pandesians, she did not want the responsibility of throwing her people into a war they could not win. Yet she also did not want to back down, to embolden the Lord's Men, to disgrace her people, make them seem weak, especially after Anvin and the others had so courageously made a stand.

Her father, she realized, was wise: by putting the decision in her hands, he made it seemed as if the decision was theirs, not the Lord's Men, and that act alone had saved his people face. She also realized he had put the decision in her hands for a reason: he must have knew this situation required an outside voice to help all parties save face—and he chose her because she was convenient, and because he knew her not to be rash, to be a voice of moderation. The more she pondered it, the more she realized that was why he chose her: not to incite a war—he could have chosen Anvin for that—but to get his people out of one.

She came to a decision.

"The beast is cursed," she said dismissively. "It nearly killed my brothers. It came from the Wood of Thorns and was killed on the eve of Winter Moon, a day we are forbidden to hunt. It was a mistake to bring it through our gates—it should have been left to rot in the wild, where it belongs."

She turned derisively to the Lord's Men.

"Bring it to your Lord Governor," she said, smiling. "You do us a favor."

The Lord's Men looked from her to the beast, and their expressions morphed; they now looked as if they had bitten into something rotten, as if they didn't want it anymore.

Kyra saw Anvin and the others looking at her approvingly, gratefully—and her father most of all. She had done it—she had allowed her people to save face, had spared them from a war—and had managed a jibe at Pandesia at the same time.

Her brothers dropped the boar to the ground and it landed in the snow with a thud. They stepped back, humbled, their shoulders clearly aching.

All eyes now fell to the Lord's Men, who stood there, not knowing what to do. Clearly Kyra's words had cut deep; they now looked at the beast now as if it were something foul dragged up from the bowels of the earth. Clearly, they no longer wanted it. And now that it was theirs, they seemed to have also lost the desire for it.

Their commander, after a long, tense silence, finally gestured to his men to pick up the beast, then turned, scowling, and marched away, clearly annoyed, as if knowing he had been outsmarted.

The crowd dispersed, the tension gone, and there came a sense of relief. Many of her father's men approached her approvingly, laying hands on her shoulder.

"Well done," Anvin said, looking at her with approval. "You shall make a good ruler someday."

The village folk went back to their ways, the hustle and bustle returning, the tension dissipated, and Kyra turned and searched for her father's eyes. She found them looking back, he standing but a few feet away. In front of his men, he was always reserved when it came to her, and this time was no different—he wore an indifferent expression, but he nodded at her ever so slightly, a nod, she knew, of approval.

Kyra looked over and saw Anvin and Vidar clutching their spears, and her heart quickened.

"Can I join you?" she asked Anvin, knowing they were heading to the training grounds, as the rest of her father's men.

Anvin glanced nervously at her father, knowing he would disapprove.

"Snow's thickening," Anvin finally replied, hesitant. "Night's falling, too."

"That's not stopping you," Kyra countered.

He grinned back.

"No, it's not," he admitted.

Anvin glanced at her father again, and she turned and saw him shake his head before turning and heading back inside.

Anvin sighed.

"They're preparing a mighty feast," he said. "You'd best go in."

Kyra could smell it herself, the air heavy with fine meats roasting, and she saw her brothers turn and head inside, along with dozens of villagers, all rushing to prepare for the festival.

But Kyra turned and looked longingly out at the fields, at the training grounds.

"A meal can wait," she said. "Training cannot. Let me come."

Vidar smiled and shook his head.

"You sure you're a girl and not a warrior?" Vidar asked.

"Can I not be both?" she replied.

Anvin let out a long sigh, and finally shook his head.

"Your father would have my hide," he said.

Then, finally, he nodded.

"You won't take no for an answer," he concluded, "and you've got more heart than half my men. I suppose we can use one more."

*

Kyra ran across the snowy landscape, trailing Anvin, Vidar and several of her father's men, Leo by her side as usual. The snowfall was thickening and she did not care. She felt a sense of freedom, of exhilaration, as she always did when passing through Fighter's Gate, a low, arched opening cut into the stone walls of the training ground. She breathed deep as the sky opened up and she ran into this place she loved most in the world, its rolling green hills, now covered in snow, encased by a rambling stone wall, perhaps a quarter mile wide and deep. She felt everything was as it should be as she saw all the men training, crisscrossing on their horses, wielding lances, aiming for distant targets and bettering themselves. This, for her, was what life was about.

This training ground was reserved for her father's men; women were not allowed here and neither were boys who had not yet reached their eighteenth year—and who had not been invited. Brandon and Braxton, every day, waited impatiently to be invited—yet Kyra suspected that they never would. Fighter's Gate was for honorable, battle-hardened warriors, not for blowhards like her brothers.

Kyra ran through the fields, feeling happier and more alive here than anywhere else on earth. The energy was intense, it packed with dozens of her father's finest warriors, all wearing slightly different armor, warriors from all regions of Escalon, all of whom had over time gravitated to her father's fort. There were men from the south, from Thebus and Leptis; from the Midlands, mostly from the capital, Andros, but also from the mountains of Kos; there were westerners from Ur; river men from Thusis and their neighbors from Esephus. There were men who lived near the Lake of Ire, and men from as far away as the waterfalls at Everfall. All wore different colors, armor, wielded different weapons, all men of Escalon yet each representing his own stronghold. It was a dazzling array of power.

Her father, the former King's champion, a man who commanded great respect, was the only man in these times, in this fractured kingdom, that men could rally around. Indeed, when the old King had surrendered their kingdom without a fight, it was her father that people urged to assume the throne and lead the fight. Over time, the best of the former King's warriors had sought him out, and now, with the force growing larger each day, Volis was achieving a strength that nearly rivaled the capital. Perhaps that was why, Kyra realized, the Lord's Men felt the need to humble them.

Elsewhere throughout Escalon, the Lord Governors for Pandesia did not allow knights to gather, did not allow such freedoms, for fear of a revolt. But here, in Volis, it was different. Here, they had no choice: they needed to allow it because they needed the best possible men to keep The Flames.

Kyra turned and looked out, beyond the walls, beyond the rolling hills of white, and in the distance, on the far horizon, even through the snowfall, she could see, just barely, the dim glow of The Flames. The wall of fire that protected the eastern border of Escalon, The Flames, a wall of fire fifty feet deep and several hundred high, burned as brightly as ever, lighting up the night, their outline visible on the horizon and growing more pronounced as night fell. Stretching nearly fifty miles wide, The Flames were the only thing standing between Escalon and the nation of savage trolls to the east.

Even so, enough trolls broke through each year to wreak havoc, and if it weren't for The Keepers, her father's brave men who kept The Flames, Escalon would be a slave nation to the trolls. The trolls, who feared water, could only attack Escalon by land, and The Flames was the only thing keeping them at bay. The Keepers stood guard in shifts, patrolled in rotation, and Pandesia needed them. Others were stationed at The Flames, too—draftees, slaves and criminals—but her father's men, The Keepers, were the only true soldiers amongst the lot, and the only ones who knew how to keep The Flames.

In return, Pandesia allowed Volis and their men their many small freedoms, like Volis, these training grounds, real weapons—a small taste of freedom to make them still feel like free warriors, even if it was an illusion. They were not free men, and all of them knew it. They lived with an awkward balance between freedom and servitude that none could stomach.

But here, at least, in Fighter's Gate, these men were free, as they had once been, warriors who could compete and train and hone their skills. They represented the best of Escalon, better warriors than any Pandesia had to offer, all of them veterans of The Flames—and all serving shifts there, but a day's ride away. Kyra wanted nothing more than to join their ranks, than to prove herself, to be stationed at The Flames, to fight real trolls as they came through and to help guard her kingdom from invasion.

She knew, of course, that it would never be allowed. She was too young to be eligible—and she was a girl. There were no other girls in the ranks, and even if there were, her father would never allow it. His men, too, had looked upon her as a child when she had started visiting them years ago, had been amused by her presence, like a spectator watching. But after the men had left, she had remained behind, alone, training every day and night on the empty fields, using their weapons, targets. They had been surprised at first to arrive the following day to find arrow marks in their targets—and even more surprised when they were in the center. But over time, they had become used to it.

Kyra began to earn their respect, especially on the rare occasions she had been allowed to join them. By now, two years later, they all knew she could hit targets most of them could not—and their tolerating her had morphed to something else: respecting her. Of course, she had not fought in battles, as these other men had, had never killed a man, or stood guard at The Flames, or met a troll in battle. She could not swing a sword or a battle axe or halberd, or wrestle as these men could. She did not have nearly their physical strength, which she regretted dearly.

Yet Kyra had learned she had a natural skill with two weapons, each of which made her, despite her size and sex, a formidable opponent: her bow, and her staff. The former she had taken to naturally, while the latter she had stumbled upon accidentally, moons ago, when she could not lift a double-handed sword. Back then, the men had laughed at her inability to wield the sword, and as an insult, one of them had chucked her a staff derisively.

"See if you can lift this stick instead!" he'd yelled, and the others had laughed. Kyra had never forgotten her shame at that moment.

At first, her father's men had viewed her staff as a joke; after all, they used it merely for a training weapon, these brave men who carried double-handed swords and hatchets and halberds, who could cut through a tree with a single stroke. They looked to her stick of wood as a plaything, and it had given her even less respect than she already had.

But she had turned a joke into an unexpected weapon of vengeance, a weapon to be feared. A weapon that now even many of her father's men could not defend against. Kyra had been surprised at its light weight, and even more surprised to discover that she was quite good with it naturally—so fast that she could land blows while soldiers were still raising their swords. More than one of the men she had sparred with had been left black and blue by it and, one blow at a time, she had fought her way to respect.

Kyra, through endless nights of training on her own, of teaching herself, had mastered moves which dazzled the men, moves which none of them could quite understand. They had grown interested in her staff, and she had taught them. In Kyra's mind, her bow and her staff complemented each other, each of equal necessity: her bow she needed for long-distance combat, and her staff for close fighting.

Kyra also discovered she had an innate gift that these men lacked: she was nimble. She was like a minnow in a sea of slow-moving sharks, and while these aging men had great power, Kyra could dance

45

around them, could leap into the air, could even flip over them and land in a perfect roll—or on her feet. And when her nimbleness combined with her staff technique, it made for a lethal combination.

"What is *she* doing here?" came a gruff voice.

Kyra, standing to the side of the training grounds beside Anvin and Vidar, heard the approach of horses, and turned to see Maltren riding up, flanked by a few of his soldier friends, still breathing hard as he held a sword, fresh from the grounds. He looked down at her disdainfully and her stomach tightened. Of all her father's men, Maltren was the only one who disliked her. He had hated her, for some reason, from the first time he'd laid eyes upon her.

Maltren sat on his horse, and seethed; with his flat nose and ugly face, he was a man who loved to hate, and he seemed to have found a target in Kyra. He had always been opposed to her presence here, probably because she was a girl.

"You should be back in your father's fort, girl," he said, "preparing for the feast with all the other young, ignorant girls."

Leo, beside Kyra, snarled up at Maltren, and Kyra laid a reassuring hand on his head, keeping him back.

"And why is that wolf allowed on our grounds?" Maltren added.

Anvin and Vidar gave Maltren a cold, hard look, taking Kyra's side, and Kyra stood her ground and smiled back, knowing she had their protection and that he could not force her to leave.

"Perhaps you should go back to the training ground," she countered, her voice mocking, "and not concern yourself with the comings and goings of a young, ignorant girl."

Maltren reddened, unable to respond. He turned, preparing to storm off, but not without taking one last jab at her.

"It's spears today," he said. "You'd best stay out of the way of real men throwing real weapons."

He turned and rode off with the others and as she watched him go, her joy at being here was tempered by his presence.

Anvin gave her a consoling look and lay a hand on her shoulder.

"The first lesson of a warrior," he said, "is to learn to live with those who hate you. Like it or not, you will find yourself fighting side-by-side with them, dependent on them for your lives. Oftentimes, your worst enemies will not come from without, but from within."

"And those who can't fight, run their mouths," came a voice.

46

Kyra turned to see Arthfael approaching, grinning, quick to take her side, as he always was. Like Anvin and Vidar, Arthfael, a tall, fierce warrior with a stark bald head and a long, stiff black beard, had a soft spot for her. He was one of the best swordsmen, rarely bested, and he always stood up for her. She took comfort in his presence.

"It's just talk," Arthfael added. "If Maltren were a better warrior, he'd be more concerned with himself than others."

Anvin, Vidar and Arthfael mounted their horses and took off with the others, and Kyra stood there watching them, thinking. Why did some people hate? she wondered. She did not know if she would ever understand it.

As they charged across the grounds, racing in wide loops, Kyra studied the great warhorses in awe, eager for the day when she might have one of her own. She watched the men circle the grounds, riding alongside the stone walls, their horses sometimes slipping in the snow. The men grabbed spears handed to them by eager squires, and as they rounded the loop, they threw them at distant targets: shields hanging from branches. When they hit, the distinct clang of metal rang out.

It was harder than it looked, she could see, to throw while on horseback, and more than one of the men missed, especially as they aimed for the smaller shields. Of those who hit, few hit in the center—except for Anvin, Vidar, Arthfael and a few others. Maltren, she noticed, missed several times, cursing under his breath and glaring over at her, as if she were to blame.

Kyra, wanting to keep warm, pulled out her staff and began spinning and twirling it in her hands, over her head, around and around, twisting and turning it like a living thing. She thrust at imaginary enemies, blocked imaginary blows, switching hands, over her neck, around her waist, the staff like a third arm for her, its wood well-worn from years of molding it.

While the men circled the fields, Kyra ran off to her own little field, a small section of the training grounds neglected by the men but which she loved for herself. Small pieces of armor dangled from ropes in a grove of trees, spread out at all different heights, and Kyra ran through and, pretending each target was an opponent, struck each one with her staff. The air filled with her clanging as she ran through the grove, slashing, weaving and ducking as they swung back at her. In her

47

mind she attacked and defended gloriously, conquering an army of imaginary foes.

"Kill anyone yet?" came a mocking voice.

Kyra turned to see Maltren ride up on his horse, laughing derisively at her, before he rode off. She fumed, wishing that someone would put him in his place.

Kyra took a break as she saw the men, done with their spears, dismount and form a circle in the center of the clearing. Their squires rushed forward and handed them wooden training swords, made of a thick oak, weighing nearly as much as steel. Kyra kept to the periphery, her heart quickening as she watched these men square off with each other, wanting more than anything to join them.

Before they began, Anvin stepped into the middle and faced them all.

"On this holiday, we spar for a special bounty," he announced. "To the victor shall go the choice portion of the feast!"

A cry of excitement followed, as the men charged each other, the click-clack of their wooden swords filling the air, driving each other back and forth.

The sparring was punctuated by the blasts of a horn, sounding every time a fighter was struck by a blow, and sending him to the sidelines. The horn sounded frequently, and soon the ranks began to thin, most of the men now standing to the side and watching.

Kyra stood on the sidelines with them, burning to spar, though she was not allowed. Yet today was her birthday, she was fifteen now, and she felt ready. She felt it was time to press her case.

"Let me join them!" she pleaded to Anvin, who was standing nearby, watching.

Anvin shook his head, never taking his eyes off the action.

"Today marks my fifteenth year!" she insisted. "Allow me to fight!"

He glanced over at her skeptically.

"This is a training ground for men," chimed in Maltren, standing on the sidelines after losing a point. "Not young girls. You can sit and watch with the other squires, and bring us water if we demand it."

Kyra flushed.

"Are you so afraid that a girl might defeat you?" she countered, standing her ground, feeling a rush of anger within her. She was her father's daughter, after all, and no one could speak to her like that.

Some of the men snickered, and this time, Maltren blushed.

"She has a point," Vidar chimed in. "Maybe we should let her spar. What's to lose?"

"Spar with what?" Maltren countered.

"My staff!" Kyra called out. "Against your wooden swords."

Maltren laughed.

"That would be a sight," he said.

All eyes turned to Anvin, as he stood there, debating.

"You get hurt, your father will kill me," he said.

"I won't get hurt," she pleaded.

He stood there for what felt like forever, until finally he sighed.

"I see no harm in it then," he said. "If nothing else, it will keep you silent. As long as these men have no objection," he added, turning to the soldiers.

"AYE!" called out a dozen of her father's men in unison, all enthusiastically rooting for her. Kyra loved them for it, more than she could say. She saw the admiration they held for her, the same love they reserved for her father. She did not have many friends, and these men meant the world to her.

Maltren scoffed.

"Let the girl make a fool of herself then," he said. "Might teach her a lesson once and for all."

A horn sounded, and as another man left the circle, Kyra rushed in.

Kyra felt all eyes on her as the men stared, clearly not expecting this. She found herself facing her opponent, a tall man of stocky build in his thirties, a powerful warrior she had known since her father's days at court. From having observed him, she knew him to be a good fighter—but also overconfident, charging in the beginning of each fight, a bit reckless.

He turned to Anvin, frowning.

"What insult is this?" he asked. "I shall not fight a girl."

"You insult yourself by fearing to fight me," Kyra replied, indignant. "I have two hands, and two legs, just as you. If you will not fight me, then concede defeat!"

He blinked, shocked, then scowled back.

"Very well then," he said. "Don't go running to your father after you lose."

He charged at full speed, as she knew he would, raised his wooden sword hard and high, and came straight down, aiming for her shoulder. It was a move she had anticipated, one she had seen him perform many times, one he clumsily foreshadowed by the motion of his arms. His wooden sword was powerful, but it was also heavy and clumsy next to her staff.

Kyra watched him closely, waited until the last moment, then sidestepped, allowing the powerful blow to come straight down beside her. In the same motion, she swung her staff around and whacked him in the side of his shoulder.

He groaned as he stumbled sideways. He stood there, stunned, annoyed, having to concede defeat.

"Anyone else?" Kyra asked, smiling wide, turning and facing the circle of men.

Most of them wore smiles, clearly proud of her, proud of watching her grow up and reach this point. Except, of course, Maltren, who frowned back. He looked as if he were about to challenge her when suddenly another soldier appeared, facing off with a serious expression. This man was shorter and wider, with an unkempt red beard and fierce eyes. She could tell by the way he held his sword that he was more cautious than her previous opponent. She took that as a compliment: finally, they were beginning to take her seriously.

He charged, and Kyra did not understand why, but for some reason, knowing what to do came easily to her. It was as if her instincts kicked in and took over for her. She found herself to be much lighter and more nimble than these men, with their heavy armor and thick, wooden swords. They all were fighting for power, and they all expected their foes to challenge and block them. Kyra, though, was happy to dodge them, and refused to fight on their terms. They fought for power—but she fought for speed.

Kyra's staff moved in her hand like an extension of her; she spun it so quickly her opponents had no time to react, they still in mid-swing while she was already behind them. Her new opponent came at her with a lunge to the chest—but she merely sidestepped and swung her staff up, striking his wrist and dislodging his sword from his grip. She then brought the other end around and cracked him on the head.

The horn sounded, the point hers, and he looked at her in shock, holding his forehead, his sword on the ground. Kyra, examining her handiwork, realizing she was still standing, was a bit startled herself.

Kyra had become the person to beat, and now the men, no longer hesitant, lined up to test their skills against her.

The snowstorm raged on as torches were lit against the twilight and Kyra sparred with one man after the next. No longer did they wear smiles: their expressions were now deadly serious, perplexed, then outright annoyed, as no one could touch her—and each ended up defeated by her. Against one man, she leapt over his head as he thrust, spinning and landing behind him before whacking his shoulder; for another, she ducked and rolled, switched hands with her staff and landed the decisive blow, unexpectedly, with her left hand. For each, her moves were different, part gymnast, part swordsman, so none could anticipate her. These men did a walk of shame to the sidelines, each amazed at having to admit defeat.

Soon there remained but a handful of men. Kyra stood in the center of the circle, breathing hard, turning in each direction to search for a new foe. Anvin, Vidar and Arthfael watched her from the sidelines, all with smiles across their faces, looks of admiration. If her father could not be there to witness this and be proud of her, at least these men could.

Kyra defeated yet another opponent, this one with a blow behind the knee, yet another horn sounded, and finally, with none left to face her, Maltren stepped out into the circle.

"A child's tricks," he spat, walking toward her. "You can spin a piece of wood. In battle, that will do you no good. Against a real sword, your staff would be cut in half."

"Would it, then?" she asked, bold, fearless, feeling the blood of her father flowing within her and knowing she had to confront this bully for all time, especially as all these men were watching her.

"Then why not try it?" she prodded.

Maltren blinked back at her in surprise, clearly not expecting that response. Then he narrowed his eyes.

"Why?" he shot back. "So you can run for your father's protection?"

"I need not my father's protection, nor anyone else's," she replied. "This is between you and me—whatever should happen."

Maltren looked over at Anvin, clearly uncomfortable, as if he had dug himself into a pit which he could not get out of.

Anvin stared back, equally disturbed.

"We spar with wooden swords here," he called out. "I won't have anyone get hurt under my watch—much less, our commander's daughter."

But Maltren suddenly darkened.

"The girl wants real weapons," he said, his voice firm, "then we shall give it to her. Perhaps she will learn a lesson for life."

Without waiting any further, Maltren crossed the field, drew his real sword from its scabbard, the sound ringing in the air, and stormed back. The tension became thick in the air, as all grew silent, none sure what to do.

Kyra faced Maltren , feeling her palms sweating despite the cold, despite a gust of wind that blew the torches sideways. She could feel the snow turning to ice, crunching beneath her boots, and she forced herself to focus, to concentrate, knowing this would be no ordinary bout.

Maltren let out a sharp cry, trying to intimidate her, and charged, raising his sword high, it gleaming in the torchlight. Maltren, she knew, was a different fighter than the others, more unpredictable, less honorable, a man who fought to survive rather than to win. She was surprised to find him swinging right for her chest.

Kyra ducked out of the way as the blade passed right by.

The crowd of men gasped, outraged, and Anvin, Vidar and Arthfael stepped forward.

"Maltren!" Anvin called out, furious, as if ready to stop it.

"No!" Kyra called back, staying focused on Maltren, breathing hard as he came at her again. "Let us fight!"

Maltren immediately spun around and swung again—and again and again. Each time, she dodged, or stepped back, or leapt over his swings. He was strong, but not as quick as she.

He then raised his sword high and brought it straight down, clearly expecting her to block and expecting to slash her staff in two.

But Kyra saw it coming and she instead sidestepped and swung her staff sideways, hitting his sword on the side of its blade, deflecting it while protecting her staff. In the same motion, she took advantage of the opening, and swung around and jabbed him in the solar plexus.

He gasped and dropped to one knee as a horn sounded.

There came a great cheer, all the men looking to her with pride as she stood over Maltren, the victor.

Maltren, enraged, looked up at her—and instead of conceding defeat as all the others had, he suddenly charged for her, raising his sword and swinging.

It was a move Kyra had not expected, assuming he would concede honorably. As he came for her, Kyra realized there were not many moves left at her disposal with such short notice. She could not get out of the way in time.

Kyra dove to the ground, rolled out of the way, and at the same time, spun around with her staff and struck Maltren behind the knees, sweeping his legs out from under him.

He landed on his back in the snow, his sword flying from his grip—and Kyra immediately gained her feet and stood over him, holding the tip of her staff down on his throat and pushing. At the same moment, Leo bounded over beside her and snarled over Maltren's face, inches away, his drool landing on Maltren's cheek, just waiting for the order to pounce.

Maltren looked up, blood on his lip, stunned and finally humbled.

"You dishonor my father's men," Kyra seethed, still enraged. "What do you think of my little stick now?"

A tense silence fell over them as she kept him pinned down, a part of her wanting to raise her staff and strike him, to let Leo loose on him. None of the men tried to stop it, or came to his aid.

Realizing he was isolated, Maltren looked up with real fear.

"KYRA!"

A harsh voice suddenly cut through the silence.

All eyes turned, and her father suddenly appeared, marching into the circle, wearing his furs, flanked by a dozen men and looking at her disapprovingly.

He stopped a few feet away from her, staring back, and she could already anticipate the lecture to come. As they faced each other, Maltren scrambled out from under her and scurried off, and she wondered why he did not rebuke Maltren instead of her. That angered her, leaving father and daughter looking at each other in a standoff of rage, she as stubborn as he, neither willing to budge.

Finally, her father wordlessly turned, followed by his men, and marched back towards the fort, knowing she would follow. The tension broke as all the men fell in behind him, and Kyra, reluctantly, joined. She began to trudge back through the snow, seeing the distant lights of the fort, knowing she'd be in for an earful—but no longer caring.

Whether he accepted her or not, on this day, she was accepted amongst his men—and for her, that was all that mattered. From this day forward, she knew, everything would change.

CHAPTER SIX

Kyra marched beside her father down the stone corridors of Fort Volis, a rambling fort the size of a small castle, with smooth stone walls, tapered ceilings, thick, ornate wood doors, an ancient redoubt that had served to house the Keepers of The Flames and protect Escalon for centuries. It was a crucial fort for their Kingdom, she knew, and yet it was also home to her, the only home she'd ever known. She would often fall asleep to the sound of warriors, feasting down the halls, dogs snarling as they fought over scraps, fireplaces hissing with dying embers and drafts of wind finding their way through the cracks. With all its quirks, she loved every corner of it.

As Kyra struggled to keep pace, she wondered what was troubling her father. They walked quickly, silently, Leo beside them, late for the feast, turning down corridors, soldiers and attendants stiffening as they went. Her father walked more quickly than usual, and though they were late, this, she knew, was unlike him. Usually he walked side-by-side with her, had a big smile ready to flash behind his beard, clasped an arm around her shoulder, sometimes told her jokes, recounted his day's events.

But now he walked somberly, his face set, several steps ahead of her, and he wore what appeared to be a frown of disapproval, one she had rarely seen him wear. He looked troubled, too, and she assumed it could only be from the day's events, her brothers reckless hunting, the Lord's Men snatching their boar—and perhaps even because she, Kyra, had been sparring. At first she had assumed he was just preoccupied with the feast—holiday feasts were always burdensome for him, having to host so many warriors and visitors well past midnight, as was ancient tradition. When her mother had been alive and hosting these events, Kyra had been told, it had been much easier on him. He was not a social creature, and he struggled to keep up with social graces.

But as their silence thickened, Kyra started to wonder if it was something else entirely. Most likely, she figured, it had something to do with her training with his men. Her relationship with her father, which used to be so simple, had become increasingly complicated as she grew up. He seemed to have a great ambivalence over what to do with her, over what kind of daughter he expected her to be. On the one hand, he often taught her of the principles of a warrior, of how a knight should think, should conduct herself. They had endless conversations about valor, honor, courage, and he oft stayed up late into the night recounting tales of their ancestor's battles, tales that she lived for, and the only tales she wanted to hear.

Yet at the same time, Kyra noticed him catching himself now when he discussed such things, silencing himself abruptly, as if he'd realized he shouldn't be speaking of it, as if he realized that he had fostered something within her and wanted to take it back. Talking about battle and valor was second nature to him, but now that Kyra was no longer a girl, now that she was becoming a woman, and a budding warrior herself, there was a part of him that seemed surprised by it, as if he had never expected her to grow up. He seemed to not quite know how to relate to a growing daughter, especially one who craved to be a warrior, as if he did not know which path to encourage her on. He did not know what to do with her, she realized, and a part of him even felt uncomfortable around her. Yet he was secretly proud, she sensed, at the same time. He just couldn't allow himself to show it.

Kyra could not stand his silence anymore—she had to get to the bottom of it.

"Do you worry for the feast?" she asked.

"Why should I worry?" he countered, not looking at her, a sure sign he was upset. "All is prepared. In fact, we are late. If I had not come to Fighter's Gate to find you, I would be at the head of my own table by now," he concluded resentfully.

So that was it, she realized: her sparring. The fact that he was angry made her angry, too. After all, she had beaten his men and she deserved his approval. Instead, he was acting as if nothing had happened, and if anything, was disapproving.

She demanded the truth and, annoyed, she decided to provoke him.

"Did you not see me beat your men?" she said, wanting to shame him, demanding the approval that he refused to give.

She watched his face redden, ever so subtly, but he held his tongue as they walked—which only increased her anger.

They continued to march, past the Hall of Heroes, past the Chamber of Wisdom, and were nearly at the Great Hall when she could stand it no more.

"What is it, Father?" she demanded. "If you disapprove of me, just say it."

He finally stopped right before the arched doors to the feasting hall, turned and looked at her, stone-faced. His look pained her. Her father, the one person she loved more than anyone in the world, who always had nothing but a smile for her, now looked at her as if she were a stranger. She could not understand it.

"I don't want you on those grounds again," he said, a cold anger in his voice.

The tone of his voice hurt her even more than his words, and she felt a shiver of betrayal rush through her. Coming from anyone else it would hardly have bothered her—but from him, this man she loved and looked up to so much, who was always so kind to her, his tone made her blood run cold.

But Kyra was not one to back down from a fight—a trait she had learned from him.

"And why is that?" she demanded.

His expression darkened.

"I do not need to give you a reason," he said. "I am your father. I am commander of this fort, of my men. And I do not want you training with them."

"Are you afraid I shall defeat them?" Kyra said, wanting to get a rise out of him, refusing to allow him to close this door on her forever.

He reddened, and she could see her words hurt him, too.

"Hubris is for commoners," he chided, "not for warriors."

"But I am no warrior, is that right, Father?" she goaded.

He narrowed his eyes, unable to respond.

"It is my fifteenth year. Do you wish me to fight against trees and twigs my whole life?"

"I do not wish you to fight at all," he snapped. "You are a girl—a woman now. You should be doing whatever women do—cooking, sewing—whatever it is your mother would have raised you to do if she were alive."

Now Kyra's expression darkened.

"I'm sorry I am not the girl you wish me to be, Father," she replied. "I am sorry I am not like all the other girls."

His expression became pained now, too.

"But I am my father's daughter," she continued. "I am the girl you raised. And to disapprove of me is to disapprove of yourself."

She stood there, hands on her hips, her light-gray eyes, filled with a warrior's strength, flashing back at his. He stared back at her with his brown eyes, behind his brown hair and beard, and he shook his head.

"This is a holiday," he said, "a feast not just for warriors but for visitors and dignitaries. People will be coming from all over Escalon, and from foreign lands." He looked her up and down disapprovingly. "You wear a warrior's clothes. Go to your chamber and change into a woman's fineries, like every other woman at the table."

She flushed, infuriated—and he leaned in close and raised a finger.

"And don't let me see you on the field with my men again," he seethed.

He turned abruptly, as servants opened the huge doors for him, and a wave of noise came tumbling out to greet them, along with the smell of roasting meat, unwashed hounds and roaring fires. Music carried in the air, and the din of activity from inside the hall was all-consuming. Kyra watched her father turn and enter, attendants following.

Several servants stood there, holding open the doors, waiting as Kyra stood there, fuming, debating what to do. She had never been so angry in her life.

She finally turned and stormed off with Leo, away from the hall, back for her chamber. For the first time in her life, she hated her father at that moment. She had thought he was different, above all this; yet now she realized he was a smaller man than she had thought—and that, more than anything, hurt her. His taking away from her what she loved most—the training grounds—was a knife in her heart. The thought of living her life confined to silks and dresses left her feeling a greater sense of despair than she had ever known.

She wanted to leave Volis—and never come back.

*

Commander Duncan sat at the head of the banquet table, in the massive feasting hall of fort Volis, and he looked out over his family, warriors, subjects, counselors, advisors and visitors—more than a hundred people, all stretched along the table for the holiday—with a heavy heart. Of all these people before him, the one most on his mind was the one he tried not to look at on principle: his daughter. Kyra. Duncan had always had a special relationship with her, had always felt the need to be both father and mother to her, to make up for the loss of her mother. But he was failing, he knew, at being her father—much less a mother, too.

Duncan had always made a point of watching over her, the only girl in a family of boys, and in a fort full of warriors—especially given that she was a girl unlike the other girls, a girl, he had to admit, who was too much like him. She was very much alone in a man's world, and he went out of his way for her, not only out of obligation, but also because he loved her dearly, more than he could say, perhaps even more, he hated to admit, than his boys. Because of all his children, he had to admit that he, oddly, even though she was a girl, saw himself most in her. Her willfulness; her fierce determination; her warrior's spirit; her refusal to back down; her fearlessness; and her compassion. She always stood up for the weak, especially her younger brother, and always stood up for what was just—whatever the cost.

Which was another reason why their conversation had irked him so badly, had left him in such a mood. As he had watched her on the training ground this evening, wielding her staff against those men with a remarkable, dazzling skill, his heart had leapt with pride and joy. He hated Maltren, a braggart and a thorn in his side, and he was elated that his daughter, of all people, had put him in his place. He was beyond proud that she, a girl of just fifteen, could hold her own with his men—and even beat them. He had wanted so badly to embrace her, to shower her with praise in front of all the others.

But as her father, he could not. Duncan wanted what was best for her and deep down, he felt she was going down a dangerous road, a road of violence in a man's world. She would be the only woman in a field of dangerous men, men with carnal desires, men who, when their blood was up, would fight to the death. She did not realize what true battle meant, what bloodshed, pain, death was like, up close. It was not the life he wanted for her—even if it were allowed. He wanted her safe and secure here in the fort, living a domestic life of peace and comfort. But he did not know how to make her want that for herself.

It had all left him feeling confused. By refusing to praise her, he figured, he could dissuade her. Yet deep down, he had a sinking feeling he could not—and that his withdrawal of praise would only alienate her further. He hated how he had to act tonight, and he hated how he felt right now. But he had no idea what else to do.

What upset him even more than all this, was what echoed in the back of his head: the prophecy proclaimed about her the day she was born. He had always disregarded it as nonsense, a witch's words; but today, watching her, seeing her prowess, made him realize how special she was, made him wonder if it could really be true. And that thought terrified him more than anything. Her destiny was fast approaching, and he had no way to stop it. How long would it be until everyone knew the truth about her?

Duncan closed his eyes and shook his head, taking a long swig from his sack of wine and trying to push it all from his mind. This was supposed to be a night of celebration, after all. The Winter solstice had arrived, and as he opened his eyes he saw the snow raging through the window, now a full-fledged blizzard, snow piled high against the stone, as if arriving on cue for the holiday. While the wind howled outside, they were all secure here in this fort, warm from the fires raging in the fireplaces, from the body heat, from the roasting food and from the wine.

Indeed, as he looked around, everyone looked happy—jugglers, bards and musicians made their rounds as men laughed and rejoiced, sharing battle stories. Duncan looked with appreciation at the awesome bounty before him, the banquet table covered with every sort of food and delicacy. He felt pride as he saw all the shields hanging high along the wall, each one hand-hammered with a different crest, each insignia representing a different house of his people, a different warrior who had come to fight with him. He saw all the trophies of war hanging, too, memories of a lifetime fighting for Escalon. He was a lucky man, he knew.

And yet as much as he liked to pretend otherwise, he had to face that his was a Kingdom under occupation. The old king, King Tarnis, had surrendered his people to all of their shame, had laid down arms without even a fight, allowing Pandesia to invade. It had spared casualties and cities—but it had also robbed their spirit. Tarnis had always argued that Escalon was indefensible anyway, that even if they held the Southern Gate, the Bridge of Sorrows, Pandesia could surround them and attack by sea. But they all knew that was a weak argument. Escalon was blessed with shores made of cliffs a hundred feet high, crashing waves and jagged rocks at their base. No ship could get close, and no army could breach them without a heavy price. Pandesia could attack by sea, but the price would be far too great, even for such a great empire. Land was the only way—and that left only the bottleneck of the Southern Gate, which all of Escalon knew was defensible. Surrendering had been a choice of pure weakness and nothing else.

Now he and all the other great warriors were king-less, each left to his own devices, his own province, his own stronghold, and each forced to bend the knee and answer to the Lord Governor installed by the Pandesian Empire. Duncan could still recall the day he had been forced to swear a new oath of fealty, the feeling he'd had when he was made to bend the knee—it made him sick to think of it.

Duncan tried to think back to the early days, when he had been stationed in Andros, when all the knights of all the houses had been together, rallied under one cause, one king, one capital, one banner, with a force ten times as great as the men he had here. Now they were scattered to the far corners of the Kingdom, these men here all that remained of a unified force.

King Tarnis had always been a weak king; Duncan had known that from the start. As his chief commander, he'd had the task of defending him, even if it was unmerited. A part of Duncan was not surprised the King had surrendered—but he was surprised at how quickly it had all fallen apart. All the great knights scattered to the wind, all returning to their own houses, with no king left to rule and all the power ceded to Pandesia. It had stripped lawfulness and had turned their Kingdom, once so peaceful, into a breeding ground for crime and discontent. It was no longer safe to even travel the roads, once so safe, outside of strongholds.

Hours passed, and as the meal wound down, food was taken away and mugs of ale refreshed. Duncan grabbed several chocolates and ate them, relishing them, as trays of Winter Moon delicacies were brought to the table. Mugs of royal chocolate were passed around, covered in the fresh cream of goats, and Duncan, head spinning from drink and needing to focus, took one in his hands and savored its warmth. He drank it all at once, the warmth spreading through his belly. The snow raged outside, stronger with each moment, and jesters played games, bards told stories, musicians offered interludes, and the night went on and on, all oblivious to the weather. It was a tradition on Winter Moon to feast past midnight, to welcome the winter as one would a friend. Keeping the tradition properly, as legend went, meant the winter would not last as long.

Duncan, despite himself, finally looked over and saw Kyra; she sat there, disconsolate, looking down, as if alone. She had not changed from her warrior's clothes, as he had commanded; for a moment, his anger flared up, but then he decided to let it go. He could see she was upset, too; she, like he, felt things too deeply.

Duncan decided it was time to make peace with her, to at least console her if he could not agree with her, and he was about to rise in his chair and go to her—when suddenly, the great doors of the banquet hall burst open.

A visitor hurried into the room, a small man in luxurious furs heralding another land, his hair and cloak covered in snow, and he was escorted by attendants to the banquet table. Duncan was surprised to receive a visitor this late in the night, especially in this storm, and as the man removed his cloak, Duncan noted he wore the purple and yellow of Andros. He had come, Duncan realized, all the way from the capital, a good three-day ride.

Visitors had been arriving throughout the night, but none this late, and none from Andros. Seeing those colors made Duncan think of the old king, of better days.

The room quieted as the visitor stood before his seat and bowed his head graciously to Duncan, waiting to be invited to sit.

"Forgive me, my lord," he said. "I meant to arrive sooner. The snow prevented that, I'm afraid. I mean you no disrespect."

Duncan nodded.

"I am no lord," Duncan corrected, "but a mere commander. And we are all equals here, high and low-born, men and women. All visitors are welcome, whatever hour they arrive."

The visitor nodded graciously and was about to sit, when Duncan raised a palm.

"Our tradition holds for visitors from far away be given an honored seat. Come, sit near me."

The visitor, surprised, nodded graciously and the attendants led him, a thin, short man with gaunt cheeks and eyes, perhaps in his forties but appearing much older, to a seat near Duncan. Duncan examined him and detected anxiety in his eyes; the man appeared to be too on-edge for a visitor in holiday cheer. Something, he knew, was wrong.

The visitor sat, head down, eyes averted, and as the room slowly fell back into cheer, the man gulped down the bowl of soup and chocolate put before him, slurping it down with a big piece of bread, clearly famished.

"Tell me," Duncan said as soon as the man finished, anxious to know more, "what news do you bring from the capital?"

The visitor slowly pushed away his bowl and looked down, unwilling to meet Duncan's eyes. The table quieted, seeing the grim look on his face. They all waited for him to respond.

Finally, he turned and looked at Duncan, his eyes bloodshot, watering.

"No news that any man should have to bear," he said.

Duncan braced himself, sensing as much.

"Out with it, then," Duncan said. "Bad news grows only more stale with time."

The man looked back down at the table, rubbing his fingers against it nervously.

"As of the Winter Moon, a new Pandesian law is being enacted upon our land: *puellae nuptias.*"

Duncan felt his blood curdle at the words, as a gasp of outrage emitted from up and down the table, an outrage he shared himself. *Puellae Nuptias.* It was incomprehensible.

"Are you certain?" Duncan demanded.

The visitor nodded.

"As of today, the first unwed daughter of every man, lord, and warrior in our Kingdom who has reached her fifteenth year can be claimed for marriage by the local Lord Governor—for himself, or for whomever he chooses."

Duncan immediately looked at Kyra, and he saw the look of surprise and indignation in her eyes. All the other men in the room, all the warriors, also turned and looked to Kyra, all understanding the gravity of the news. Any other girl's face would have been filled with terror, but she appeared to wear a look of vengeance.

"They shall not take her!" Anvin called out, indignant, his voice rising in the silence. "They shall not take any of our girls!"

Arthfael drew his dagger and stabbed the table with it.

"They can take our boar, but we shall fight to the death before they take our girls!"

The warriors let out a shout of approval, their anger fueled, too, by their drink. Immediately, the mood in the room had turned rotten.

Slowly Duncan stood, his meal spoiled, and the room quieted as he rose from the table. All the other warriors stood as he did, a sign of respect.

"This feast is over," he announced, his voice heavy. Even as he said the words, he noted it was not yet midnight—a terrible omen for the Winter Moon.

Duncan walked over to Kyra in the thick silence, passing rows of soldiers and dignitaries. He stood over her chair, and looked her in the eye, and she stared back, strength and defiance in her eyes, a look which filled him with pride. Leo, beside her, looked up at him, too.

"Come, my daughter," he said. "You and I have much to discuss."

CHAPTER SEVEN

Kyra sat in her father's chamber, a small stone room on the upper floors of their fort with high, tapered ceilings and a massive marble fireplace, blackened from years of use, and they each stared in the gloomy silence. They sat on opposite sides of the fire, each on a pile of furs, staring at the crumbling logs as they crackled and hissed.

Kyra's mind spun from the news as she stroked Leo's fur, curled up at her feet, and it was still hard to believe it was true. Change had finally come to Escalon, and it felt as if this were the day her life had ended. She stared into the flames, wondering what was left to live for if Pandesia would snatch her away from her family, her fort, from all she knew and loved and wed her to some grotesque Lord Governor. She would rather die.

Kyra usually took comfort in being here, this room, where she had spent countless hours reading, getting lost in tales of valor and sometimes of legends, tales which she never quite knew were fact or fantasy. Her father liked to comb his ancient books and read them aloud, sometimes into the early hours of the morning, chronicles of a different time, a different place. Most of all, Kyra loved the stories of the warriors, of the great battles. Leo was always at her feet and Aidan often joined them; on more than one sunrise, Kyra would return bleary-eyed to her chamber, drunk on the stories. She loved to read even more than she loved weapons, and as she looked at the walls of her father's chamber, lined with bookcases, filled with scrolls and leather-bound volumes passed down for generations, she wished she could get lost in them now.

But as she glanced at her father, his grim face, it brought back their awful reality. This was no night for reading. She had never seen her father look so disturbed, so conflicted, as if for the first time he was unsure what action to take. Her father, she knew, was a proud man—all of his men were proud—and in the days when Escalon had a king, a capital, a court to rally around, all would have given up their lives for their freedom. It was not her father's way to surrender, to barter. But the old King had sold them out, had surrendered on their behalf, had left them all in this terrible position. As a fragmented, dispersed army, they could not fight an enemy already lodged in their midst.

"It would have been better to have been defeated that day in battle," her father said, his voice heavy, "to have faced Pandesia nobly and lost. The old King's surrender was a defeat anyway—just a long, slow, cruel one. Day after day, year after year, one freedom after the next is taken from us, each one making us slightly less of a man."

Kyra knew he was right; yet she could also understand King Tarnis's decision: Pandesia covered half the world. With their vast army of slaves they could have laid waste to Escalon until there was nothing left. They never would have backed down, however many millions of men it took. At least now Escalon was intact, its people alive—if one could call this life.

"For them, this is not about taking our girls," her father continued, his speech punctuated by the crackling fire. "This is about power. About subjugation. About crushing what is left of our souls."

Her father stared into the flames and she could see he was staring into his past and his future all at once. Kyra prayed that he would turn and tell her that the time had come to fight, to stand up for what they all believed in, to make a stand. That he would never let her be taken away.

But instead, to her increasing disappointment and anger, he sat there silently, staring, brooding, not offering her the assurances she needed. She had no idea what he was thinking, especially after their earlier argument.

"I remember a time when I served the King," he said slowly, his deep, strong voice setting her at ease, as it always had, "when all the land was one. Escalon was invincible. We had only to man The Flames to hold back the trolls and the Southern Gate to hold back Pandesia. We were a free people for centuries, and that was always how it was supposed to be."

He fell silent for a long time, the fire crackling, and Kyra waited impatiently for him to finish, stroking Leo's head.

"If Tarnis had commanded us to defend the gate," he continued, "we would have defended it to the last man. All of us would have gladly died for our freedom. But one morning we all woke to find out

66

lands already filled with men," he said, his eyes widening with agony as if reliving it again before his eyes.

"I know all of this," Kyra reminded, impatient, tiring of hearing the same story.

He turned to her, his eyes filled with defeat.

"When your own king has given up," he asked, "when the enemy is already amongst you, what is there left to fight for?"

Kyra fumed.

"Maybe kings do not always merit the title," she said, no longer having patience. "Kings are just men, after all. And men make mistakes. Perhaps, sometimes, the most honorable route is to defy your king."

Her father sighed, staring into the fire, not really hearing her.

"We here, of Volis, have lived well compared to the rest of Escalon. They allow us to keep weapons—*real* weapons—unlike the others, who are stripped of all steel under penalty of death. They let us train, they give us the illusion of freedom—just enough to keep us complacent. Do you know why they have?" he asked, turning to her.

"Because you were the King's greatest knight," she replied. "Because they want to afford you honors befitting your rank."

He shook his head.

"No," he replied. "It is only because they need us. They need Volis to man The Flames. We are all that stands between Marda and them. Pandesia fears Marda more than we. It is only because we are the Keepers. They patrol The Flames with their own men, their own draftees, but none are as vigilant as we."

Kyra thought about that.

"I always thought we were above it all, above the reach of Pandesia. But tonight," he said gravely, turning to her, "I realize that is not true. This news…I have been waiting for something of the sort for years. I did not realize how long. And despite all those years of preparation, now that it has arrived…there is nothing I can do."

He hung his head and she stared back at him, appalled, feeling indignation welling within her.

"Are you saying you will let them take me?" she asked. "Are you saying you would not fight for me?"

His face darkened.

"You are young," he said, angry, "naïve. You don't understand the way of the world. You look at this one fight—not the greater kingdom. If I fight for you, if my men fight for you, we might win one battle. But they will come back, not with a hundred men, or a thousand, or ten thousand—but a sea of men. If I fight for you, I commit all of my people to death."

His words cut into her like a knife, left her shaking inside, not only his words, but the despair behind them. A part of her wanted to storm out of here, sickened, so disappointed in this man she had once idolized. She felt like crying inside at such betrayal.

She stood, trembling, and scowled down at him.

"*You*," she seethed, "*you*, the greatest fighter of our land—yet afraid to protect the honor of his own daughter?"

She watched his face redden, humiliated.

"Watch yourself," he warned darkly.

But Kyra would not back down.

"I *hate* you!" she shouted.

Now it was his turn to stand.

"Do you want all of our people killed?" he yelled back. "All for your honor?"

Kyra could not help herself. For the first time in as long as she could member, she burst into tears, so deeply wounded by her father's lack of caring for her.

He stepped forward to console her, but she lowered her head and turned away as she cried. Then she caught hold of herself and quickly turned and wiped her tears away, looking to the fire with watery eyes.

"Kyra," he said softly.

She looked up at him and saw that his eyes were watering, too.

"Of course I would fight for you," he said. "I would fight for you until my heart stopped beating. I, and all of my men, would die for you. In the war that followed, you would die, too. Is that what you want?"

"And my slavery?" she shot back. "Is that what *you* want?"

Kyra knew she was being selfish, that she was putting herself first, and that was not her nature. Of course she would not allow all of her people to die on her behalf. But she just wanted to hear her father say the words: *I will fight for you. Whatever the consequences. You come first. You matter most.*

68

But he remained silent, and his silence hurt her more than anything.

"*I* shall fight for you!" came a voice.

Kyra turned, surprised, to see Aidan entering the room, holding a small spear, trying to put on his bravest look.

"What are you doing here?" her father snapped. "I am speaking with your sister."

"And I overheard it!" Aidan said, marching inside, as Leo ran over to him, licking him.

Kyra could not help but smile. Aidan shared the same streak of defiance as she, even if he was too young and too small for his prowess to match his will.

"I will fight for my sister!" he added. "Even against all the trolls of Marda!"

She reached over and hugged him and kissed his forehead.

She then wiped her tears and turned back to her father, her glare darkening. She needed an answer; she needed to hear him say it.

"Do I not matter to you more than your men?" she asked him.

He stared back, his eyes filled with pain.

"You matter more to me than the world," he said. "But I am not merely a father—I am a Commander. My men are my responsibility, too. Can't you understand that?"

She frowned.

"And where is that line drawn, Father? When exactly do your people matter more than your family? If the abduction of your only daughter is not that line, then what is? I am sure if it were one of your *sons* taken, you would go to war."

He scowled.

"This is not about that," he snapped.

"But isn't it?" she shot back, determined. "Why is a boy's life worth more than a girl's?"

Her father fumed, breathing hard, and loosed his vest, more agitated than she'd ever seen him.

"There is another way," he finally said.

She stared back, puzzled.

"Tomorrow," he said slowly, his voice taking on a tone of authority, as if he were talking to his councilmen, "you shall choose a boy. Any boy you like from amongst our people. You shall wed by

69

sundown. When the Lord's Men come, you will be wed. Untouchable. You will be safe, here with us."

Kyra stared back, aghast.

"Do you really expect me to marry some strange boy?" she asked. "To just pick someone, just like that? Someone I don't love?"

"You *will!*" her father yelled, his face red, equally determined. "If your mother were alive, she would handle this business—she would have handled it long ago, before it came to this. But she is not. You are not a warrior—you are a girl. And girls wed. And that is the end of the matter. If you have not chosen a husband by day's end, I will choose one for you—and there is nothing more to say on the matter!"

Kyra stared back, disgusted, enraged—but most of all, disappointed.

"So is that how the great Commander Duncan wins battles?" she asked, wanting to hurt him. "Finding loopholes in the law to hide from his occupier?"

Kyra did not wait for a response, but turned and stormed from the room, Leo at her heels, and slammed the thick oak door behind her.

"KYRA!" her father yelled—but the slam muffled his voice.

Kyra marched down the corridor, feeling her whole world shifting beneath her, as if she were no longer walking on steady ground. She realized, with each passing step, that she could no longer stay here. That her presence would endanger them all. And that was something she could not allow.

Kyra could not fathom her father's words. She would never, *ever*, marry someone she did not love. She would never just give in and live a domestic life like all the other women. She would rather die first. Didn't he know that? Did he not know his own daughter at all?

Kyra stopped by her chamber, put on her winter boots, draped herself with her warmest furs, grabbed her bow and staff, and kept walking.

"KYRA!" her father's angry voice echoed from somewhere down the corridor.

She would not give him a chance to catch up. She kept marching, turning down corridor after corridor, determined to never see Volis again. Whatever lay out there, out in the real world, she would face it head on. She might die, she knew—but at least it would be *her* choice. At least she wouldn't live according to someone else's designs.

Kyra reached the main doors to the fort, Leo beside her, and the servants, standing there beneath the dying torches, stared back at her, puzzled.

"My lady," one said. "It is late. The storm rages."

But Kyra stood there, determined, until finally they realized she would not back down. They exchanged an unsure look, then each reached out and slowly pulled back the thick door.

The moment they did, a freezing gale of wind howled and struck her in the face, the wind carrying whipping snow. She pulled her furs tighter as she looked down and saw snow up to her shins.

Kyra stepped out into the snow, knowing it was unsafe out here at night, the woods filled with creatures, seasoned criminals, and sometimes trolls. Especially on this night of all nights, the Winter Moon, the one night of the year one was supposed to stay indoors, to bar the gates, the night when the dead crossed worlds and anything could happen. Kyra looked up and saw the huge, blood-red moon hanging on the horizon, as if tempting her.

Kyra breathed deep, took the first step and did not turn back, ready to face whatever the night had in store.

CHAPTER EIGHT

Alec sat in his father's forge, the great iron anvil before him, well-nicked from years of use, lifted his hammer and pounded on the glowing-hot steel of a sword, freshly removed from the flames. He sweated, frustrated, as he tried to hammer out his fury. Having just reached his sixteenth year, shorter than most boys his age yet stronger than them, too, with broad shoulders, already emerging muscles, and a big mat of wavy black hair that fell past his eyes, Alec was not one to give up easily. His life had been hard-forged, like this iron, and as he sat beside the flames, wiping hair from his eyes continually with the back of his hand, he brooded, contemplating the news he had just received. He had never felt such a sense of despair. He smashed the hammer again and again, and as sweat poured down his forehead and hissed on the sword, he wanted to hammer away all his troubles.

His entire life, Alec had been able to control things, to work however hard he needed to to make things right. But now, for the first time in his life, he would have to sit back and watch as injustice came to his town, to his family—and there was nothing he could do about it.

Alec hammered again and again, the metal ringing in his ears, sweat stinging his eyes and not caring. He wanted to pound this iron until there was nothing left, and as he pounded he thought not of the sword but of Pandesia. He would kill them all if he could, these invaders who were coming to take away his brother. Alec slammed the sword, imagining it was their heads, wishing he could grab fate by the hands and shape it to his will, wishing he were powerful enough to stand up to Pandesia himself.

Today, Winter Moon, was his most hated day, the day when Pandesia scoured all the villages across Escalon and rounded up all eligible boys who had reached their eighteenth year for service at The Flames. Alec, two years shy, was still safe. But his brother, Ashton, having turned eighteen last harvest season, was not. Why Ashton, of all people? He wondered. Ashton was his hero. Despite being born with a club foot, Ashton always had a smile on his face, always had a

72

cheerful disposition—more cheerful than Alec—and had always made the best of life. He was the opposite of Alec, who felt everything very deeply, who was always caught up in a storm of emotions. No matter how hard he tried to be happy, like his brother, Alec could not control his passions, and often caught himself brooding. He had been told that he took life too seriously, that he should lighten up; but for him, life was a hard, serious affair, and he simply did not know how.

Ashton, on the other hand, was calm, levelheaded and happy despite his position in life. He was also a fine blacksmith, like their father, and he was now single-handedly providing for their family, especially since their father's malady. If Ashton were taken away, their family would fall into poverty. Worse, Alec would be crushed, for he had heard the stories, and he knew that life as a draftee would mean death for his brother. With Ashton's club foot, it would be cruel and unjust for Pandesia to take him. But Pandesia was not famed for its compassion, and Alec had a sinking feeling that today could be the last day his brother lived at home.

They were not a rich family and did not live in a rich village. Their home was simple enough, a small, single-story cottage with a forge attached, in the fringes of Soli, a day's ride north of the capital and a day's ride south of Whitewood. It was a landlocked, peaceful village, in a rolling countryside, far from most things—a place most people looked over on the way to Andros. Their family had just enough bread to get through each day, no more, no less—and that was all they wished for. They used their skills to bring iron to market, and it was just enough to provide them what they needed.

Alec did not wish for much in life—but he did crave justice. He shuddered at the thought of his brother being snatched away to serve Pandesia. He had heard too many tales of what it was like to be drafted, to serve guard duty at The Flames that burned all day and all night, to become a Keeper. The Pandesian slaves who manned The Flames, Alec had heard, were hard men, slaves from across the world, draftees, criminals, and the worst of the Pandesian soldiers. Most of them were not noble Escalon warriors, not the noble Keepers of Volis. The greatest danger at The Flames, Alec had heard, was not the trolls, but your fellow Keepers. Ashton, he knew, would be unable to protect himself; he was a fine blacksmith, but not a fighter.

"ALEC!"

His mother's shrill tone cut through the air, rising even over the sound of his hammering.

Alec put down his hammer, breathing hard, not realizing how much he had worked himself up, and wiped his forehead with the back of his hand. He looked over to see his mother sticking her head disapprovingly through the door frame.

"I have been calling for ten minutes now!" she said harshly. "Dinner's past ready! We haven't much time before they arrive. We are all waiting for you. Come in at once!"

Alec snapped out of his reverie, laid down his hammer, rose reluctantly, and weaved his way through the cramped workshop. He could no longer prolong the inevitable.

He stepped back into their cottage through the open doorway, past his disapproving mother, and he stopped and looked at their dinner table, set with their finest, which wasn't much. It was a simple slab of wood and four wooden chairs, and one silver goblet had been placed in its center, the only nice thing the family owned.

Seated around the table, looking up at him, waiting, sat his brother and father, bowls of stew before them.

Ashton was tall and thin with dark features, while their father, beside him, was a large man, twice as wide as Alec, with a growing belly, a low brow, thick eyebrows, and the callused hands of a blacksmith. They resembled each other—and neither resembled Alec, who had always been told, with his unruly, wavy hair and flashing green eyes, that he looked like his mother.

Ashton looked at them and noted immediately the fear in his brother's face, the anxiety in their father's, both of them looking as if they were on a deathwatch. He felt a pit in his own stomach upon entering the room. Each had a bowl of stew set before them, and as Alec sat down across from his brother, his mother set a bowl before him, then sat down with one for herself.

Even though it was past dinner and by this time he was usually starving, Alec could barely even smell it, his stomach churning.

"I'm not hungry," he muttered, breaking the silence.

His mother gave him a sharp look.

"I care not," she snapped. "You will eat what is given you. This may well be our last meal together as a family—do not disrespect your brother."

74

Alec turned to his mother, a plain-looking woman in her fifties, her face lined from a life of hardship, and he saw the determination in her green eyes flashing back at him, the same determined look he wore himself.

"Shall we just pretend then that nothing is happening?" he asked.

"He is our son, too," she snapped. "You are not the only one here."

Alec turned to his father, feeling a sense of desperation.

"Will you let it happen, Father?" he asked.

His father frowned but remained silent.

"You're ruining a lovely meal," his mother said.

His father raised his hand, and she fell silent. He turned to Alec and gave him a look.

"What would you have me do?" he asked, his voice serious.

"We have weapons!" Alec insisted, hoping for a question such as this. "We have steel! We are one of the few that do! We can kill any soldier that comes near him! They'll never expect it!"

His father shook his head disapprovingly.

"Those are the dreams of a young man," he said. "You, who have never killed a man in your life. Let's pretend you kill the soldier that grabs Ashton—and what of the two hundred behind him?"

"Let us hide Ashton, then!" Alec insisted.

His father shook his head.

"They have a list of every boy in this village. They know he's here. If we don't turn him over, they will kill each and every one of us." He sighed, annoyed. "Do you not think I haven't thought through these things, boy? Do you think you're the only one who cares? Do you think I want my only son to be shipped off?"

Alec paused, puzzled by his words.

"What do you mean, *only* son?" he asked.

His father flushed.

"I did not say *only*—I said *eldest*."

"No, you said *only*," Alec insisted, wondering.

His father reddened and raised his voice.

"Stop harping on points!" he shouted. "Not at a time like this. I said *eldest* and that's what I meant and that's the end of it! I do not want my boy taken, just as much as you don't want your brother taken!"

"Alec, relax," came a compassionate voice, the only calm one in the room.

Alec looked across the table to see Ashton smiling back at him, even-keeled, well composed as always.

"It will be fine, my brother," Ashton said. "I shall serve my duty and I shall return."

"Return?" Alec repeated. "They take Keepers for seven years."

Ashton smiled.

"Then I shall see you in seven years," he replied, and smiled wide. "I suspect you shall be taller than me by then."

That was Ashton, always trying to make Alec feel better, always thinking of others, even in a time like this.

Alec felt his heart breaking inside.

"Ashton, you can't go," he insisted. "You won't survive The Flames."

"I—" Ashton began.

But his words were interrupted by a great commotion outside. There came the sound of horses charging into the village, of men clamoring. The whole family looked at each other, in fear. They sat there, frozen, as people began rushing to and fro outside the window. Alec could already see all the boys and families lining up outside.

"No sense prolonging it now," his father said, standing, placing his palms on the table, his voice breaking the silence. "We should not suffer the indignity of their coming into our house and dragging him off. We shall line up outside with the others and stand proudly, and let us pray that when they see Ashton's foot, they shall do the humane thing and skip him over."

Alec rose reluctantly from the table as the others all shuffled outside the house.

As he stepped outside into the cold night, Alec was struck at the sight: there was a commotion in his village like never before. The streets were aglow with torches, and all boys over eighteen were lined up, all their families standing by nervously, watching. Clouds of dust filled the streets as a caravan of Pandesians charged into town, dozens of soldiers in the scarlet armor of Pandesia, riding chariots driven by large stallions. Behind them they towed carriages made of iron bars, jolting roughly on the road.

Alec examined the carriages and saw they were filled with boys from across the land, staring out with scared and hardened faces. He gulped at the sight, imagining what lay in store for his brother.

They all came to a stop in the village, and a tense silence fell, as everyone waited, breathless.

The commander of the Pandesian soldiers jumped down from his carriage, a tall soldier with no kindness in his black eyes and a long scar across one eyebrow. He walked slowly, surveying the ranks of boys, the town so quiet that one could hear his spurs jingling as he went.

The soldier looked over each boy, lifting their chins and looking them in the eyes, poking their shoulders, giving each a small shove to test their balance. He nodded as he went, and as he did, his soldiers in waiting quickly grabbed the boys and dragged them to the cart. Some boys went silently; some protested, though, and these were quickly beat down by clubs and thrown into the carriage with the others. Sometimes a mother cried or a father yelled out—but nothing could stop the Pandesians.

The commander continued, emptying the village of its most prized assets, until finally he came to a stop before Ashton, at the end of the line.

"My son is lame," their mother quickly called out, pleading desperately. "He'd be useless to you."

The soldier looked Ashton up and down, and stopped at his foot.

"Roll up your pants," he said, "and take off your boot."

Ashton did so, leaning on Alec for balance, and as Alec watched him, he knew his brother well enough to know he was humiliated; his foot had always been a source of shame for him, smaller than the other, twisted and mangled, forcing him to hobble as he walked.

"He also works for me in the forge," Alec's father chimed in. "He is our only source of income. If you take him, our family will have nothing. We won't be able to survive."

The commander, finished looking at his foot, gestured for Ashton to put his boot back on. He then turned and looked at their father, his black eyes cold and firm.

"You live in our land now," he said, his voice like gravel, "and your son is our property to do with as we wish. Take him away!" the commander called out, and as he did, soldiers rushed forward.

"NO!" Alec's mother cried out in grief. "NOT MY SON!"

She rushed forward and grabbed Ashton, clinging to him, and as she did, a Pandesian soldier stepped forward and backhanded her across the face.

Alec's father grabbed the soldier's arm and as he did several soldiers pounced and pummeled him to the ground.

As Alec stood there, watching the soldiers drag Ashton away, he could stand it no more. The injustice of it all killed him—he knew he would be unable to live with it for the rest of his days. The image of his brother being dragged away would be imprinted in his mind forever.

Something within him snapped.

"Take me instead!" Alec found himself crying out, involuntarily rushing forward and standing between Alec and the soldiers.

They all stopped and looked at him, clearly caught off guard.

"We are brothers of the same family!" Alec continued. "The law says to take one boy from each family. Let me be that boy!"

The commander came and looked him over warily.

"And how old are you, boy?" he demanded.

"I've passed my sixteenth year!" he exclaimed proudly.

The soldiers laughed, while their commander sneered.

"You're too young for drafting," he concluded, dismissing him.

But as he turned to go, Alec rushed forward, refusing to be dismissed.

"I am a greater soldier than he!" Alec insisted. "I can throw a spear further and cut deeper with a sword. My aim is truer, and I am stronger than boys twice my age. *Please*," he pleaded. "Give me a chance."

As the commander stared back, Alec, despite his feigned confidence, was terrified inside. He knew he took a great risk: he could easily be imprisoned or killed for this.

The commander stared him down for what felt like an eternity, the entire village silent, until finally, he nodded back at his men.

"Leave the cripple," he commanded. "Take the boy."

The soldiers shoved Ashton, reached forward and grabbed Alec, and within moments, Alec felt himself being dragged away. It all happened so quickly, it was surreal.

"NO!" cried Alec's mother.

He saw her weeping as he felt himself being dragged and then tossed roughly into the iron carriage full of boys.

"No!" Ashton cried out. "Leave my brother alone! Take me!"

But there was no more listening. Alec was shoved deep inside the carriage, which stank of body odor and fear, stumbling over other boys who shoved him back rudely, and the iron door was slammed behind him, echoing. Alec felt a great sense of relief at having saved his brother's life, greater even than his fear. He had given his life up for his brother's—and whatever should come next would matter little next to that.

As he sat on the floor and settled back against the iron bars, the carriage already moving beneath him, he knew that he probably would not survive this. He met the angry eyes of the other boys, summing him up in the blackness, and as they jolted along the road, he knew that on the journey to come, there would be a million ways to die. He wondered which would be his. Singed by The Flames? Stabbed by a boy? Eaten by a troll?

Or would the least likely thing of all happen: would he somehow, against all odds, survive?

CHAPTER NINE

Kyra hiked through the blinding snow, Leo leaning against her leg, the feel of his body the only thing grounding her in a sea of white. Snow whipping in her face, she could see hardly more than a few feet, the only light that from the blood-red moon, glowing eerily against the clouds when they did not consume the moon completely. The cold bit her to the bone, and only hours from home, she already missed the warmth of her father's fort. She imagined sitting by the fireplace now, in a pile of furs, drinking melted chocolate and lost in a book.

Kyra forced those thoughts from her mind and instead doubled her efforts, determined. She would get away from the life her father had carved out from her, whatever the cost. She would not be forced to marry a man she did not know or love, especially to appease Pandesia. She would not be ordered to a life by a hearth, would not be forced to give up on her dreams. She would rather die out here in the cold and the snow than live a life that other people had planned for her.

Kyra trekked on, wading through snow up to her knees, heading deeper into the black night, in the worst weather she had ever been in. It felt surreal. She could feel a special energy in the air on this night, when the dead were said to share the earth with the living, when others feared to leave their homes, when villagers boarded windows and doors, even in the best of weather. The air felt thick, and not only with snow: she could feel the spirits all around her. It felt as if they were watching her, as if she were walking into her destiny—or to her death.

Kyra crested a hill and caught a glimpse of the horizon, and for the first time in this trek, she was filled with hope. There, in the distance, lighting the sky despite the storm, sat The Flames, the only beacon in a world of white. In this black night they summoned her like a magnet, this place which she had wondered about her entire life and which her father had strictly forbidden her to go. She was surprised she had hiked this far, and she wondered if she had been unconsciously marching towards it since she'd set out.

Kyra stopped, gasping for breath, and took it in. The Flames. The great wall of fire that stretched fifty miles across the eastern border of Escalon, the only thing blocking her country from the vast lands of Marda, the kingdom of the trolls. The place where her father and his father before him had served dutifully, protecting their homeland, where all of her father's men, all of the Keepers, went to serve their duty in rotation.

They were higher, brighter, than she had imagined—all the men had boasted of and more—and she wondered what magical force kept them lit, how they could burn all day and night, if they would ever burn out. Seeing them in person only raised more questions than it answered.

Kyra knew thousands of men were stationed along The Flames, all sorts of men, the professionals from Volis, but also Pandesians, slaves, draftees, and criminals. All of them, technically, were Keepers, though none of the others had the skill her father's people had, having manned The Flames for generations. On the other side lurked thousands of trolls, desperate to break through. It was a dangerous place. A mystical place. A place for the desperate, the bold, and the fearless.

Kyra had to see it, up close. If nothing else, she needed to get her bearings in this storm, to warm her hands, and to decide where to go next.

Kyra hiked downhill through the snow, using her staff to steady herself, Leo beside her, marching for The Flames. Though it could hardly have been a mile away, it felt like ten, and what should have been a ten-minute hike took her over an hour as the snow worsened, the cold biting her to the bone. She turned and looked back for Volis, but it was long gone, lost in a world of white. She was too cold to make it back anyway.

Legs trembling from the cold, her toes growing numb, her hand stuck to the staff, Kyra finally stumbled down the hill and felt a sudden burst of heat as The Flames spread out before her. The sight took her breath away. Hardly a hundred yards away, the light was so bright that it lit up the entire night, making it feel like day, and The Flames rose so high, when she looked up, she could not see the end. The heat was so strong that even from here it warmed her, her body slowing coming back to life as she felt her hands and toes again. The crackling and hissing noise of the fire was so intense, it drowned out even the howl of the wind.

Mesmerized, Kyra came closer, feeling more and more warmth, as if walking towards the surface of the sun. She felt herself thaw as she approached, began to feel her toes and fingers again, tingling as the feeling came back. It was like standing before a huge fireplace, and she felt it bring her back to life. She stood before it, hypnotized, like a moth to a flame, staring at this wonder of the world, the greatest wonder in their land, the one thing keeping them safe—and the one thing no one understood. Not the historians, not the kings, and not even the sorcerers. When had it begun? What kept it going? When would it end?

It was said the Watchers knew the answers. But they, of course, would never reveal them. Legend had it the Sword of Fire, closely guarded in one of the two towers—no one knew which—kept The Flames alive. The Towers, guarded by a cult-like group of men, the Watchers, an ancient order, part man, part something else, were each well-hidden and guarded on two opposite ends of Escalon, one on the far western shore, in Ur, and the other in the southeastern corner of Kos. The Watchers were joined, too, by the finest knights the kingdom had to offer, all intent on keeping the Sword of Fire hidden and The Flames alive.

More than one troll, her father had told her, who breached The Flames had tried to find the towers, to steal the Sword—but none had ever been successful. The Watchers were too good at what they did. After all, even Pandesia, with all its might, dared not try to occupy the Towers, dared not risk angering the Watchers and lowering The Flames.

Kyra detected motion, and in the distance spotted soldiers on patrol, carrying torches in the night, pacing along The Flames, swords at their hips. They were spread out every fifty yards or so, with such vast territory to cover. Her heart beat faster as she watched them. She had really made it.

Kyra stood there, feeling alive, knowing anything could happen at any time. At any moment, a troll could burst through those flames, she knew. Of course, the fire killed most of them, but some, using shields, managed to burst through and live, at least long enough to kill as many soldiers as they could. Sometimes a troll even survived the passage and roamed the woods and terrorized villages. She remembered once when one of her father's men brought back a troll's head; it was a sight she would never forget.

As Kyra stared into The Flames, so mysterious, she wondered at her own fate, so far from home. What would become of her now?

"Hey, what are you doing here?" shouted a voice.

A soldier, one of her father's men, had spotted her, and was walking towards her.

Kyra did not want a confrontation. She was warm again, her spirits restored, and it was time to move on.

She whistled to Leo, and the two of them turned and headed back into the storm, towards the distant wood. She did not know where she would go next, but, inspired by The Flames, she knew that her destiny lay out there somewhere, even if she could not see it yet.

*

Kyra stumbled through the night, chilled to the bone, glad Leo was with her and wondering how much longer she could go on. She had searched everywhere for shelter, for escape from the biting wind and snow, and despite the risks, she had found herself gravitating toward the Wood of Thorns, the only place in sight. The Flames were far behind her by now, their glow no longer visible on the horizon, and the blood-moon had long ago been swallowed by the clouds, leaving her no light to see by. Fingers and toes numb again, her situation seemed to grow more dire by the moment. She began to wonder if it had been foolish to leave the fort at all. She wondered if her father, willing to give her away, would even care.

Kyra felt a fresh burst of anger as she continued through the snow, marching she was not sure where, but determined to get away from the life waiting for her. As another gale of wind passed and Leo whined, Kyra looked up and was surprised to see she had made it: before her lay the towering Wood of Thorns.

Kyra paused, feeling apprehensive, knowing how dangerous it was—even in the day, even in a group. To come here alone, and at night—and on Winter Moon, when spirits roamed—would be reckless. Anything, she knew, could happen.

But another gale whipped through, sending snow down the back of her neck and chilling her to the bone, and it drove Kyra forward, past the first tree, its branches heavy with snow, and into the wood.

As she entered, Kyra immediately felt relief. The thick branches sheltered her from the wind, and it was quieter in here. The raging snow was but a flurry in here, its fall broken by the thick branches, and for the first time since being outside, Kyra could see again. Even Already, she felt warmer.

Kyra used the opportunity to shake the snow off her arms and shoulders and hair, while Leo shook himself, too, snow flying everywhere. She reached into her sack and pulled out a piece of dried meat for him, and he snatched it eagerly as she stroked his head.

"Don't worry, I'll find us shelter, my friend," she said.

Kyra continued deeper into the wood, looking for any shelter she could find, realizing she'd need to stay the night here to wait out the storm, wake to a new day, and continue her trek in the morning. She searched for a boulder to take shelter against, or the nook of a tree, or ideally a cave—anything—but found none.

Kyra trekked deeper, snow up to her knees, brushing against snowy branches in the thick wood; as she went, strange animal noises cried out all around her. She heard a deep purring noise beside her and she spun and peered into the thick branches—but it was too dark to see anything. Kyra hurried on, not wanting to contemplate what beasts might be lurking here, and in no mood for a confrontation. She clutched her bow tightly, unsure if she could even use it, given how numb her hands were.

Kyra ascended a gentle slope and as she crested it, she stopped and looked out, afforded a view down below as moonlight momentarily shone through an opening in the trees. Down below, before her, sat a glistening lake, its waters ice-blue, translucent, and she recognized it immediately: the Lake of Dreams. Her father had brought her here once, when she was a child, and they had lit a candle and placed it on a lily pad, in honor of her mother. This lake was rumored to be a sacred place, a vast mirror that allowed one to look into both life above and life below. It was a mystical place, a place you did not come without good reason, a place where heartfelt wishes could not be ignored.

Kyra hiked for the lake, feeling drawn to it. She stumbled down the steep hill, using her staff to steady herself, weaving between trees, slipping and steadying herself, until she reached its shore. Oddly enough, its shore, made of a fine white sand, was free of snow. It was magical.

Kyra knelt by the water's edge, shivering from the cold, and looked down. In the moonlight, she saw her reflection, her blonde hair falling by her cheeks, her light gray eyes, her high cheekbones, her delicate features, looking nothing like her father or brothers, staring back at her. In her eyes, she was surprised to see a look of defiance, the eyes of a warrior.

As she looked at her reflection, she recalled her father's words from so many years ago: *a heartfelt prayer at the Lake of Dreams cannot be refused.*

Kyra, at a crossroads in her life as never before, needed guidance now more than ever. She had never felt more confused as to what to do, where to go, next. She closed her eyes and prayed with all her might.

God, I don't know who you are. But I ask your help. Give me something, and I shall give you whatever you ask in return. Show me which path to take. Give me a life of honor and courage. Of valor. Allow me to become a great warrior, to be at the mercy of no man. Allow me to have the freedom to do as I choose—not as someone else would choose for me.

Kyra knelt there, numb to the cold, at her wits' end, with nowhere left to turn in the world, praying with all her heart and all her soul. She lost all sense of time and place.

Kyra had no idea how much time had passed when she opened her eyes, snowflakes on her eyelids. She felt changed somehow, she did not know how, as if an inner peace had settled over her. She looked down into the lake, and this time, what she saw took her breath away.

Staring back up at her she did not see her own reflection—but the reflection of a dragon. It had fierce, glowing yellow eyes, and ancient red scales, and she felt her blood run cold as it opened its mouth and roared at her.

Kyra, startled, wheeled, expecting to see a dragon standing over her. She looked everywhere, but saw nothing.

It was only her, and Leo, who whined softly.

Kyra turned and looked down at the lake again, and this time, saw only her face staring back.

Her heart slammed in her chest. Had it been some trick of the light? Of her own imagination? Of course, it could not have been possible—dragons had not visited Escalon in a thousand years. Was she losing her mind? What could this all mean?

Kyra flinched as she suddenly heard a terrifying noise from far off in the woods, something like a howl, or possibly a cackle. Leo heard it, as he turned and snarled, his hair rising. Kyra searched the woods and in the distance saw a faint glow from behind the tree line. It was as if there were a fire—but there was no fire. Only an eerie, white glow.

Kyra felt the hair rise on the back of her neck as she felt as if another world were beckoning her. She felt as if she had opened a portal to the other world. As much as every part of her screamed to turn and run, she found herself mesmerized, found her body acting for her as she got up and began to make her way inextricably toward the light.

Kyra hiked up the hill with Leo, the glow getting brighter as she weaved between the trees. Finally she reached the ridge, and as she did, she stopped short, aghast. Before her, in a small clearing, was a sight she could have never expected—and one she would never forget.

An old woman, face whiter than the snow, grotesque, covered in warts and scars, stared down at what appeared to be a fire below her, holding her wrinkled hands to it. But the fire burned a bright white, and there were no logs beneath it. She looked up at Kyra with ice-blue eyes, eyes with no whites, all color, and no pupils. It was the scariest thing Kyra had ever seen, and her heart froze within her. Everything within her told her to turn and run, but she could not help herself as she stepped closer.

"The Winter Moon," the old lady said, her voice unnaturally deep, as if a bullfrog had spoken. "When the dead are not quite alive and the alive not quite dead."

"And which are you?" Kyra asked, stepping forward.

The woman cackled, a horrific sound that sent a chill up her spine. Beside her, Leo snarled.

"The question is," the woman said, "which are *you*?"

Kyra frowned.

86

"I am alive," she insisted.

"Are you? In my eyes, you are more dead than me."

Kyra wondered what she meant, and she sensed it was a rebuke, a rebuke for not going forth boldly and following her own heart.

"What is it you seek, brave warrior?" the woman asked

Kyra's heart quickened at the term, and she felt emboldened.

"I want a bigger life," she said. "I want to be a warrior. Like my father."

The old woman looked back down into the light, and Kyra was relieved to have her eyes off of her. A long silence fell over them as Kyra waited, wondering.

Finally, as the silence stretched forever, Kyra's heart fell in disappointment. Perhaps the woman would not respond. Or perhaps her wish was not possible.

"Can you help me?" Kyra asked, finally. "Can you change my destiny?"

The women looked back up, her eyes aglow, intense, scary.

"You've picked a night when all things are possible," she replied slowly. "If you want something badly enough, you can have it. The question is: what are you willing to sacrifice for it?"

Kyra thought, her heart pounding with the possibilities.

"I will give anything," she said. "*Anything*."

There came another long silence as the wind howled. Leo began to whine.

"We are each born with a destiny," the old woman finally said. "Yet we must also choose it for ourselves. Fate and free-will, they perform a dance, your whole life long. There is a constant tug of war between the two. Which side wins…well, that depends."

"Depends on what?" Kyra asked.

"Your force of will. How desperately you want something—and how graced you are by God. And perhaps most of all, what you are willing to give up."

"I will sacrifice," Kyra said, feeling the strength rising up within her. "I will sacrifice *everything* not to live the life that others have chosen for me."

In the long silence that followed, the woman stared into her eyes with such an intensity, Kyra nearly had to turn away.

"Vow to me," the old woman said. "On this night, vow to me that you will pay the price."

Kyra stepped forward solemnly, her heart pounding, feeling her life was about to change.

"I *vow*," she proclaimed, meaning it more than any words she had uttered in her life.

The certainty of her tone cut through the air, her voice carrying an authority which surprised even her.

The old woman looked at her, and for the first time, she nodded, as her face morphed into what appeared to be a look of respect.

"You will be a warrior—and more," the woman proclaimed loudly, raising her palms out to her side, her voice booming, louder and louder as she continued. "You will be the greatest of all warriors. Greater than your father. More than this, you will be a great ruler. You will achieve power beyond what you could dream. Entire nations will look to you."

Kyra's heart was slamming in her chest as she listened to the woman's proclamation, spoken with such authority, as if it had already happened.

"Yet you will also be tempted by darkness," the woman continued. "There will be a great struggle within you, darkness battling light. If you can defeat yourself, then the world will be yours."

Kyra stood there, reeling, hardly believing it all. How was it possible? Surely, she must have the wrong person. No one had ever told her she would be important, that she would be anything special. It all seemed so foreign to her, so unattainable.

"How?" Kyra asked. "How is this possible? I am but a girl."

The woman smiled, an awful, evil smile that Kyra would remember for the rest of her life. She stepped in close, so close that Kyra shook with fear.

"Sometimes," the old woman grinned, "your fate is waiting for you just around the corner, with your very next breath."

There came a sudden flash of light, and Kyra shielded her eyes as Leo snarled and pounced for the old woman.

When Kyra opened her eyes, the light was gone. The woman was gone, Leo leaping at thin air. The forest clearing held nothing but blackness.

Kyra looked everywhere, baffled. Had she imagined the whole thing?

Suddenly, as if to answer her thoughts, there came a horrific, primordial shriek, as if the heavens themselves had cried out. Kyra stood there, frozen in place, and she thought of the lake. Of her reflection

Because, although she had never set eyes upon one, she knew, she just *knew* that was the shriek of a dragon. That it was waiting for her, just beyond the clearing.

Standing there alone, the woman gone, Kyra felt herself reeling as she tried to process what just happened, what it all could mean. Most of all, she tried to understand that noise. It was a roar, a sound unlike any she had ever heard, so primal, as if the earth were being born. It at once terrified her and drew her in, leaving her no place else to go. It resonated through her in a way she could not understand, and she realized it was a sound she had been hearing somewhere in the back of her head her entire life.

Kyra tore through the woods, Leo beside her, stumbling knee-deep in the snow, branches snapping her in the face and she not caring, feeling an urgency to reach it. For as it screeched again, Kyra knew it was a sound of distress.

The dragon, she knew, was dying—and it desperately needed her help.

CHAPTER TEN

Merk stood in the forest clearing, one man dead at his feet, and stared back at the seven other thieves, who gaped back. They now had a look of respect—and fear—in their eyes, clearly realizing they had made a mistake in taking him for just another vulnerable traveler.

"I'm tired of killing," Merk said to them calmly, a smile on his face, "so today is your lucky day. You have one chance to turn and run."

A long, tense silence fell over them as they all looked to each other, clearly debating what to do.

"That's our friend you killed," one seethed.

"Your *ex*-friend," Merk corrected. "And if you keep talking, it will be you, too."

The thief scowled and raised his club.

"There are still seven of us and one of you. Lay that knife down real slow and raise your hands, and maybe we won't cut you to pieces."

Merk smiled wider. He was tired, he realized, of resisting the urge to kill, of resisting who he was. It was so much easier just to stop fighting it, to become the old killer he was.

"You had your warning," he said, shaking his head.

The thief charged, raising his club high and swinging wildly.

Merk was surprised. For a big man, he swung quicker than he would have imagined. Yet he was clumsy, and Merk merely ducked, stabbed him in the gut, and stepped aside, letting him fall face-first into the dirt.

Another thief charged, raising his dagger, aiming for Merk's shoulder, and Merk grabbed his wrist, re-directed it, and plunged the man's own dagger into his heart.

Merk saw a thief raise a bow and take aim, and he quickly grabbed another thief charging him, spun him around, and used him as a human shield. His hostage cried out as the arrow pierced his chest instead.

Merk then shoved the dying man forward, right into the one with the bow, blocking his shot, then raised his dagger and threw it. It spun end over end, crossing the clearing until it impaled in the man's neck, killing him.

That left three of them, and they now looked back at Merk with uncertain faces, as if debating whether to charge or run.

"There are three us and one of him!" one called out. "Let's charge together!"

They all charged him at once, and Merk stood there, waiting patiently, relaxed. He was unarmed, and that was how he wanted it; often, he found, the best way to defeat foes, especially when outnumbered, was to use their weapons against them.

Merk waited for the first one to slash at him, an oaf of a boy who charged clumsily with a sword, all power and no technique. Merk stepped aside, grabbed the boy's wrist, snapped it, then disarmed him and sliced his throat. As the second attacker came, Merk spun backwards and slashed him across the chest. He then turned and faced the third thief and threw the sword—a move the man did not expect. It spun end over end and entered the man's chest, sending him flat on his back.

Merk stood there, looking around at the eight dead men, taking stock of his work with a professional assassin's eye. As he did he noticed one of them—the one with the club—was still alive, squirming on his stomach. The old Merk took over, and he could not help himself as he walked over to the man, still unsatisfied. *Leave no enemies alive. Ever. Never let them see your face.*

Merk walked casually over to the thief, reached out with his boot, and kicked him over, until he lay on his back. The thief looked up, bleeding from his mouth, eyes filled with fear.

"Please…don't do it," he begged. "I would have let you go."

Merk smiled.

"Would you?" he asked. "Was that before you tortured me, or after?"

"Please!" the man called out, starting to cry. "You said you had renounced violence!"

Merk leaned back and thought about that.

"You're right," he said.

The man blinked up at him, hope in his eyes.

"I have," Merk added. "But the thing is, you stirred something up in me today, something I would have quite rather suppressed."

"Please!" the man shrieked, sobbing.

"I wonder," Merk said, reflective, "how many innocent women, children, you have killed on this road?"

The man continued to sob.

"ANSWER ME!" Merk yelled.

"What does it matter?" the man called back, between sobs.

Merk lowered the tip of his sword to the man's throat.

"It matters to me," Merk said, "a great deal."

"Okay, okay!" he called out. "I don't know. Dozens? Hundreds? It is what I have been doing my whole life."

Merk thought about that; at least it was an honest response.

"I myself have killed many men in my lifetime," Merk said. "Not all I am proud of—but all for a cause, a purpose. Sometimes I was duped into killing an innocent—but in that case, I always killed the person who hired me. I never killed women, and I never killed children. I never preyed on the innocent, or the defenseless. I never robbed and I never cheated. I guess that makes me something of a saint," Merk said, smiling at his own humor.

He sighed.

"But *you*," he continued, "you are scum."

"Please!" the man shouted. "You can't kill an unarmed man!"

Merk thought about that.

"You're right," he said, and looked about. "See that sword lying next to you? Grab it."

The man looked over, fear in his eyes.

"No," he cried, trembling.

"Grab it," Merk said, pushing the tip of his sword to the man's throat, "or I will kill you."

The thief finally reached over, grabbed the hilt of the sword, and held it with trembling hands.

"You can't kill me!" the man shouted again. "You vowed to never kill again!"

Merk smiled wide, and in one quick motion, he plunged his sword into the man's chest.

"The nice thing about starting over," Merk said, "is that there's always tomorrow."

CHAPTER ELEVEN

Kyra raced through the snow, brushing back the thick branches in her way, the dragon's cry still echoing in her ears, and burst into a clearing, when she suddenly stopped short. All of her anticipation could not prepare her for what she saw before her.

Her breath was taken away—not by the blizzard or the cold or the wind—but this time by the sight, unlike anything she'd seen in her life. She had heard the tales, night after night in her father's chamber, the ancient legends of dragons, and had wondered if they were true. She had tried to imagine them in her mind's eye, had stayed up many a sleepless night trying visualize, and yet still she could not believe it was true.

Not until now.

For before her, hardly twenty feet away, Kyra was stunned to find herself standing face to face with a real, breathing dragon. It was terrifying—yet magnificent. It screeched as it lay on its side, trying to get up but unable, one wing flapping and the other appearing to be broken. It was huge, massive, each of its scarlet-red scales the size of her. Krya noticed the dozens of flattened trees, and realized it must have fallen from the sky, creating this clearing. It lay on a steep snow bank, close to a gushing river.

As she stared, agape, Kyra tried to process the sight before her. A dragon. Here, in Escalon. In Volis, in the Wood of Thorns. It wasn't possible. Dragons, she knew, lived on the other side of the world, and never in her life, or her father's time, or her father's father's time, had one been spotted in Escalon—much less near Volis. It made no sense.

She blinked several times and rubbed her eyes, thinking it must be an illusion.

And yet there it was, shrieking again, digging its claws in the snow, stained red with its blood. It was definitely wounded. And it was definitely a dragon.

Kyra knew she should turn and flee, and a part of her wanted to; after all, this dragon could surely kill her with a single breath, much less a stroke of its claws. She had heard tales of the damage a dragon could do, of their hatred for mankind, of their ability to tear a person to shreds in the blink of an eye, or wipe out an entire village with a single breath.

But something within Kyra made her hold her ground. She did not know if it was courage or foolishness or her own desperation—or something deeper. For deep down, as crazy as it was, she felt a primal connection to this creature she could not understand.

It blinked, slowly, staring back at her with equal surprise and as it did, what terrified Kyra most were not its fangs or its claws or its size—but its eyes. They were huge, glowing yellow orbs, so fierce, so ancient, so soulful and they looked right into hers. The hair raised on her arms as she realized they were the exact eyes she had seen in her own reflection in the Lake of Dreams.

Kyra braced herself, expecting to be killed—but the dragon did not breathe fire. Instead, it just stared at her. It was bleeding, its blood running down the snow bank into the river, and it pained Kyra to see it. She wanted to help it, and even more so, she was obliged to. Every clan in the kingdom had an oath they lived by, a sacred family law they had to uphold, at the risk of bringing a curse on their family. Her family's law, passed down for generations, was to never kill a wounded animal—indeed, it was the very insignia of her father's house: a knight holding a wolf. Her family had taken it further over the generations, taking it upon themselves as a law to help any wounded animal they encountered.

As Kyra watched its labored breathing, gasping, her heart went out to it and she thought of her family's obligation. She knew that to turn her back on it would bring a terrible curse upon her family, and she was determined to make it well again, whatever the risk.

As Kyra stood there, transfixed, unable to move, she realized she could not walk away for another reason: she felt a stronger connection to this beast than she had to any animal she had ever encountered, more so even than to Leo, who was like a brother to her. She felt as if she had just been reunited with a long-lost friend. She could sense the dragon's tremendous power and pride and fierceness, and just being around it inspired her. It made her feel as if the world were so much bigger.

As Kyra stood at the edge of the clearing, debating what action to take, she was startled by the snap of a branch, followed by laughter—a cruel man's laughter. As she watched, she was shocked to see a soldier, dressed in the scarlet armor and important furs of the Lord's Men, saunter into the clearing, wielding a spear and standing over the dragon.

Kyra flinched as the soldier suddenly jabbed the dragon in its ribcage, making it shriek and curl up; she felt as if she had been stabbed herself. Clearly the soldier was taking advantage of this wounded beast, preparing to kill it but torturing it first. The thought pained Kyra to no end.

"My ax, boy!" the soldier yelled.

A boy, perhaps thirteen, warily entered the clearing, leading a horse. He looked like a squire, and he seemed terrified as he approached, eyeing the dragon warily. He did as commanded and drew a long ax from the saddle and placed it in his master's hand.

Kyra watched with a sense of dread as the soldier came closer, the blade glistening in the moonlight.

"I'd say this will make a fine trophy," he said, clearly proud of himself. "They will sing songs of me for generations, this kill of all kills."

"But you did not kill it!" the squire protested. "You discovered it wounded!"

The soldier turned and raised the blade to the boy's throat threateningly.

"I *killed* it, boy, do you understand?"

The boy gulped, and slowly nodded.

The soldier turned back to the beast, raised his ax, and studied the dragon's exposed neck. The dragon struggled to get away, to lift itself up, but it was helpless.

The dragon suddenly turned and looked directly at Kyra, as if remembering her, its yellow eyes aglow, and she could feel it pleading to her.

Kyra could hold herself back no longer.

"NO!" she cried.

Without thinking, Kyra ran into the clearing, rushing down the slope, slipping in the snow, Leo at her side. She did not stop to consider that confronting a Lord's Man was a crime punishable by death, or that she was alone out here, exposed, that her actions could likely get her killed. She thought only of saving the dragon's life, of protecting what was innocent.

As she rushed forward, she instinctively pulled the bow from her shoulder, placed an arrow, and aimed for the Lord's Man.

The soldier looked truly stunned to see another person out here, in the middle of nowhere—much less a girl, and holding a bow at him. He stood holding his ax, frozen in midair, then slowly lowered it as he turned and faced her.

Kyra's arms shook as she held the bowstring and aimed at the man's chest, not wanting to fire if she didn't have to. She had never killed a man before, and was not sure if she could.

"Lower your ax," she commanded, trying to use her fiercest voice. She wished, at a time like this, that she possessed the deep, commanding voice of her father.

"And who commands me?" the man called back in a mocking voice, appearing amused.

"I am Kyra," she called out, "daughter of Duncan, *Commander* of Volis." She added the last bit with emphasis, hoping to scare him into backing down.

But he only grinned wider.

"An empty title," he countered. "You are serfs to Pandesia, as the rest of Escalon. You answer to the Lord Governor—like everybody else."

He looked her up and down and licked his lips, then took a threatening step toward her, clearly unafraid.

"Do you know the penalty for aiming a weapon at a Lord's Man, girl? I could imprison you and your father and all of your people just for this."

The dragon suddenly breathed hard, labored, gasping, and the soldier turned back and glanced at it, remembering. It was clearly trying to breathe fire, but unable to.

The soldier glanced back at Kyra.

"I have work to do!" he snapped at her, impatient. "This is your lucky day. Run off now, back to your father, and count your blessings I let you live. Now piss off!"

He turned his back on her derisively, ignoring her completely, as if she were harmless. He raised his ax again, took a step forward, and held it over the dragon's throat.

Kyra felt herself flush with rage.

"I will not warn you again!" she called out, her voice lower this time, filled with meaning, surprising even her.

She drew her bow further back, and the soldier turned and looked at her, and this time he did not smile, as if realizing she were serious. Kyra was puzzled as she saw him look over her shoulder, as if watching something behind her. Just then she suddenly detected motion out of the corner of her eye—but it was too late.

Kyra felt herself slammed from the side. She went flying sideways and dropped her bow, its arrow shooting harmlessly up in the air, as a heavy body landed on top of her and tackled her down to the ground. She landed in snow so deep she could hardly breathe.

Disoriented, Kyra struggled her way back to the surface to find a soldier on top of her, pinning her down. She saw four of the Lord's Men standing over her, and she realized: there had been more of them, hiding in the wood. How stupid of her, she realized, for assuming that solider was alone. These other men must have been lurking out there all that time. That's why, she realized now, the first soldier had been so brazen, even with a bow trained on him.

Two of the men roughly dragged her to her feet, while the other two stepped in close. They were cruel-looking men, with boorish faces, unshaven, eager for bloodlust—or worse. One began to unbuckle his belt.

"A girl with a little bow, are you?" asked one, mocking.

"You should have stayed home in your daddy's fort," said another.

Barely had he finished speaking when there came a snarling noise—and Leo leapt through the snow, pouncing on one and pinning him down.

Another one of the men turned and kicked Leo, but Leo turned and bit his ankle, felling him. Leo went back and forth between the two soldiers, snarling and biting as they kicked him back.

The two other soldiers, though, stayed focused on Kyra, and with Leo tied up, she felt a wave of panic. Strangely enough, though, despite her circumstances, she realized she did not feel panic for herself but for the dragon. Out of the corner of her eye, she saw the first soldier once again raise his ax high and turn and approach the beast, and she knew that in a moment, it would be dead.

Kyra reacted instinctively. As one of the soldiers momentarily loosened his grip on her arm, caught off guard by Leo, she reached behind her, drew the staff sheathed to her back, and brought it down on an angle with lightning speed. She struck one of them perfectly in the pressure point in his temple, felling him before he could react.

She then pulled back the staff, slid her grip all the way up so she could use it at close range and jabbed the other soldier on the bridge of the nose. He shrieked, gushing blood, and dropped to his knees.

Kyra knew this was her chance to finish these two men. They were now prone, and Leo had the other two pinned down and struggling.

But her heart was still with the dragon—it was all she could think of—and she knew there wasn't time. So she instead ran for her bow, picked it up, placed an arrow, and with barely time to think, much less to aim, she prepared to fire. She had one shot, she knew, and it had to be true. It would be the first shot she had ever taken in action, in real battle, in the dark, in the blinding snow and wind, between trees and branches and with a target twenty yards off. It would be the first shot she had taken with her life at stake.

Kyra summoned all of her training, all of her long days and nights of shooting, everything she had within her, and forced herself to focus. She forced herself to become one with her weapon.

Kyra drew and released, and time slowed as she watched the arrow fly, hearing its whistle, unsure if it would hit. There were too many variables at play, from a gust of wind to the swaying branches to her frozen hands, to the movement of the soldier.

Kyra heard the satisfying thump of the arrow finding its mark, and she heard the soldier cry out. She watched his face in the moonlight, contorted in pain, and watched as he dropped the ax harmlessly at his side and collapsed, dead.

The dragon looked over at Kyra and their eyes met. Its huge yellow eyes, glowing even in the night, seemed to acknowledge what she had done, and in that moment she felt as if it knew she had saved it, and that they had just made a connection for life.

98

Kyra stood there in shock, hardly believing what she had done. Had she really just killed a man? And not just any man—but a Lord's Man. She had broken Escalon's sacred law. It was an act from which there was no return—an act which would spark a war and embroil all of her people. What had she done?

Yet somehow, she had no regrets, no doubts about what she had done. She felt as if she had stepped into destiny.

A searing pain on her jaw line snapped her out of it, as Kyra felt thick, calloused knuckles smash into her skin. Her world was filled with pain as she stumbled, punched in the face, and fell in the snow to her hands and knees, seeing stars, her world spinning. Before she could collect herself she felt a kick in the ribs, then felt a second soldier tackling her and pinning her face in the snow.

Kyra gasped for breath as a soldier jerked her to her feet. She stood there, facing the two men she had let live. Leo snarled, but he still struggled with the other two. One soldier bled from his nose and the other from his temple, and Kyra realized she should have killed them when she'd had the chance. She struggled with all her might to break free from their grip, but to no avail. She could see the look of death in their eyes.

One of them glanced back at his dead commander, then stepped in close and sneered.

"Congratulations," he hissed. "By morning, your fort, your people, will be razed to the ground."

He backhanded her, and her face filled with pain as she went stumbling back.

The other soldier grabbed her firmly and pushed his dagger to her throat, while the other reached for his belt buckle.

"Before you die, you're going to remember us," he said. "It will be the last memory of your short life."

Kyra heard a whining and looked over her shoulder to see one of the soldiers stab Leo. She winced as if she herself had been stabbed, though Leo, fearless, turned and sunk his teeth into the soldier's wrist.

Kyra felt the blade at her throat, and she knew she was on her own. Yet instead of fear, she felt liberated. She felt her anger, her desire for vengeance against the Lord's Men, well up inside her. In this man, she had the perfect target. She might go down, but she would not do down without a fight.

99

She waited until the last moment as the soldier stepped closer, grabbing at her clothes—then she planted one foot, leaned back, and used her great flexibility to kick straight up, with all her might.

Kyra felt her foot connect between the man's legs with a great force and as she watched him cry out and drop to his knees, knowing it was a perfect blow. At the same moment, Leo shook off his attackers and turned and lunged for the man she felled, pouncing and sinking his fangs into his throat.

She turned to face the other soldier, the last one standing, and he drew a sword and faced her. Kyra picked up her staff from the snow and faced off with him—and he laughed.

"A staff against a sword," he mocked. "Better to give up now—your death won't be so painful."

He charged and swung at her, and as he did, Kyra's instincts took over; she imagined herself back in the training ground. As he swung, she dodged left and right, using her speed to her advantage. The soldier was big and strong and he wielded a heavy sword—yet she was light and unencumbered, and as he came down with a particularly fierce blow meant to chop her in half, she sidestepped and left him off balance; she swung around with her staff and cracked him on the back of his wrist and he dropped his sword, losing it in the snow.

He looked back at her, shocked, then sneered and charged her with his bare hands, as if to tackle her. Kyra waited, then at the last moment crouched low and brought the tip of her staff straight up, connecting with his chin. The blow snapped his neck back and sent him landing flat on his back, unmoving. Leo pounced on him and sank his fangs into his throat, making sure he was dead.

Kyra, assuming all her attackers were dead, was confused to hear movement behind her. She turned to see one of the two soldiers Leo had attacked somehow back on his feet, limping to his horse, drawing a sword from its saddle. The soldier rushed Leo, who still had his fangs in the other soldier's throat, his back to him.

Kyra's heart slammed in her chest; she was too far away to reach him in time.

"LEO!" she cried out.

But Leo, too busy snarling, did not realize.

Kyra knew she had to take drastic action or else watch Leo be killed before her eyes. Her bow was still in the snow, too far away from her.

She thought quick. She raised her staff and broke it over her knee and it broke in two. She took one of the halves, its tip jagged, took aim, leaned back and hurled it like a spear.

It whistled through the air and she prayed it find its target.

Kyra breathed with relief as she watched it pierce the soldier's throat right before he reached Leo. The man stumbled and fell at Leo's feet, dead.

Kyra stood there in the silence, breathing hard, seeing the carnage all around her, the five Lord's Men sprawled out in the snow, staining it red, and she could hardly believe what she had done. But before she could finish processing it, she suddenly detected motion out of the corner of her eye. She turned to see the squire, running for his horse.

"Wait!" Kyra called out.

She knew she had to stop him. If he made it back to the Lord Governor he would tell them what had happened. They would know it was she who had done this, and her father and her people would be killed.

Kyra picked up her bow, took aim, and waited until she had a good shot. Finally, the boy broke into the clearing, and as the clouds opened and the moon shone down, she had her chance.

But she could not take the shot. The boy had not done anything, after all, and something within her just could not kill an innocent boy.

Kyra lowered her bow with shaking hands and watched him ride off, feeling sick, knowing it would be her death sentence. Surely, a war would come for this.

With the squire on the run, Kyra knew her time was short. She should run back through the wood, for her father's fort, and alert them all as to what had happened. They would need time to prepare for war, to seal the fort—or to flee for their lives. She felt a terrible sense of guilt, yet also, of duty.

Yet Kyra could go nowhere. Instead, she stood there and watched, mesmerized, as the dragon flapped its good wing and stared back at her. She felt she had to be by its side.

Kyra hiked quickly through the snow, down the bank, toward the gushing river, until she stood before the dragon. It lifted its neck just a

101

bit and stared at her, their eyes meeting, and the dragon stared back at her with an inscrutable expression. In its look Kyra thought she spotted gratitude—yet also, fury. She did not understand.

Kyra stepped closer, Leo snarling beside her, until she stood but a few feet away. Her breath caught in her throat. She could hardly believe she was standing so close to such a magnificent creature. She knew how dangerous this was, knew this dragon could kill her at any moment if it chose.

Kyra slowly lifted her hand, even as the dragon appeared to be frowning and, heart pounding with fear, reached out and touched its scales. Its skin was so rough, so thick, so primordial—it was like touching the beginning of time. Her hand trembled as her fingertips stroked it, and not from the cold.

Its presence here was such a mystery, and her mind raced with a million questions.

"What hurt you?" Kyra asked, stroking its scales. "What are you doing on this side of the world?"

There came a sound like a growling from deep within its throat, and Kyra withdrew her hand, afraid. She could not read this beast, and even though she had just saved its life, Kyra suddenly felt it was a very bad idea to be so close to it.

The dragon looked at Kyra and slowly raised a sharpened claw until it touched Kyra's throat. Kyra stood there, frozen, terrified, wondering whether it would slice her throat.

Something flashed in its eyes and it seemed to change its mind. It withdrew its claw and then, to her surprise, in one quick motion slashed down.

Kyra felt a searing pain on her face and she cried out as the claw grazed her cheek, drawing blood. It was just a scratch, but it was enough, Kyra knew, to leave her with a scar.

Kyra reached up and touched the wound, saw the fresh blood in her hands, and felt a deep sense of betrayal and confusion. She looked back into the dragon's glowing yellow eyes, filled with defiance, and she was at a loss to understand this creature. Did it hate her? Had she made a mistake to save its life? Why had it only scratched her when it could have killed her?

"Who are you?" she asked softly, afraid.

She heard a voice, an ancient voice, rumbling in her mind's eye:

Theos.

She was shocked. She was sure it was the dragon's voice.

Kyra waited, hoping it would tell her more—but then suddenly, without warning, Theos shattered the silence by shrieking, rearing its head, and struggling to get away from her. It flopped and spun wildly, trying desperately to lift off.

Kyra could not understand why.

"Wait!" Kyra cried out. "You are wounded! Let me help you!"

It pained her to see him flopping so much, blood dripping from its wound, unable to get one wing to work. He was so massive that each flop raised a great cloud of snow, shaking the ground, making the earth rumble and shattering the stillness of this snowy night. He tried so hard to lift off into the air, but could not.

"Where is it you want to go?" Kyra called out.

Theos flopped again and this time he rolled down the steep, snowy bank, rolling, again and again, out of control, unable to stop itself. He rolled right for the gushing rapids.

Kyra watched with horror, helpless, as the dragon splashed into the raging waters of the river below.

"NO!" she cried out, rushing forward.

But there was nothing she could do. The great rapids carried Theos, flailing, screeching, downriver, winding through the forest, around a bend and out of sight.

Kyra watched him disappear and as she did, her heart broke inside her. She had sacrificed everything, her life, the destiny of her people, to save this creature—and now he was gone. What had it all been for? Had any of it even been real?

Kyra turned and looked out and saw the five dead men, still lying in the snow, saw Leo, wounded, beside her; she reached up and felt the sting on her cheek, saw the blood—and knew it had all been very real. She had survived an encounter with a dragon. She had killed five of the Lord's Men.

After tonight, she knew, her life would never be the same again.

Kyra noticed the horse's trail, winding into the wood, and she remembered the boy, riding to alert his people. She knew the Lord's Men would be coming for her people.

Kyra turned and sprinted into the wood, Leo at her side, determined to make it back to Volis, to alert her father and all her people—if it were not already too late.

CHAPTER TWELVE

Vesuvius, King of the Trolls and Supreme Ruler of Marda, stood in the enormous cave beneath the earth, on a stone balcony a hundred feet high, and he looked down, surveying the work of his army of trolls beneath him. Thousands of trolls labored in this huge cavernous underground, hammering away at rock with pickaxes and hammers, chopping away at earth and stone, the sound of mining heavy in the air. Endless torches lined the walls while streams of lava crisscrossed the floor, sparking, emitting a glow, brightening the cave and keeping it hot while trolls sweated and gasped in the heat below.

Vesuvius smiled wide, his troll face grotesque, misshapen, twice the size of a human's, with two long fangs, like tusks, that emerged from his mouth, and beady red eyes which enjoyed watching people suffer. He wanted them his people to toil, to work harder than they'd ever had, for he knew it was only through extreme toil that he would achieve what his fathers could not. Twice the size of a typical troll, and three times the size of a human, Vesuvius was all muscle and rage, and he knew he was different, knew he could achieve what none before him had. He had hatched a plan that even his ancestors could not conceive, a plan that would bring glory to his nation forever. It would be the greatest tunnel ever created, a tunnel to bring them beneath The Flames, all the way into Escalon—and with each fall of the hammer, the tunnel became just a little bit deeper.

Not once, in centuries, had his people figured out how to cross The Flames en masse; individual trolls were able to pass through here and there, but most died on these suicide missions. What Vesuvius needed was an entire army of trolls to cross together, at once, to destroy Escalon once and for all. His fathers could not understand how to do it, and they had become complacent, resigned to a life here in the wilds of Marda. But not he. He, Vesuvius, was wiser than all his fathers, tougher, more determined—and more ruthless. One day, while brooding, he had thought, if he could not go through The Flames, or over them, then perhaps he could go under them. Captivated by the idea, he had set his plan into motion at once and had not stopped since, rallying thousands of his soldiers and slaves to build what would be the greatest creation of the troll kingdom: a tunnel beneath The Flames.

Vesuvius watched with satisfaction as one of his taskmasters whipped a human slave, one they had captured from the West, chained to the hundreds of other slaves. The human cried out and fell, and he was lashed until he died. Vesuvius grinned, pleased to see the other humans work harder. His trolls were nearly twice the size of the humans, much more grotesque-looking, too, with bulging muscles and misshaped faces, filled with a bloodlust that was insatiable. The humans, he'd found, were a good way for his people to vent their violence.

Yet as he watched, Vesuvius was still frustrated: no matter how many people he enslaved, how many of his soldiers he put to work, no matter how hard he lashed them, how much he tortured or killed his own people to motivate them, the progress remained too slow. The rock was too hard, the job too massive. At this rate, he knew, they would never complete this tunnel in his lifetime, and his dream of invading Escalon would remain but a dream.

Of course, they had more than enough room here in Marda—but it was not room that Vesuvius wanted. He wanted to kill, to subjugate all humans, to take all that was theirs, just for the fun of it. He wanted it all. And he knew that if he was to get there, the time had come for more drastic measures.

"My Lord and King?" came a voice.

Vesuvius turned to see several of his soldiers standing there, wearing the distinctive green armor of the troll nation, their insignia— a roaring boar's head with a dog in its mouth—emblazoned across the front. His men lowered their heads out of deference, looking to the ground, as they had been trained to do when in his presence.

Vesuvius saw they were holding a troll soldier between them, wearing tattered armor, his face covered in dirt and ash and spotted with burn marks.

"You may address me," he commanded.

Slowly, they raised their chins and looked him in the eye.

"This one was captured inside Marda, in Southwood," one reported. "He was caught returning from beyond The Flames."

Vesuvius looked over the captive soldier, shackled, and was filled with disgust. Every day he sent men west, across Marda, on a mission to charge through The Flames and emerge on the other side, in Escalon. If they survived the journey, they were ordered to wreak terror amongst as many humans as they could. If they survived that, their orders were to seek out the two Towers and steal the Sword of Fire, the mythical weapon that supposedly held up The Flames. Most of his trolls never returned from the journey—they were either killed by the passage through the Flames or eventually, by the humans in Escalon. It was a one-way mission: they were commanded *never* to return—unless they came back with the Sword of Fire in hand.

But once in a while some of his trolls sneaked back, mostly disfigured from their journey through The Flames, unsuccessful in their mission but seeking to return anyway, for safe harbor back in Marda. Vesuvius had no stomach for these trolls, whom he considered to be deserters.

"And what news do you bring from the West?" he asked. "Did you find the Sword?" he added, already knowing the answer.

The soldier gulped, looking terrified.

He slowly shook his head.

"No, my Lord and King," he said, his voice broken.

Vesuvius raged in the silence.

"Then why did you return to Marda?" he demanded.

The troll kept his head lowered.

"I was ambushed by a party of humans," he said. "I was lucky to escape and make it back here."

"But why did you come back?" Vesuvius pressed.

The soldier looked at him, puzzled and nervous.

"Because my mission was over, my Lord and King."

Vesuvius fumed.

"Your mission was to find the Sword—or die trying."

"But I made it through The Flames!" he pleaded. "I killed many humans! And I made it back!"

"And tell me," Vesuvius said kindly, stepping forward and laying a hand on the troll's shoulder as he slowly walked with him toward the edge of the balcony. "Did you really think, upon coming back, that I would let you live?"

Vesuvius suddenly grabbed the troll by the back of his shirt, stepped forward, and hurled him over the edge.

The soldier flailed, shrieking through the air as much as his shackles would allow. All the workers down below stopped and looked up, watching as he fell. He tumbled a hundred feet then finally landed with a splat on the hard rock below.

The workers all looked up at Vesuvius, and he glared back down at them, knowing this would be a good reminder to all who failed him.

They quickly went back to work.

Vesuvius, still in a rage and needing to let it out on someone, turned from the balcony and strutted down the winding stone steps carved into the canyon wall, followed by his men. He wanted to see their progress himself, up close—and while he was down there, he figured he could find a pathetic slave to beat to a pulp.

Vesuvius wound his way down the stairs, carved into the black rock, descending flight after flight, all the way down to the base of this vast cave, which became hotter the lower he went. Dozens of his soldiers fell in behind him as he strutted across the cave floor, weaving his way between the streams of lava, between hordes of workers. As he went, thousands of soldiers and slaves stopped working and parted ways for him, bowing their heads differentially.

It was hot down here, the base heated not only from the sweat of men, but from the streaks of lava that crisscrossed the room and oozed from the walls, from the sparks flying off the rocks as men struck them everywhere with axes and picks. Vesuvius marched across the vast cave floor, until finally he reached the entrance of the tunnel. He stood before it and stared: a hundred feet wide and fifty feet tall, the tunnel was being dug so that it sloped down gradually, deeper and deeper beneath the earth, deep enough to be able to support an army when the time came to burrow under The Flames. One day they would penetrate Escalon, rise above the surface, and take thousands of human slaves. It would, he knew, be the greatest day of his life.

Vesuvius marched forward, snatched a whip from a soldier's hands, reached high, and began lashing soldiers left and right. They all went back to work, striking the rock twice as fast, smashing the hard black rock until clouds of dust filled the air. He then made his way to the human slaves, men and women they had abducted from Escalon and had managed to bring back. Those were the missions he relished most of all, missions solely for the sake of terrorizing the West. Most humans died on the passage back, but enough survived, even if badly burnt and maimed—and these he worked to the bone in his tunnels.

Vesuvius zeroed in on them. He thrust the whip into a human's hand and pointed at a woman.

"Kill her!" he commanded.

The human stood there, shaking, and merely shook his head.

Vesuvius snatched the whip back from his hand and instead lashed the man, again and again, until he finally stopped resisting, dead.

The others went back to work, averting his gaze, while Vesuvius threw down the whip, breathing hard, and stared back into the mouth of the cave. It was like staring at his nemesis. It was a half-formed creation, going nowhere. It was all happening too slowly.

"My Lord and King," came a voice behind him.

Vesuvius turned slowly to see several soldiers from the Mantra, his elite division of trolls, dressed in the black and green armor reserved for his best troops. They stood their proudly, holding halberds at their sides. These were the few trolls Vesuvius respected, and seeing them made his heart quicken. It could only mean one thing: they had brought news.

Vesuvius had dispatched the Mantra on a mission many moons ago: to find the giant that lurked in Great Wood, rumored to have killed thousands of trolls. His dream was to capture this giant, bring it back, and use its brawn to complete his tunnel. Vesuvius had sent mission after mission, and none had come back. All had been discovered dead, killed by the giant.

As Vesuvius stared at these men, his heart beat faster with hope.

"Speak," he commanded.

"My Lord and King, we have found the giant," one reported. "We have cornered him. Our men await your command."

Vesuvius grinned slowly, pleased for the first time in as along as he could recall. His smile grew wider as a plan hardened in his mind. Finally, he realized, it would all be possible; finally, he would have a chance to breach The Flames.

He stared back at his commander, filled with resolve, ready to do what he had to.

"Lead me to him."

CHAPTER THIRTEEN

Kyra stumbled through the snow, now past her knees, trekking her way through the Wood of Thorns as she leaned on her staff, trying to fight her way through what had become a full-fledged blizzard. The storm raged so strongly now, it had even penetrated the thick branches of the wood, blowing back these huge trees, gusts of wind so strong that they nearly bent them in half. Gusts of wind and snow whipped her face, making it hard to see again—hard to even keep her footing. As the wind continually picked up, it took all her might just to walk a few steps.

The blood-red moon was long gone, as if it had been swallowed up by the storm, and now she had no light left to navigate by. Even if she had, she could barely see a thing. All she had left to ground her was Leo, walking slowly, wounded, leaning against her, his presence her only solace. With each step her feet seemed to sink deeper and she wondered if she were even making any progress. She felt an urgency to get back to her people, to warn them, making each step all the more frustrating.

Kyra tried to look up, squinting into the wind, hoping to find some distant landmark—anything—trying to see if she was even going the right way. But she was lost in a world of white. Her cheek burned from the dragon's scratch, feeling as if it were on fire. She reached up and touched it, and her hand was dotted with blood, the only warm thing left in the universe. Her cheek throbbed, nonetheless, as if the dragon had infected her.

As a particularly strong gust of wind knocked her backwards, Kyra finally realized she could not go on; they had to find shelter. She was desperate to reach Volis before the Lord's Men, but she knew that if she continued hiking like this, she knew she would die out here. Her only comfort was the fact that the Lord's Men would not be able to attack in this weather—if the squire even made it home.

Kyra looked around, this time for shelter—but even finding that proved elusive. Seeing nothing but white, the wind howling so loudly she could barely think, Kyra began to panic, to have visions of herself and Leo being found frozen out here in the snow, never discovered at all. She knew if she did not find something soon, they would certainly be dead by morning. This situation had crept up on her, and now it had become desperate. Of all nights to leave Volis, she realized now, she had picked the worst one.

As if sensing her new intention, Leo began to whine and he suddenly turned and ran away from her. He crossed a clearing and as he reached the other side, began to dig fiercely at a mound of snow.

Kyra watched curiously as Leo howled, scratching wildly, digging deeper and deeper in the snow, wondering what he had found. Finally, it gave way, and she was surprised to see he had unearthed a small cave, carved into the side of a huge boulder. Heart pounding with hope, she hurried over and crouched down and saw it was just wide enough to shelter them. It was also, she was thrilled to see, dry—and protected from the wind.

She leaned down and kissed his head.

"You did it, boy."

He licked her back.

She knelt down and crawled into the cave, Leo beside her, and as she entered, she had an immediate sensation of relief. Finally, it was quiet; the wind's noise was muted and for the first time it was not stinging her face, her ears; for the first time, she was dry. She felt like she could breathe again.

Kyra crawled on pine needles, deeper and deeper into the cave, wondering how deep it went, until finally she reached the back wall. She sat and leaned against it and looked out. Occasional bursts of snow came in here, but the cave remained mostly dry, none reaching as deep as she. For the first time, she could truly relax.

Leo crawled up beside her, snuggling his head in her lap, and she hugged him to her chest as she leaned back against the stone, shivering, trying to keep warm. She brushed the snowflakes off of her furs and off his coat, trying to get them dry, and she examined his wound. Luckily, it wasn't deep.

Kyra used the snow to clean it out and he whined as she touched it.

"Shhh," she said.

She reached into her pocket and gave him her last piece of dried meat; he ate it greedily.

As she leaned back and sat there in the dark, listening to the raging wind, watching the snow begin to pile up again, blocking her view, Kyra felt as if it were the end of the world. She tried to close her eyes, feeling bone weary, frozen, desperately needing to rest, but the scratch on her cheek kept her awake, throbbing.

Eventually, her eyes grew heavy and began to shut on her. The pine beneath her felt oddly comfortable, and as her body morphed into the rock, she soon found herself, despite her best efforts, succumbing to the embrace of sweet sleep.

*

Kyra flew on the back of a dragon, hanging on for dear life, moving faster than she knew was possible, as it screeched and flapped its wings. They were so wide and magnificent, and they grew wider as she watched them, seeming as if they would stretch over the world.

She looked down and her stomach dropped as she saw, far below, the rolling hills of Volis. She had never seen it from this angle, so high up. They flew over a lush countryside, with rolling green hills, stretches of woods, gushing rivers, and fertile vineyards. It was familiar terrain, and soon Kyra recognized her father's fort, rambling, its ancient stone walls blanketing the countryside, sheep roaming outside of it.

But as the dragon dove down, Kyra sensed immediately that something was wrong. She saw smoke rising—not the smoke of chimneys, but black, thick smoke. As she looked closer, she was horrified to see it was her father's fort aflame, waves of flame engulfing everything. She saw an army of the Lord's Men, stretching to the horizon, surrounding the fort, torching it, and as she heard the screams, she knew that everyone she knew and loved in the world was being slaughtered.

"NO!" she tried to shout.

But the words, stuck in her throat, would not come out.

The dragon craned its neck, turned it all the way back and looked her in the eye—and Kyra was surprised to see it was the same dragon she had saved, its piercing yellow eyes staring right back at her. Theos.

112

You saved me, she heard it say in her mind's eye. *Now I shall save you. We are one now, Kyra. We are one.*

Suddenly, Theos turned sharply, and Kyra lost her balance and fell.

She shrieked as she plummeted through the air, the ground coming for her fast.

"NO!" Kyra shrieked.

Kyra sat up shrieking in the blackness, unsure of where she was. Breathing hard, she looked all around, until she finally realized: she was in the cave.

Leo whined beside her, his head in her lap, licking her hand. She breathed deep, trying to remember where she was. It was still dark out, and outside the storm still raged, the winds howled, and the snow piled up. The throbbing in her cheek was worse, and she reached up and looked at her fingers and saw fresh blood. She wondered if it would ever stop bleeding.

"Kyra!" called out a mystical voice, sounding almost like a whisper.

Kyra, startled, wondering who could be in this cave with her, peered into the blackness, on alert. She looked up to see an unfamiliar figure standing over her in the cave. He wore a long, black robe and cloak and he held a staff; he appeared to be an older man, with white hair peeking out of his hood. His staff glowed, emitting a soft light in the blackness.

"Who are you?" she asked, sitting up straight, on guard. "How did you get in here?"

He took a step forward, and she wanted to see his face, but he was still obscured in shadow.

"What is it that you seek?" he asked, his ancient voice somehow putting her at ease.

She thought about that, trying to understand.

"I seek to be free," she said. "I seek to be a warrior."

Slowly, he shook his head.

"You forget something," he said. "The most important thing of all. What is it that you seek?"

Kyra stared back, confused.

Finally, he took another step forward.

"You seek your destiny."

Kyra wondered at his words.

"And more," he said, "you seek to know who you are."

He stepped forward again, standing so close, yet still obscured in shadow.

"Who are you, Kyra?" he asked.

She stared back blankly, wanting to answer, but in that moment she had no idea. She was no longer sure of anything.

"*Who are you*?" he demanded, his voice so loud, echoing off the walls, hurting her eardrums.

Kyra raised her hands to her face, bracing herself as he came closer.

Kyra opened her eyes again and she was shocked to see that no one was there. She couldn't understand what was happening. She slowly lowered her hands, and as she did, she realized that this time, she was fully awake.

Bright sunlight shone into the cave, light reflecting off the snow, off the cave walls, blinding. She squinted, disoriented, trying to collect herself. The raging wind was gone; the blinding snow was gone. Instead, there was snow partially blocking the entrance and beyond it a world with a crystal blue sky, birds singing. It was as if the world had been reborn.

Kyra could hardly fathom it: she had survived the long night.

Leo gently bit at her pants leg and prodded her, impatient.

Disoriented, Kyra slowly stood and as she did, she immediately reeled from the pain. Not only was her entire body sore from the fighting, the blows she had received, but most of all, her cheek burned as if it were on fire. She recalled the dragon's claw, and she reached up and felt it; although just a scratch, it was still mysteriously moist, caked with blood.

As she stood she felt lightheaded , and she did not know if it was from her exhaustion, her hunger, or the dragon's scratch. She walked on unsteady legs, feeling unlike herself, as she followed Leo, who led the way impatiently out of the cave and back into day, clawing at the snow to widen their exit.

Kyra crouched down and stepped outside and as she stood, found herself immersed in a world of blinding white. She raised her hands to her eyes, her head splitting at the sight. It had warmed considerably, the wind was gone, birds chirped, and the sun filtered

114

through trees in the forest clearing. She heard a whoosh and turned to see a huge clump of snow slide off a heavy pine and make its way to the forest floor. She looked down and saw she stood in snow up to her thighs.

Leo led the way, bounding through the snow, back in the direction of Volis, she was sure. She followed him, struggling to keep up.

Kyra, though, found herself struggling with each step she took. She licked her lips and felt more and more lightheaded. The blood pulsed in her cheek, and she began to wonder if the wound had infected her. She felt herself changing. She could not explain it, but she felt as if the dragon's blood were pulsing through her.

"Kyra!"

There came a distant shout, sounding as if it were a world away. It was followed by several other voices, shouting her name, their cries absorbed by the snow and the pines. It took her a moment to realize, to recognize the voices: her father's men. They were out here, searching for her.

Kyra felt a surge of relief.

"Here!" she called out, thinking she was shouting, but surprised to hear her own voice was barely above a whisper. At that moment, she realized just how weak she was. Her wound was doing something to her, something she did not understand.

Suddenly, her knees buckled out from under her, and Kyra found herself falling into the snow, helpless to resist.

Leo yelped, then turned and ran for the distant voices.

She wanted to call to him, to call to all of them, but she was too weak now. She lay there, deep in the snow, and looked up at a world of white, at the blinding winter sun, and closed her eyes as a slumber she could no longer resist carried her away.

CHAPTER FOURTEEN

Alec held his head in his hands, trying to stop his headache, as the carriage, packed with boys, jolted roughly along the country road, as it had been doing all night long. The bumps and ditches never seemed to end, and this primitive wooden cart, with its iron bars and wooden wheels, seemed to have been constructed to inflict the maximum possible discomfort. With each bump, Alec's head slammed into the wood behind him. After the first bump, he had been sure it could not go on like this for long, that the road must end sometime soon.

But hour after hour had passed, and if anything, the road only seemed to worsen. He had been awake all night long, with no hope of sleep, if not from the bumps then from the stink of the other boys, from their elbowing and jostling him awake. All night long the cart made stops in villages, picking up more and more boys, cramming them all in here in the blackness. Alec could feel them looking him over, summing him up, a sea of dejected faces staring back at him, their eyes filled with wrath. They were all older, miserable, and looking for a victim.

Alec had at first assumed that, since they were all in this together, all drafted against their will to serve at The Flames, there would be a solidarity amongst them. But he'd learned quickly that was not the case. Each boy was his own island, and if Alec received any sort of communication, it was only hostility. They were rough faces, unshaven, scars across them, noses that looked like they had been broken in too many fights, and it was beginning to dawn on Alec that not every boy in this carriage had just reached his eighteenth year—some were older, more broken down by life, looking like criminals, thieves, rapists, murderers, thrown in with the others, all of them being sent to keep The Flames.

Alec, sitting on the hard wood, jammed in, feeling as if he were on a journey to hell, was certain it could not get any worse; but the carriage stops never ended, and to his amazement, they crammed more and more boys in here. When he had first entered, a dozen boys had seemed tight, with no room to maneuver; but now, with over two dozen and counting, Alec could barely breathe. The boys who piled in after him were all forced to stand, trying to grab onto the ceiling, to anything, but mostly slipping and falling onto each other with each bump of the cart. More than one angry boy shoved back, and endless scuffles broke out, all night long, boys constantly elbowing and shoving each other. Alec watched in disbelief as one boy bit another's ear off. The only saving grace was that they had no room to maneuver, to even bring their shoulders back to throw a punch, so the fights had no choice but to defuse quickly, with vows to continue at a later time.

Alec heard birds chirping, and he looked out, bleary-eyed, to spot the first light of dawn creeping through the iron bars. He marveled that day had broke, that he had survived this, the longest night of his life.

As the sun lit the carriage, Alec began to get a better look at all the new boys that had come in. He was by far the youngest of the lot—and, it appeared, the least dangerous. It was a savage group of muscle-bound, irascible boys, all scarred, some tattooed, looking like the forgotten boys of society. They were all on edge, bitter from the long night, and Alec felt the carriage was ripe for an explosion.

"You look too young to be here," came a deep voice.

Alec looked over to see a boy, perhaps a year or two older, sitting beside him, shoulder to shoulder. He was the presence, Alec realized, that he had felt squished up against him all night long, a boy with broad shoulders, strong muscles and the innocent, plain face of a farmer. His face was unlike the others, open and friendly, perhaps even a bit naïve, and Alec sensed in him a kindred soul.

"I took my brother's slot," Alec replied flatly, wondering how much to tell him.

"He was afraid?" the boy asked, puzzled.

Alec shook his head.

"Lame," Alec corrected.

The boy nodded, as if understanding, and looked at Alec with a new respect.

They fell into silence, and Alec looked the boy over.

"And you?" Alec asked. "You don't appear to be eighteen, either."

"Seventeen," the boy said.

Alec wondered.

"Then why are you here?" he asked.

"I volunteered."

Alec was stunned.

"*Volunteered*? But why?"

The boy looked at the floor and shrugged.

"I wanted to get away."

"To get away from what?" Alec asked, baffled.

The boy fell silent and Alec could see a gloom pass over his face. He fell silent and he did not think he would respond—but finally, the boy mumbled: "Home."

Alec saw the sadness in his face, and he understood. Clearly, something had gone terribly wrong at this boy's home, and from the bruises on the boy's arms, and the look of sadness mixed with anger, Alec could only guess.

"I am sorry," Alec replied.

The boy looked at him with a surprised expression, as if not expecting any compassion in this cart. Suddenly, he extended a hand.

"Marco," he said.

"Alec."

They shook hands, the boy's twice as large as Alec's, with a strong grip that left his hand hurting. Alec sensed he had met a friend in Marco, and it was a relief, given the sea of faces before him.

"I suspect you are the only one who volunteered," Alec said.

Marco looked around and shrugged.

"I suspect you're right. Most of these were drafted or imprisoned."

"Imprisoned?" Alec asked, surprised.

Marco nodded.

"The Keepers are comprised not only of draftees, but a good amount of criminals, too."

"Who you calling a criminal, boy?" came a savage voice.

They both turned to see one of the boys, prematurely aged from his hard life, looking forty years old though not older than twenty, with a pockmarked face and beady eyes. He squatted down low, and stared into Marco's face.

"I wasn't talking to you," Marco replied, defiant.

"Well, now you are," the boy seethed, clearly looking for a fight. "Say it again. You want to call me a criminal to my face?"

Marco reddened and clenched his jaw, getting angry himself.

"If the shoe fits," Marco said.

The other boy flushed with rage, and Alec admired Marco's defiance, his fearlessness. The boy lunged at Marco, wrapping his hands around his throat and squeezing with all his might.

It all happened so fast, Marco was clearly caught off guard—and in these close quarters, he had little room to maneuver. His eyes bulged wide as he was losing air, trying unsuccessfully to pry the boy's hands off. Marco was bigger, but the boy had wiry hands, calloused, probably from years of murdering, and Marco could not loosen his grip.

"FIGHT! FIGHT!" the other boys called out.

The others looked over, half-heartedly watching the violence, one of a dozen fights that had erupted throughout the night.

Marco, struggling, leaned forward quickly and head-butted the other boy, smashing him in the nose. There came a cracking noise and blood gushed from the boy's nose.

Marco tried to stand to get better leverage—but as he did, a big boot pressed down on his shoulder from a different boy, pinning him down. At the same moment, the first boy, blood still gushing from his nose, reached into his waist and pulled out something shiny. It flashed in the pre-morning light, and Alec realized, shocked, it was a dagger. It was all happening so quickly, there was no time for Marco to react.

The boy thrust it forward, aiming for Marco's heart.

Alec reacted. He lunged forward, grabbed the boy's wrist with two hands, and pinned them down to the floor, sparing Marco from the deadly blow a moment before the blade touched his chest. The blade still grazed Marco, tearing open his shirt, but not touching his skin.

Alec and the boy went down to the wood, struggling for the blade, while Marco managed to reach up and twist the ankle of his other attacker, snapping it with a crack.

Alec felt greasy hands on his face, felt the first boy's long fingernails scratching him, reaching for his eyes. Alec knew he had to act quick, and he let go of the hand with the dagger, spun around and threw his elbow, feeling a satisfying crunch as his elbow connected with the boy's jaw.

The boy spun off of him, face-first to the ground.

Alec, breathing hard, his face stinging from the scratches, managed somehow to jump to his feet, as Marco stood beside him, sandwiched between all the other boys. The two stood side by side, looking down at their attackers lying on the floor, motionless. Alec's heart slammed in his chest, and as he stood there, he decided he no longer wanted to sit; it left him too vulnerable to attack from above. He would rather stand the rest of the way, however long the journey was.

Alec looked out and saw all the hostile eyes glaring at him, and this time, instead of looking away he met them back, realizing he needed to project confidence if he were to survive amongst this lot. Finally, they all seemed to give him a look, something like respect, and then they looked away.

Marco looked down, examining the tear in his shirt where the dagger had almost punctured his heart. He looked at Alec, his face filled with gratitude.

"You have a friend for life," Marco said sincerely.

He reached out for Alec's arm and Alec clasped it, and it felt good. A friend: that was exactly what he needed.

CHAPTER FIFTEEN

Kyra opened her eyes slowly, disoriented, wondering where she was. She saw a stone ceiling high above her, torchlight bouncing off its walls, and she felt herself lying in a bed of luxurious furs. She couldn't understand; last she remembered, she had been falling in the snow, sure she was going to die.

Kyra lifted her head and looked all around, expecting to see the snowy forest all around her. But instead, she was shocked to see a group of familiar faces crowding around her—her father, her brothers Brandon and Braxton and Aidan, Anvin, Arthfael, Vidar, and a dozen of her father's best warriors. She was back in the fort, in her chamber, in her bed, and they all looked down at her with concern. Kyra felt pressure on her arm, and she looked over to see Lyra, the court healer, with her large hazel eyes and long, silver hair, standing over her, examining her pulse.

Kyra opened her eyes fully, realizing she was not in the wood anymore. Somehow, she had made it back. She heard a whining beside her, felt Leo's nose on her hand, and she realized: he must have led them to her.

"What has happened?" she asked, still confused, trying to piece it all together.

The crowd seemed vastly relieved to see her awake, speaking, and her father stepped closer, his face filled with remorse and relief as he held her hand firmly. Aidan rushed forward and grabbed her other hand, and she smiled to see her younger brother at her side.

"Kyra," her father said, his voice filled with compassion. "You are home now. Safe."

Kyra saw the guilt in her father's face, and it all came back to her: their argument the night before. She realized he must have felt responsible. It was his words, after all, that had driven her away.

Kyra felt a sting and she cried out in pain as Lyra reached up and touched a cool cloth to her cheek; it had some sort of ointment in it, and her wound burned and then cooled.

"Water of the Lily," Lyra explained soothingly. "It took me six ointments to figure out what would cure this wound. You are lucky we can treat it—the infection was bad already."

Her father looked down at her cheek with an expression of concern.

"Tell us what happened," he said. "Who did this to you?"

Kyra propped herself up on one elbow, her head spinning as she did, feeling all the eyes on her, all the men riveted, waiting in silence. She tried to remember, to piece it all together.

"I remember..." she began, her voice hoarse. "The storm....The Flames...the Wood of Thorns."

Her father's brow furrowed in concern.

"Why did you venture there?" he asked. "Why did you hike so far on such a night?"

She tried to remember.

"I wanted to see The Flames for myself," she said. "And then...I needed shelter. I remember...the Lake of Dreams...and then...a woman."

"A woman?" he asked. "In the Wood of Thorns?"

"She was...ancient...the snow did not reach her."

"A witch," gasped Vidar.

"Such things venture out on Winter Moon," added Arthfael.

"And what did she say?" her father demanded, on edge.

Kyra could see the confusion and concern in all the faces, and she decided to refrain, not to tell them of the prophecy, of her future. She was still trying to process it all herself, and she feared that if they heard it, they might she think was crazy.

"I....can't remember," she said.

"Did she do this to you?" her father asked, looking at her cheek.

Kyra shook her head and swallowed, her throat dry, and Lyra rushed forward and gave her water from a sack. She drank it, realizing how parched she was.

"There was a cry," Kyra continued. "Unlike any I had heard."

She sat up, feeling more lucid as it all rushed back to her. She looked her father directly in the eye, wondering how he would react.

"A dragon's cry," she said flatly, bracing herself for their reaction, wondering if they would even believe her.

The room broke into an audible gasp of disbelief, all the men gaping at her. An intense silence fell over the men, all of them looking more stunned than she had ever seen.

No one spoke for what felt like an eternity.

Finally, her father shook his head.

"Dragons have not visited Escalon for a thousand years," he said. "You must have heard something else. Perhaps your ears played tricks on you."

Thonos, the old king's historian and philosopher and now a resident of Volis, stepped forward, with his long gray beard, leaning on his cane. He spoke rarely, and when he did, he always commanded great respect, a vault of forgotten knowledge and wisdom.

"On the Winter Moon," he said, his voice frail, "such things are possible."

"I saw it," Kyra insisted. "I saved it."

"*Saved* it?" her father asked, looking at her as if she were mad. "*You*, saved a dragon?"

All the men looked back at her as if she had lost her mind.

"It was the injury," Vidar said. "It has touched her mind."

Kyra blushed, desperately wanting them to believe her.

"It has *not* touched my mind," she insisted. "I do not lie!"

She searched all their faces, desperate.

"When have any of you known me to lie?" she demanded.

They all stared back, unsure.

"Give the girl a chance," Vidar called out. "Let's hear her tale."

Her father nodded back at her.

"Go on," he prodded.

Kyra licked her lips, sitting upright.

"The dragon was wounded," she recalled. "The Lord's Men had it cornered. They were going to kill it. I could not let it die—not like that."

"What did you do?" Anvin asked, sounding less skeptical than the others.

"I killed them," she said, staring into space, seeing it again, her voice heavy, realizing how crazy her story sounded. She barely believed herself. "I killed them all."

Another long silence fell over the room, even graver than the first.

"I know you won't believe me," she finally added.

Her father cleared his throat and squeezed her hand.

"Kyra," he said, somber. "We found five dead men near you—Lord's Men. If what you say is true, do you realize how serious this is? Do you realize what you have done?"

"I had no choice, Father," she said. "The sigil of our house—we are forbidden to leave a wounded animal to die."

"A dragon is not an animal!" he countered angrily. "A dragon is a...."

But his voice trailed off, he clearly unsure what to say as he stared off into space.

"If the Lord's Men are all dead," chimed in Arthfael, breaking the silence, rubbing his beard, "what does it matter? Who's to know the girl killed them? How shall the trail lead back to us?"

Kyra felt a pit in her stomach, but knew she had to tell them the complete truth.

"There was one more," she added, reluctant. "A squire. A boy. He witnessed it. He escaped, on horseback."

They stared at her, their faces somber.

Maltren stepped forward, frowning.

"And why did you let this one live, then?" he demanded.

"He was just a boy," she said. "Unarmed. Riding off, his back to me. Should I have put an arrow in it?"

"I doubt you put an arrow in any of them," Maltren snapped. "But if so, is it better to let a boy live and leave us all to die?"

"No one has left us to die," her father scolded Maltren, defending her.

"Hasn't she?" he asked. "If she is not lying, then the Lord's Men are dead, Volis is to blame, they have a witness, and we are all finished."

Her father turned to her, his face heavier than she had ever seen.

"This is grave news indeed," he said, sounding a million years old.

"I am sorry, Father," she said. "I did not mean to cause you trouble."

"Did not mean to?" Maltren countered. "No, you just accidentally killed five of the Lord's Men? And all for what?"

"I told you," she said. "To save the dragon."

"To save an imaginary dragon," Maltren snickered. "That makes it all worth it. One that, if it existed, would have gladly torn you apart."

"It did not tear me apart," she countered.

"No more talk of this dragon nonsense," her father said, his voice rising, agitated. "Tell us now the truth. We are all men here. Whatever happened, tell us. We shall not judge you."

She felt like crying inside.

"I have already told you," she said.

"I believe her," Aidan said, standing by her side. She so appreciated him for that.

But as she looked back out at the sea of faces, it was clear that no one else did. A long silence fell over the room.

"It is not possible, Kyra," her father finally said softly.

"It *is*," suddenly came a dark voice.

They all turned as the door to the chamber slammed open and in marched several of her father's men, brushing the snow off their furs and hair. The man who spoke, face still red from cold, looked at Kyra as if awestruck.

"We found prints," he said. "By the river. Near where the bodies were found. Prints too large for anything that walks this earth. Prints of a dragon."

The men all looked back at Kyra, now unsure.

"And where is this dragon then?" Maltren said.

"The trail leads to the river," the man reported.

"It couldn't fly," Kyra said. "It was wounded, like I said. It rolled into the rapids and I saw it no more."

The room fell into a long silence, and now, it was clear, they all believed her. They looked at her in awe.

"You say you saw this dragon?" her father asked.

She nodded.

"I came as close to it as you and I are now," she replied.

"And how did you survive?" he asked.

She gulped, unsure herself.

"It was how I received this wound," she said, touching her cheek.

They all looked at her cheek in a new light, all seeming stunned.

As Kyra ran her fingers along it, she sensed that it would scar, that it would change her appearance forever; yet somehow, strangely, she did not care.

"But I don't think it meant to hurt me," she added.

They stared at her as if she were mad. She wanted to explain to them the connection she had with the creature, but she did not think they would understand.

They all stared at her, all these grown men stumped, and finally her father asked:

"Why would you risk your life to save a dragon? Why would you endanger us all?"

It was a good question, one which Kyra did not have the answer to. She wished she did. She could not put into words the feelings, the emotions, the sense of destiny she had when near the beast—and she did not think these men would ever understand. Yet she knew she had endangered them all, and she felt terribly for it.

All she could do was hang her head and say: "Forgive me, Father."

"It is not possible," Maltren said, agitated. "It is impossible to confront a dragon and live."

"Unless," Anvin said, looking at Kyra strangely, then turned to her father. "Unless your daughter is the—"

Her father suddenly shot Anvin a look, and Anvin immediately stopped himself.

Kyra looked back and forth between the two, puzzled, wondering what Anvin was about to say.

"Unless I am *what?*" Kyra demanded.

But Anvin looked away and would say no more. Indeed, the entire room fell silent, and as she searched all the faces she realized that all the men averted their gaze from her, as though they were all in on some secret about her.

Her father suddenly rose from her bedside and released his grip on her hand. He stood erect, in a way that signaled that the meeting was over.

"You must rest now," he said. Then he turned gravely to his men. "An army comes," he said gravely, his voice filled with authority. "We must prepare."

CHAPTER SIXTEEN

Kyra stood alone in the warm, summer field, in awe at the world around her. Everything was in bloom, in dazzling color, the hills so green, so vibrant, dotted with glowing yellow and red flowers. Trees were in bloom everywhere, their foliage so thick, swaying in the wind, heavy with fruit. The hills rolled with vineyards, ripe, and the smell of flowers and grapes hung heavy in the summer air. Kyra wondered where she was, where her people had gone—where winter had gone.

There came a screech, high in the sky, and Kyra looked up to see Theos circling overhead. He swooped down, landing in the grass but a few feet away, and stared back at her with his intense, glowing yellow eyes. Something unspoken passed between them, their connection so intense, as if no words need be said.

Theos suddenly reared his head, shrieked, and breathed fire, right for her.

For some reason, Kyra was unafraid. She did not flinch as the flames approached her, somehow knowing he would never harm her. The fire forked, spreading out to the left and right of her, igniting the landscape all around her yet leaving her unscathed.

Kyra turned and was horrified to see the flames spread across the countryside, to see all the lush green, all the summer bounty, turn to black. The landscape changed before her eyes, the trees burned to a crisp, the grass replaced with soil.

The flames rose higher and higher, spread farther, faster, and in the distance, she watched with horror as they consumed Volis—until there was nothing left but rubble and ash.

Theos finally stopped, and Kyra turned and stared back at him. Kyra stood there, in the dragon's shadow, humbled by its massive size and she did not know what to expect. He wanted something from her, but she could not sense what it was.

Kyra reached out to touch its scales, and suddenly it raised a claw, screeched, and sliced open her cheek.

Kyra sat up in bed, shrieking, clutching her cheek, the awful pain spreading through her. She flailed, trying to get away from the dragon—but was surprised to feel human hands on her instead, calming her, trying to restrain her.

Kyra blinked and looked up to see a familiar face standing over her, holding a compress to her cheek.

"Shh," said Lyra, consoling her.

Kyra looked around, disoriented, and finally realized she had been dreaming. She was home, in her father's fort, still in her chamber.

"Just a nightmare," Lyra said.

Kyra realized she must have fallen back asleep, how long ago, she did not know. She checked the window and saw the sunlight had been replaced by blackness. She sat bolt upright, alarmed.

"What time is it?" she asked.

"Late in the night, my lady," Lyra replied. "The moon has already risen and set."

"And what of the coming army?" she asked, her heart pounding.

"No army has come, my lady," she replied. "The snow is still high, and it was nearly dark when you woke. No army can march in this. Don't worry—you have only slept for hours. Rest now."

Kyra leaned back and exhaled; she felt a wet nose on her hand and she looked over to see Leo, licking her hand.

"He hasn't left your bedside, my lady," Lyra smiled. "And neither has he."

She gestured and Kyra looked over and was touched to see Aidan lying there, slumped in a pile of furs beside the fire, a leather-bound book in his hand, fast asleep.

"He read to you while you slept," she added.

Kyra was overwhelmed with love for her younger brother—and it made her all the more alarmed at the trouble to come.

"I can feel your tension," Lyra added as she pressed a compress on her cheek. "You dreamt troubled dreams. It is the mark of a dragon."

Kyra saw her looking back meaningfully, in awe, and she wondered.

"I don't understand what is happening to me," Kyra said. "I have never dreamt before. Not like this. They feel like more than dreams—it is as if I am really there. As if I am seeing through the dragon's eye."

The nurse looked at her with her soulful eyes, and laid her hands in her lap.

128

"Is a very sacred thing to be marked by an animal," Lyra said. "And this is no ordinary animal. If a creature touches you, then you share a synergy—forever. You might see what it sees, or feel what it feels, or hear what it hears. It may happen tonight—or it may be next year. But one day, it shall happen."

Lyra looked at her, searching.

"Do you understand, Kyra? You are not the same girl you were yesterday, when you set out from here. That is no mere mark on your cheek—it is a sign. You now carry within you the mark of a dragon."

Kyra furrowed her brow, trying to understand.

"But what does that mean?" Kyra asked, trying to make sense of it all.

Lyra sighed, exhaling a long time.

"Time will show you."

Kyra thought of the Lord's Men, of the coming war, and she felt a wave of urgency. She threw off her furs and rose to her feet and as she did, she felt wobbly, unlike herself. Lyra rushed over and held her shoulder, steadying her.

"You must lie down," Lyra urged. "The fever is not yet past."

But Kyra felt a pressing urgency to help and she could stay in bed no longer.

"I shall be fine," she replied, grabbing her cloak and draping it over her shoulders to ward off the draft. As she moved to go, she felt a hand on her shoulder.

"Drink this, at least," Lyra urged, handing her a mug.

Kyra looked down and saw a red liquid inside.

"What is it?"

"My own concoction," she replied with a smile "It will calm the fever, and relieve the pain."

Kyra took a long sip, holding it with both hands, and it felt thick as it went down, hard to swallow. She made a face and Lyra smiled.

"It tastes like earth," Kyra observed.

Lyra smiled wider. "It's not known for its taste."

But already Kyra felt better from it, her whole body immediately warmer.

"Thank you," she said. She went over to Aidan, leaned over and kissed his forehead, careful not to wake him. She then turned and hurried from the room, Leo beside her.

Kyra twisted and turned down Volis's endless corridors, all dim, lit only by the flickering torches along the walls. Only a few men stood guard at this late hour, the rest of the fort quiet, fast asleep. Kyra ascended the spiral, stone staircase and stopped before her father's chamber, blocked by a guard. He looked at her, something like reverence in his eyes, and she wondered how far the story had already spread. He nodded to her.

"My lady," he said.

She nodded back.

"Is my father in his chamber?"

"He could not sleep. Last I saw he was pacing toward his study."

Kyra hurried down the stone corridors, ducking her head beneath a low, tapered archway and down a spiral staircase until finally she made her way to the far end of the fort. The hall ended in the thick, arched wooden door to his library, and she reached out to open them, but found the doors already ajar. She stopped herself as she heard urgent, strained voices coming from inside.

"I tell you that is *not* what she saw," came the angry voice of her father.

He was heated, and she stopped herself from entering, figuring it would be best to wait. She stood there, waiting for the voices to stop, curious who he was speaking to and what they were talking about. Were they talking about her? she wondered.

"If she did indeed see a dragon," came a crackly voice, which Kyra immediately recognized as Thonos, her father's oldest advisor, "there remains little hope for Volis."

Her father muttered something she could not understand, and there followed a long silence, as Thonos sighed.

"The ancient scrolls," Thonos replied, his voice labored, "tell of the rise of the dragons. A time we shall all be crushed under their flames. We have no wall to keep them out. We have nothing but hills and sky. And if they have come, they are here for a reason."

"But what reason?" her father asked. "What would compel a dragon to cross the world?"

"Perhaps a better question, Commander," Thonos replied, "is what could wound it?"

A long silence followed, punctuated only by the crackling of the fire, until finally Thonos spoke again.

"I suspect it is not the dragon that troubles you most, is it?" Thonos asked.

There followed another long silence, and Kyra, though she knew she should not listen in, leaned forward, unable to help herself, and peered through the crack. Her heart felt heavy to see her father sitting there, head in his hands, brooding.

"No," he said, his voice thick with exhaustion. "It is not," he admitted.

Kyra wondered what they could be talking about.

"You dwell on the prophecies, do you not?" he asked. "The time of her birth?"

Kyra leaned in, her heart pounding in her ears, sensing they were speaking about her, but not understanding what they meant.

There came no response.

"I was there, Commander," Thonos finally said. "As were you."

Her father sighed, but would not raise his head.

"She is your daughter. Do you not think it fair to tell her? About her birth? Her mother? Does she not have a right to know who she is?"

Kyra's heart slammed in her chest; she hated secrets, especially about her. She was dying to know what they meant.

"The time is not right," her father finally said.

"But the time is never right, is it?" the old man said.

Kyra breathed sharply, feeling stung.

She suddenly turned and ran off, a heaviness in her chest as her father's words rang in her ears. They hurt her more than a million knives, more than anything the Lord's Men could throw at her. She felt betrayed. He was withholding a secret from her, some secret he'd been hiding her entire life. He had been lying to her.

Does she not have a right to know who she is?

Her entire life Kyra had felt that people had looked at her differently, as if they knew something about her which she did not, as if she were an outside, and she had never understood why. Now, she understood. She didn't just feel different than everyone else—she *was* different. But how?

Who was she?

131

CHAPTER SEVENTEEN

Vesuvius marched, a hundred trolls on his heels, through Great Wood, up the sharply rising terrain, too steep for the horses to follow. He marched with a sense of determination, and for the first time, optimism. He hacked through the thick brush with his blade and knew he could have passed through without cutting them, but he wanted to: he enjoyed killing things.

With each passing step Vesuvius heard the roar of the captured giant, growing louder, making the ground beneath them tremble. He noted the fear in the faces of his fellow trolls—and it made him smile. That fear was what he had been hoping to see for years—it meant that finally, after all the rumors, the giant had been found.

He chopped through the last of the brush and crested the ridge, and as he did, the forest opened up into a vast clearing before him. Vesuvius stopped in his tracks, caught off guard by the sight. At the far side of the clearing lay a huge cave, its arched opening a hundred feet high, and chained to its rock, by chains fifty feet long and three feet thick, one to each ankle and wrist, was the most immense, hideous creature he had ever laid eyes upon. It was a true giant, a nasty piece of creation, standing at least a hundred feet high and thirty feet wide, with a body built like a man but with four eyes, no nose, and a mouth that was all jaw and teeth. It opened its mouth in a roar, an awful sound, and Vesuvius, who feared nothing, who had faced the most gruesome creatures alive, had to admit that even *he* was afraid. It opened its mouth wider and wider, its teeth sharpened to a point five feet long, and looked as if it were ready to swallow the world.

It also looked enraged. It roared again and again, stomping its feet, fighting at the chains that bound it, and the ground shook, the cave shook, the entire mountainside shook. It was as if this beast, with all its power, was moving the entire mountain by itself, as if it had so much energy that it could not be contained. Vesuvius grinned; this was exactly what he needed. A creature like this could blast through the tunnel, could do what an army of trolls could not.

132

Vesuvius stepped forward and entered the clearing, noticing the dozens of dead soldiers, their corpses littering the ground, and as he did, his hundreds of waiting soldiers lined up at attention. He could see the fear in all their faces, as if they had no idea what to do with the giant now that they had captured him.

Vesuvius stopped at the edge of the clearing, just out of range of the giant's chains, not wanting to end up like the corpses, and as he did, it turned and charged for him, swiping at him with its long claws and missing by only a few feet.

Vesuvius stood there, staring back at it, while his commander came running up beside him, keeping his distance along the perimeter so as to be out of the giant's range.

"My Lord and King," the commander said, bowing deferentially. "The giant has been captured. It is yours to bring back. But we cannot bind it. We have lost many soldiers trying. We are at a loss for what to do."

Vesuvius stood there, hands on his hips, feeling the eyes of all his trolls on him as he surveyed the beast. It was an awesome specimen of creation, and as it glared down and snarled at him, anxious to tear him apart, Vesuvius could see what the problem was. He realized at once, as he usually did, how to fix it.

Vesuvius lay a hand on his commander's shoulder and leaned in close.

"You are trying to approach it," he said softly. "You must let it come to you. You must catch it off guard, and only then can you bind it. You must give it what it wants."

His commander looked back, confused.

"And what is it that it wants, my Lord and King?"

Vesuvius began to walk, leading his commander forward as they stepped deeper into the clearing, toward the giant.

"Why, *you*," Vesuvius finally replied, as if it were the most obvious thing in the world—and then shoved his commander with all his might, sending the unsuspecting soldier stumbling forward into the clearing.

Vesuvius backed up, safely out of range, and watched as the giant blinked down, surprised. The soldier leapt to his feet, trying to run, but the giant reacted immediately, swooping down with its claws, scooping him up and squeezing his hands around his waist as he raised him to eye level. He pulled him close and bit off the troll's head, swallowing his screams.

Vesuvius smiled, pleased to be rid of an inept commander.

"If I need to teach you what to do," he said to the corpse that was once his commander, "then why bother having a commander?"

Vesuvius turned and looked over the rest of his soldiers, and they all stood there, petrified, staring back in shock. He pointed to a soldier standing nearby.

"You," he said.

The troll stared back nervously.

"Yes, my Lord and King?"

"You are next."

The troll's eyes widened, and he dropped to his knees and clasped his hands out before him.

"I cannot, my Lord and King!" he wept. "I beg you! Not me! Choose someone else!"

Vesuvius stepped forward and nodded amicably.

"Okay," he replied. He stepped forward and sliced the troll's throat with his dagger, and the troll fell face-first, dead, at his feet. "I will."

Vesuvius turned to his other soldiers.

"Pick him up," he commanded, "and throw him in the giant's range. When it approaches, have your ropes ready. You will bind him as he goes for the bait."

A half dozen soldiers grabbed the corpse, rushed forward, and threw him into the clearing. The other soldiers followed Vesuvius's command, rushing forward on either side of the clearing with their massive ropes at the ready.

The giant studied the fresh troll at its feet, as if debating. But finally, as Vesuvius had gambled, it exhibited its limited intelligence and lunged forward, grabbing the corpse—exactly as Vesuvius knew it would.

"NOW!" he shrieked.

The soldiers threw the ropes, casting them over the back of the giant, grabbing hold on either side and pulling, pinning it down. More soldiers rushed forward and threw more ropes, dozens of them, again and again, binding its neck, its arms, its legs. They pulled with all their might as they encircled it, and the beast strained and struggled and

134

roared in fury—but there was soon nothing it could do. Bound by dozens of thick ropes, held down by hundreds of men, it lay face down in the dirt, roaring helplessly.

Vesuvius walked close and stood over it, unimaginable just moments ago, and looked down, satisfied at his conquest.

Finally, after all these years, he grinned wide.

"Now," he said slowly, savoring each word, "Escalon is mine."

CHAPTER EIGHTEEN

Kyra stood at the window of her chamber watching dawn break over the countryside with a sense of anticipation and dread. She had spent a long night plagued by nightmares, tossing and turning after overhearing her father's conversation. She could still hear the words ringing in her head:

Does she not have a right to know who she is?

All night long she had dreamt of a woman with an obscured face, wearing a veil, a woman she felt certain was her mother. She reached for her, again and again, only to wake grasping at the bed, at nothing.

Kyra no longer knew what was real and what was a dream, what was a truth and what was a lie. How many secrets had they been keeping from her? What couldn't they tell her?

Kyra finally woke at dawn, clutching her cheek, still stinging from the wound, and she wondered about her mother. All of her life she had been told that her mother had died in childbirth, and she had no reason to believe otherwise. Kyra felt she did not really resemble anyone in her family or in this fort, and the more she thought about it, the more she realized that everyone had always looked at her a bit differently, as if she didn't quite belong here. But she had never imagined that there was anything to it, that her father had been lying to her, keeping some secret from her. Was her mother still alive? Why did they have to hide it from her?

Kyra stood at the window, trembling inside, marveling at how her life had changed so drastically in the last day. She also felt a fire burning in her veins, running from her cheek to her shoulder and down to her wrist, and she knew she was not the same person she was. She could sense the warmth of the dragon coursing through her, pulsating inside her. She wondered what it all meant. Would she ever be the same person again?

Kyra looked down at the people below, hundreds hurrying to and fro so early, and she marveled at all the activity. Usually this time of day was quiet. But not now. The Lord's Men were coming for them, like a brewing storm, and her people knew there would be retribution. The spirit in the air was different this time, too. Her people had always been quick to back down. But their spirit seemed to have hardened this time, and she was thrilled to see them preparing to fight. Scores of her father's men were securing the earthen banks, doubling the guard at the gates, lowering the portcullis, taking positions on the ramparts, barring windows and digging ditches. Men selected and sharpened weapons, filled quivers with arrows, prepared horses, and assembled in the courtyard nervously. They were all preparing.

Kyra could hardly believe she was the catalyst for all this; she felt a sense of guilt and of pride all at once. Most of all, she felt dread. Her people, she knew, could not survive a direct attack by the Lord's Men, whom, after all, had the Pandesian Empire behind them. They could put up a stand, but when Pandesia arrived with all its might, they would all surely die here.

"Glad to see you're up," came a cheerful voice.

Kyra spun, startled, as did Leo beside her, not realizing anyone else was awake in the fort this early, and she was relieved to see Anvin standing in the doorway, a grin on his face, joined by Vidar, Arthfael, and several more of her father's men. As the group stood looking back at her, she could see they looked at her differently this time. There was something different in their eyes: respect. They no longer looked at her as if she were a young girl, an observer, but rather, as if she were one of them. An equal.

That look restored her heart, made her feel as if it had all been worth it. There was nothing she had ever wanted more than to gain the respect of these men.

"You're better, then?" asked Vidar.

Kyra thought about that, and as she opened and closed her fists and stretched her arms, she realized she was, indeed, better—in fact, stronger than ever before. As she nodded back to them, she could see they also looked at her with something else: a touch of fear. As if she held some sort of power they did not know or trust.

"I feel reborn," she replied.

Anvin grinned wide.

"Good," he said. "You're going to need it. We'll need every hand we can get."

She looked back, surprised and thrilled.

137

"Are you offering me a chance to fight with you?" she asked, her heart thumping. No news could be more thrilling to her.

Arthfael smiled and stepped forward, clasping her shoulder.

"Just don't tell your father," he said.

Leo stepped forward and licked these men's hands and they all stroked his head.

"We have a little present for you," Vidar said.

Kyra was surprised.

"A present?" she asked.

"Consider it a homecoming," Arthfael said, "just a little something to help you forget that scratch on your cheek."

He stepped aside, as did the others, and Kyra realized they were inviting her to follow. There was nothing she wanted more. She smiled back, joyful for the first time in as long as she could remember.

"Is that what it takes to be invited to join your lot?" she asked with a smile. "I had to kill five of the Lord's Men?"

"Three," Arthfael corrected. "As I recall, Leo here killed two of them."

"Yes," Anvin said. "And surviving an encounter with a dragon counts for something, too."

*

Kyra marched with the men across the grounds of her father's fort, Leo at her side, their boots crunching on the snow, energized by the industry all around her, the fort so busy, filled with a sense of purpose, stunningly alive in the dawn. She passed carpenters, cobblers, saddlers, masons, all hard at work on their craft, while endless men sharpened swords and other blades along stones. As they walked, Kyra sensed people stopped and staring at her; her ears burned. They all must have known why the Lord's Men were coming, what she had done. She felt so conspicuous, and feared her people would hate her.

But she was surprised to see that they looked at her with admiration—and something else, perhaps fear. They must have discovered she'd survived an encounter with a dragon, and it seemed they did not know what to make of her.

Kyra looked up and searched the skies, hoping beyond hope that she might see Theos, recovered, flying high, circling her. But as she searched the skies, she saw nothing. Where was he? she wondered. Had he survived? Would he ever fly again? Was he already halfway across the world?

As they walked, crossing the fort, Kyra became curious as to where they were leading her and what gift they could possibly have in store for her.

"Where are we going?" she asked Anvin, as they turned down a narrow cobblestone street. They passed villagers digging out from the snow, while huge slabs of ice and snow slid off clay roofs. Smoke rose from chimneys all throughout the village, the smell of it crisp on the winter day.

They turned down another street and Kyra spotted a wide, low stone dwelling, covered in snow, with a red oak door, one set apart from the others, which she recognized immediately.

"Is that not the blacksmith's forge?" she asked.

"It is," Anvin replied, still walking.

"But why do you lead me here?" she asked.

They reached the door, and Vidar smiled as he opened the door and stepped aside.

"You shall see."

Kyra ducked through the low doorway then stood up straight in the forge, Leo following, the others filing in behind her, and as she entered, she was struck by the heat, the fires from the forge making it warm in here. She immediately noticed all the weapons laid out on the blacksmith's anvils, and she studied them with admiration: swords and axes still in progress, some still red-hot, still being molded.

The blacksmith sat there with his three apprentices, faces covered in soot, and looked up, expressionless, through his thick black beard. His place was packed with weapons—laid out on every surface, on the floor, hanging from hooks, and it appeared he was working on dozens at once. Kyra knew Brot, the blacksmith, a short man, stocky, with a low brow perpetually furrowed in concentration, to be a serious man who spoke few words, and who lived for his weapons. He was known to be gruff, not to care much for men—only for a piece of steel.

The few times Kyra had spoken with him, though, Brot had proved, beneath his gruff exterior, to be a kindhearted man, and passionate when talking about weaponry. He must have recognized a kindred soul in Kyra, as they had a mutual love for weaponry.

"Kyra," he said, seeming pleased to see her. "Sit."

She sat across form him at the empty bench, her back to the forge, feeling its heat. Anvin and the others crowded around them, and they all watched as Brot tinkered with his weaponry: a lance, a sickle, a mace in progress, its chain still waiting to be hammered out. Kyra saw a sword, its edges still rough, waiting to be sharpened. Behind him his apprentices worked, the noise of their tools filling the air. One hammered away at an ax, sparks flying everywhere, while another reached out with his long tongs and pulled a strip of white-hot steel from the forge, laying it on the anvil and preparing to hammer. The third used his tongs to take a halberd off his anvil and place it in the large, iron slack tub, its waters hissing the second it was submerged and emitting a cloud of steam.

For Kyra, this forge had always been the most exciting place in Volis.

As she watched him, her heart beat faster, wondering what present these men had in store.

"I heard of your exploits," Brot said, not meeting her eye, looking down at a long sword as he examined it, testing its weight. It was one of the longest swords she had ever seen, and he frowned and narrowed his eyes as he held its blade, seeming unsatisfied.

She knew better than to interrupt him, and she waited patiently in the silence for him to continue.

"A shame," he finally said.

Kyra stared back, confused.

"What?" she asked.

"That you did not kill the boy," he said. "We wouldn't all be in this mess if you had, would we?"

He still did not meet her eyes, weighing the sword, and she flushed, knowing he was right but not regretting her actions.

"A lesson for you," he added. "Kill them all, always. Do you understand me?" he asked, his tone hard as he looked up and met her eyes, dead serious. "*Kill them all.*"

Despite his harsh tone and blunt quality, Kyra admired Brot for always saying what he believed, and what others were afraid to say. She also admired him for his fearlessness: owning weapons of steel was outlawed by Pandesia, on punishment of death. Her father's men's weapons were sanctioned only because they kept The Flames—

140

but Brot also illegally forged weapons for dozens of others, helping to supply a secret army. He could be caught and killed at any moment, and yet he never flinched in the face of duty.

"Is that why you've summoned me?" she asked, puzzled. "To give me advice on killing men?"

He hammered away at a sword on the anvil before him, working for a while, ignoring her until he was ready. Still looking down, he said:

"No. To help you kill them."

She blinked, confused, and Brot reached back and gestured to one of his apprentices, who rushed over and handed him an object.

Brot looked at her.

"I heard you lost two weapons last night," he said. "A bow and a staff, was it?"

She nodded, wondering where he was going with this.

Brot shook his head disapprovingly.

"That is because you play with sticks. A child's weapons. You've killed five of the Lord's Men and have faced off with a dragon and lived, and that is more than anyone in this room. You are a warrior now, and you deserve a warrior's weapons."

He reached back as one of his apprentices handed him something, then turned back and laid a long object down on the table, covered in a red, velvet cloth.

She looked up at him questioningly, her heart beating with anticipation, and he nodded back.

Kyra reached out, slowly removed the red cloth, and gasped at what she saw: before her lay a beautiful longbow, its handle carved, ornate, and covered in a paper-thin sheet of shiny metal. It was unlike any bow she had ever seen.

"Alkan steel," he explained, as she hoisted it and admired how light it was. "The strongest in the world—and also the lightest. Very scarce, used by kings. These men here have paid for it—and my men have been pounding it all night."

Kyra turned and saw Anvin and the others looking back, smiling, and her heart filled with gratitude.

"Feel it," Brot urged. "Go ahead."

Kyra held up the bow and weighed it in her hand, in awe at how it fit in her hand.

"It is even lighter than my wood one," she said, confused.

"That's Beechum wood beneath," he said. "Stronger than what you had—and lighter, too. This bow will never break—and your arrows shall go much further."

She admired it, speechless, realizing this was the nicest thing anyone had ever done for her. Brot reached out and handed her a quiver filled with arrows, all with shiny new heads, and as she fingered one she was amazed at how sharp they were. She inspected their intricate design.

"Barbed broadhead," Brot said proudly. "You land one of these, and the head will not come out. They are designed to kill."

Kyra looked up at Brot and the others, overwhelmed, not knowing what to say. What meant most to her were not the weapons but that these great men thought enough of her to go out of their way.

"I don't know how to thank you," she said. "I shall do my best to honor your work, and to be worthy of this weapon."

"I'm not done yet," he said, gruffly. "Hold out your arms."

She did, puzzled, and he stepped forward and examined them, rolling up her sleeves and checking her forearms. He finally nodded, satisfied.

"That's about right," he said.

Brot nodded to an apprentice, who stepped forward holding two shiny objects and clasped them to her forearms. As the cold metal touched her skin, Kyra was shocked to see that they were bracers, long, thin forearm guards. They ran from her wrist to her elbow, and as they were clasped into place with a click, they fit perfectly.

Kyra bent her elbows in wonder, examining the bracers, and as she did, she felt invincible, as if they were a part of her new skin. They were so light, yet so strong, protecting her from wrist to elbow.

"Bracers," Brot said. "Thin enough to allow you to move, yet strong enough to withstand the blow of any sword." He looked right at her. "These are not only for protection from the string when firing that bow—these are extra-long, also made of Alkan steel. They are meant to replace a shield. This shall be your armor. If an enemy comes at you with a sword, you now have the means to defend yourself."

He suddenly grabbed a sword off the table, raised it high, and brought it down right for her head.

142

Kyra, shocked, reacted, raising her forearms with her new bracers—and she was amazed as she stopped the blow, sparks flying.

Brot smiled, lowering his sword, pleased.

Kyra examined her bracers and felt an overwhelming joy.

"You have given me all I could ever want," Kyra said, getting ready to embrace them.

But Brot held up a hand and stopped her.

"Not *all*," he corrected.

Brot gestured to his third apprentice, who brought forth a long object wrapped in a black velvet cloth.

Kyra looked at it curiously, then draped the bow over her shoulder and reached out and took it. She unwrapped it slowly, and when she finally saw what was beneath it, she was breathless.

It was a staff, a work of beauty, even longer than her old one, and, most amazing of all, shiny. Like the bow, it was covered in a plate of Alkan steel, pounded paper-thin, light reflecting off of it. Yet even with all this metal, as she weighed it in her hands, it was lighter than her old staff.

"Next time," Brot said, "when they strike your staff, it won't break. And when you hit a foe, the blow will be more severe. It is a weapon and a shield in one. And that's not all," he said, pointing at it.

Kyra looked down, confused, not understand what he was pointing at.

"Twist it," he said.

She did as he told her and as she did, to her shock, the staff unscrewed and split in two equal halves. In each end was embedded a pointy blade, several inches long.

Kyra looked up, agape, and Brot smiled.

"Now you have more ways to kill a man," he said.

She looked up at the glistening blades, the finest work she had ever seen, and she was in awe. He had custom-forged this weapon for her, giving her a staff that doubled as two short spears, a weapon uniquely suited for her strengths. She twisted it closed again, smoothly locking it into place, so seamless she could not even tell there was a concealed weapon within.

She looked up at Brot, at all of the men, tears in her eyes.

"I shall never be able to thank you," she said.

"You already have," Anvin said, stepping forward. "You have brought a war upon us—a war that we ourselves were afraid to start. You have done us a great favor."

Before she could process his words, suddenly, a series of horns sounded in the distance, one after the next, echoing off the fort.

All of them exchanged a glance, all knowing what this meant: battle had come.

The Lord's Men were here.

CHAPTER NINETEEN

Merk hiked and hiked on the forest trail, the shadows getting long as he wound his way through Whitewood, the dead thieves now a good day's hike behind him. He hadn't stopped hiking since, trying to clear his mind of the incident, to get back to the peaceful place he had once inhabited. It wasn't easy. His legs growing weary, Merk was more anxious than ever to find the Tower of Ur, to walk into his new life as a Watcher, and he scanned the horizon, trying to catch a glimpse of it through the trees.

But there was no sign of it. This trek was beginning to feel more like a pilgrimage, one that would never end. The Tower of Ur was more remote, more well-hidden, than he had imagined.

Encountering those thieves had awakened something deep within him, had made Merk realize how hard it might be to shake off his old self. He did not know if he had the discipline. He only hoped that the Watchers would accept him in their order; if not, with nowhere else to turn, he would surely go back to being the man he once was.

Up ahead, Merk saw the wood change, saw a grove of ancient white trees, trunks as wide as ten men, reaching high into the sky, their branches spreading out like a canopy with shimmering red leaves. One of the trees, with a broad, curved trunk, looked particularly inviting, and Merk, feet aching, sat down beside it. He leaned back and felt an immediate sense of relief, felt the pain leaving his back and legs from hours of hiking. He kicked off his boots and felt the pain throbbing in his feet, and he sighed as a cool breeze soothed him, leaves rustling above.

Merk reached into his sack and extracted what remained of the dried strips of meat from the rabbit he had caught the other night. He took a bite and chewed slowly, closing his eyes, resting, wondering what the future had in store for him. Sitting here, against this tree, beneath these rustling leaves, felt good enough for him.

Merk's eyes felt heavy and he let them close, just for a moment, needing the rest.

When he opened them, Merk was surprised to see the sky had grown darker, to realize that he had fallen asleep. It was already twilight, and he realized with a start that he would have slept all night—if he had not been awakened by a noise.

Merk sat up and took stock, immediately on guard as his instincts kicked in. He clutched the hilt of his dagger, hidden in his waist, and waited. He did not want to resort to violence—but until he reached the Tower, he was starting to feel that anything was possible.

The rustling became louder, and it sounded like someone running, bursting through the forest. Merk was puzzled: what was someone else doing out here, in the middle of nowhere, in twilight? From the sound of the leaves, Merk could tell it was one person, and that it was light. Maybe a child, or a girl.

Sure enough, a moment later there burst into his sight a girl, emerging from the forest, running, crying. He watched her, surprised, as she ran, alone, stumbled, and fell, but feet away from him. She landed face-first in the dirt. She was pretty, perhaps eighteen, but disheveled, her hair a mess, dirt and leaves in it, her clothes ragged and torn.

Merk stood, and as she scrambled to get back to her feet she saw him and her eyes widened in panic.

"Please don't hurt me!" she cried, standing, backing away.

Merk raised his hands.

"I mean you no harm," he said slowly, standing to his full height. "In fact, I was just about to be on my way."

She backed up several feet in terror, still crying, and he could not help but wonder what had happened. Whatever it was, he did not want to get involved—he had enough problems of his own.

Merk turned back on the trail and began to walk away, when her voice cried out behind him:

"No, wait!"

He turned and saw her standing there, desperate.

"Please. I need your help," she pleaded.

Merk looked at her and saw how beautiful she was beneath her disheveled appearance, with unwashed blonde hair, light blue eyes, and a face with perfect features, covered in tears and in dirt. She wore simple farmer's clothes, and he could tell she was not rich. She looked as if she had been on the run for a long time.

He shook his head.

"You don't have the money to pay me," Merk said. "I cannot help you, whatever it is you need. Besides, I'm on my way for my own mission."

"You don't understand," she begged, stepping closer. "My family—our home was raided this morning. Mercenaries. My father's been hurt. He chased them away, but they'll be back soon—and with a lot more men—to kill him, to kill my whole family. They said they will burn our farm to the ground. Please!" she begged, stepping closer. "I'll give you anything. *Anything!*"

Merk stood there, feeling sorry for her, but determined not to get involved.

"There are many problems in the world, miss," he said. "And I can't fix them all."

He turned once again to walk away, when her voice rang out again:

"Please!" she cried. "It is a *sign*, don't you see? That I would run into you here, in the middle of nowhere? I expected to find no one—and I found you. You were meant to be here, meant to help me. God is giving you a chance for redemption. Don't you believe in signs?"

He stood there and watched her sobbing, and he felt guilty, but mostly detached. A part of him thought of how many people he'd killed in his lifetime, and wondered: what's a few more? But there were always just a few more. It never seemed to end. He had to draw the line somewhere.

"I'm sorry, miss," he said. "But I am not your savior."

Merk turned again and began to walk off, determined this time not to stop, to drown out her sobs and grief by rustling the leaves loudly with his feet, blocking out the noise.

But no matter how hard he rustled the leaves, her cries continued, ringing somewhere in the back of his head, summoning him. He turned and watched her run off, disappearing back into the wood, and he wanted to feel a sense of relief. But more than anything, he felt haunted—haunted by a cry he did not want to hear.

He cursed as he hiked, enraged, wishing he'd never met her. Why? he wondered. Why him?

It kept gnawing away at him, would not let him be, and he hated the feeling. Was this what it was like, he wondered, to have a conscience?

CHAPTER TWENTY

Kyra's heart pounded as she walked with her father and brothers, Anvin and all the warriors, all marching solemnly through the streets of Volis, all preparing for war. There was a solemn silence in the air, the skies heavy with gray, a light snow falling once again as their boots crunched through the snow, approaching the main gate of the fort. Horns sounded again and again, and her father led his men stoically, Kyra surprised at how calm he was, as if he had done this a thousand times before.

Kyra looked straight ahead, and through the iron bars of the lowered portcullis she caught a glimpse of the Lord Governor, leading his men, a hundred of them, dressed in their scarlet armor, the yellow and blue Pandesian banners flapping in the wind. They galloped through the snow on their massive black horses, wearing the finest armor and donning the finest weaponry, all heading directly for the gates of Volis. The rumble of their horses was audible from here, and Kyra felt the ground tremble beneath her.

As Kyra marched, her heart pounding, she held her new staff, had her new bow strapped over her shoulder, and she wore hew new bracers—and she felt reborn. Finally, she felt like a *real* warrior, with real weapons. She was elated to have them.

As they marched, Kyra was pleased her to see her people rallying, unafraid, all joining them on their march to meet the enemy. She saw all the village folk looking to her father and his men with hope, and she was honored to be marching with them. They all seemed to have an infinite trust in her father, and she suspected that if they were under any other leadership, the village folk would not be as calm.

The Lord's Men came closer, a horn sounded yet again, and Kyra's heart slammed.

"No matter what happens," Anvin said, coming up beside her, talking quietly, "no matter how close they get, do not take any action without your father's command. He is your commander now. I speak to you not as his daughter, but as one of his men. One of *us*."

She nodded back, honored.

"I do not wish to be the cause of death for our people," she said.

"Don't worry," Arthfael said, coming up on her other side. "This day has been a long time coming. You didn't start this war—they did. The second they crossed the Southern Gate and invaded Escalon."

Kyra, reassured, tightened her grip on her staff, ready for whatever might come. Perhaps the Lord Governor would be reasonable. Perhaps he would negotiate a truce?

Kyra and the others reached the portcullis, and they all stopped and looked to her father.

He stood there, looking out, expressionless, his face hard, ready. He turned to his men.

"We shall not cower behind iron gates in fear of our enemies," he boomed, "but meet them, as men, beyond the gate. Raise it!" he commanded.

A groaning noise followed as soldiers slowly raised the thick iron portcullis. Finally, it stopped with a bang, and Kyra joined the others as they all marched through.

They marched across the hollow wood bridge, their boots echoing, crossed over the moat, and all came to a stop at the opposite side, waiting.

A rumble filled the air as the Lord's Men came to a stop a few feet before them. Kyra stood several feet behind her father, grouped in with the others, and she pushed her way to the front lines, wanting to stand by his side—and to stare down the Lord's Men, face to face.

Kyra saw the Lord Governor, a middle-aged, balding man with wisps of gray hair and a large belly, sitting smugly on his horse a dozen feet away, staring down at all of them as if he were too good for them. A hundred of his men sat on horseback behind him, all wearing serious expressions and bearing serious weaponry. These men, she could see, were all prepared for war and death.

Kyra was so proud to see her father standing there, before all his men, unflinching, unafraid. He wore the face of a commander at war, one she had never seen before. It was not the face of the father she knew, but the face he reserved for his men.

A long, tense silence filled the air, punctuated only by the howling of the wind. The Lord Governor took his time, examining them for a full minute, clearly trying to intimidate them, to force her people to

150

look up and take in the awesomeness of their horses and weapons and armor. The silence stretched so long that Kyra started to wonder if anyone would break it, and she began to realize that her father's silence, his greeting them silently, coldly, standing with all his men at arms, was in itself an act of defiance. She loved him for it. He was not a man to back down to anyone, whatever the odds.

Leo was the only one to make a sound, snarling quietly up at them.

Finally, the Lord Governor cleared his throat, as he stared at her father.

"Five of my men are dead," he announced, his voice nasally. He remained on his horse, not coming down to meet them at their level. "Your daughter has broken the sacred Pandesian law. You know the consequence: touching a Lord's Man means pain of death."

He fell silent, and her father did not respond. As the snow and wind picked up, the only sound that could be heard was the flapping of the banners in the wind. The men, equally numbered on both sides, stared at each other in a tense silence.

Finally, the Lord Governor continued.

"Because I am a merciful Lord," he said, "I will not execute your daughter. Nor will I kill you and your men and your people, which is my right. I am, in fact, willing to put all this nasty business behind us."

The silence continued as the Governor, taking his time, slowly surveyed all their faces, until he stopped on Kyra. She felt a chill as his greedy, ugly eyes settled on her.

"In return, I will take your daughter, as is my right. She is unwed, and of age, and as you know, Pandesian law permits me. Your daughter—*all* of your daughters—are our property now."

He sneered at her father.

"Consider yourself lucky I do not exact a harsher punishment," he concluded.

The Lord Governor turned and nodded to his men, and two of his soldiers, fierce-looking men, dismounted and began to cross the bridge, their boots and spurs echoing over the hollow wood as they went.

Kyra's heart slammed in her chest as she saw them coming for her; she wanted to take action, to draw her bow and fire, to wield her staff. But she recalled Anvin's words about awaiting her father's command, about how disciplined soldiers should act, and as hard as it was, she forced herself to wait.

As they came closer, Kyra wondered what her father would do. Would he give her away to these men? Would he fight for her? Whether they won or lost, whether they took her or not, did not matter to her—what mattered more to her was that her father cared enough to make a stand.

As they neared, though, her father did not react. Kyra's heart pounded in her throat. She felt a rush of disappointment, realizing he was going to let her go. It made her want to cry.

Leo snarled furiously, standing out in front of her, hair raised; yet still they didn't stop. She knew that if she commanded him to pounce, he would; yet she did not want him to be harmed by those weapons, and she did not want to defy her father's command and spark a war.

The men were but a few feet away from her when, suddenly, at the last second, her father nodded to his men, and six of them stepped forward, Kyra was elated to see, and lowered their halberds, blocking the soldiers' approach.

The soldiers stopped short, their armor clanging against the metal halberds, and they looked to her father with surprise, clearly not expecting this.

"You'll be going no further," he said. His voice was strong, dark, a voice no one would dare defy. It carried the tone of authority—not of a serf.

In that moment, Kyra loved him more than she'd ever had.

He turned and looked out at the Lord Governor.

"We are all free men here," he said, "men and women, old and young alike. The choice is hers. Kyra," he said, turning to her, "do you wish to leave with these men?"

She stared back at him, suppressing a smile.

"No," she answered firmly.

He turned back to the Lord Governor.

"There you have it," he said. "The choice is hers to make. Not yours, and not mine. If you wish to have some property or gold of mine as recompense for your loss," he said to the Governor, "then you may have it. But you shall not have my daughter—or any of our daughters—regardless of what a scribe has set down as Pandesian law."

The Lord Governor glowered down at him, shock in his face, clearly not used to being spoken to that way—or defied. He looked like he did not know what to do. Clearly, this was not the reception he had been expecting.

"You dare to block my men?" he asked. "To turn down my offer?"

"It is no offer at all," Duncan replied.

"Think carefully, serf," he chided. "I shall not offer it twice. If you refuse me, you will face death—you and all of your people. Surely you know that I am not alone—I speak for the vast Pandesian army. Do you imagine you can face Pandesia alone—when your own King has surrendered your kingdom? When the odds are so stacked against you?"

Her father shrugged.

"I don't fight for odds," he replied. "I fight for causes. Your number of men does not matter to me. What matters is our freedom. You may win—but you will never take our spirit."

The governor's face hardened.

"When all your women and children are taken from you screaming," he said, "remember the choice you made today."

The Lord Governor turned, kicked his horse, and rode off, followed by several attendants, heading back on the road on which he'd came, into the snowy countryside.

His soldiers, though, remained behind, and their commander raised his banner high and ordered: "ADVANCE!"

The Lord's Men all dismounted, lined up in a row, and marched in perfect discipline, over the bridge and right for them.

Kyra, heart pounding, turned and looked at her father, as did all the others, awaiting his command—and suddenly he raised one fist high, and with a fierce battle cry, lowered it.

Suddenly, the sky filled with arrows. Kyra looked over her shoulder to see several of her father's archers take aim from the battlements and fire. Arrows whizzed by her ear and she watched as they hit the Lord's Men left and right.

Cries filled the air as men died all around her. It was the first time she had seen so many men die up close, and the sight stunned her.

Her father, at the same time, drew a short sword from each side of his waist, stepped forward, and stabbed the two soldiers who had come for his daughter, each dropping, dead, at his feet.

At the same moment, Anvin, Vidar, and Arthfael raised spears and hurled them, each felling a soldier who charged across the bridge. Brandon and Braxton stepped forward and hurled spears, too, one grazing a soldier's arm and the other grazing a soldier's leg, wounding them, at least.

More men charged and Kyra, inspired, set aside her staff, raised her new bow for the first time, placed an arrow, and fired. She aimed for the commander, leading his men in a charge on horseback, and she watched with great satisfaction as her arrow sailed through the air and impaled his chest. It was her first shot with the new bow, and her first time killing a man in formal combat—and as their commander fell to the ground, she looked down in shock at what she had just done.

At the same time, a dozen of the Lord's Men raised their bows and fired back, and Kyra watched in horror as arrows whizzed by her from the opposite direction—and as some of her father's men cried out, wounded, dropping all around her.

"FOR ESCALON!" her father yelled.

He drew his sword and led a charge across the bridge, into the thick of the Lord's Men. His soldiers followed close behind, and Kyra drew her staff and joined in, too, exhilarated at rushing into battle and wanting to be by her father's side.

As they charged, the Lord's Men prepared another round of arrows and fired once again—and soon a wall of arrows came at them.

But then, to Kyra's surprise, her father's men raised their large shields, creating a wall as they all squatted down together, perfectly disciplined. She squatted behind one of them, and heard the thwack as deadly arrows were stopped.

They all jumped to their feet and charged again, and she realized her father's strategy—to get close enough to the Lord's Men to render their arrows useless. They soon reached the wall of soldiers and there came a great clang of metal as men clashed in battle, swords meeting swords, halberds meeting shields, spears meeting armor. It was terrifying and exhilarating at the same moment.

Squeezed into the bridge with nowhere to go, the men fought hand-to-hand, groaning, slashing and blocking, the clang of metal deafening. Leo lunged forward and sunk his teeth into a man's foot, while one of her father's men cried out beside her and she looked over to see him stabbed by a sword, blood dripping from his mouth.

Kyra watched Anvin head-butt a man, then plunge a sword into his gut. She watched her father use his shield as a weapon, smashing two men so hard he knocked them over the bridge and into the moat. She'd never before seen her father in action, and he was a fierce thing to watch. Even more impressive was how his men formed around him, and it was clear they had fought by each other's sides for years. They had a camaraderie she envied.

Her father's men fought so well, they caught the Lord's Men off guard, who clearly had not expected an organized resistance. The Lord's Men fought for their Governor, who had already left them— while her father's men fought for their home, their families and their very lives, all right here. Their passion, their stakes, gave them momentum.

In close quarters with little room to maneuver, Kyra saw a soldier come at her, sword raised high, and she immediately grabbed her staff with both hands, turned it sideways and raised it overhead as a shield. The man came at her with a long sword, and she prayed Brot's Alkan steel would hold.

The sword clanged off the staff as it would against a shield, and to her relief, the staff did not break.

Kyra spun the staff around and smashed the soldier in the side of the head. He stumbled back, and she then kicked him, sending him tumbling backwards, shrieking, into the moat.

Another soldier charged her from the side, swinging a flail, and she realized she wouldn't be able to react in time. But Leo rushed forward and pounced on his chest, pinning him down on all fours.

Another soldier came at her with an ax, swinging sideways at her; she barely had time to react, as she spun and used her staff to block it. She held her staff vertically, barely able to keep back the soldier's strength, as the ax came closer to her. She gained a valuable lesson, realizing she should not try to meet these men head on. She could not overpower them; she had to fight to her strength, not to theirs.

Losing strength as the ax blade came closer, Kyra remembered Brot's contraption. She twisted the staff, it split into two pieces, and she stepped back as the ax came whizzing past, missing her. The soldier was stunned, clearly not expecting this, and in the same motion, Kyra raised the two halves of the staff and plunged the blades into the soldier's chest, killing him.

There came a shout, a rallying cry from behind her—and Kyra turned to see a mob of village folk—farmers, masons, blacksmiths, armorers, butchers—all wielding weapons—sickles, hatchets, anything and everything—racing for the bridge. Within moments they joined her father's men, all of them ready to take a stand.

Kyra watched as Thomak the butcher used a cleaver to sever a man's arm, while Brine the mason smashed a soldier in the chest with a hammer, felling him. The village folk brought a fresh burst of energy to the battle, and as clumsy as they were, they caught the Lord's Men off guard. They fought with passion, releasing years of pent-up anger at their servitude. Now, finally, they had a chance to stand up for themselves—a chance for vengeance.

They pushed back the Lord's Men as they hacked their way through with brute force, felling men—and their horses—left and right. But after a few minutes of intense fighting these amateur warriors began to fall, the air filled with their cries as the better armed and better trained soldiers cut them down. The Lord's Men pushed back, and the momentum swung back the other way.

The bridge became more crowded as more of the Lord's Men reinforcements charged onto it. Her father's men, slipping in the snow, were tiring, more than one crying out and falling, killed by the Lord's Men. The tide of battle was turning against them, and Kyra knew she had to do something quickly.

Kyra eyed her surroundings and had an idea: she jumped up on the stone rail at the edge of the bridge, gaining the vantage point she needed, several feet above the others, exposing herself but no longer caring. She was the only one of them nimble enough to leap all the way up here, and she drew her bow, took aim, and fired.

With her superior angle, Kyra was able to take out one soldier after the next. She took aim at one of the Lord's Men, bringing a hatchet down for her unsuspecting father's back, and hit him in the neck, felling him right before he put a blade in her father's back. She then fired at a soldier swinging a flail, hitting him in the ribs right before he could impact Anvin's head.

Firing arrow after arrow, Kyra felled a dozen men—until she was finally spotted. She felt an arrowed whizz by her face, and she looked out to see archers firing back at her. Before she could react, she gasped in horrific pain as an arrow grazed her arm, drawing blood.

Kyra jumped down from the rail and back into the fray. She rolled to her hands and knees, and she knelt there, breathing hard, her arm killing her, and looked up and saw more reinforcements arriving onto the bridge. She watched her people get driven back, and watched as one of them, right beside her, a man she had known and loved, was stabbed in the gut and tumbled over the railing, into the moat, dead.

As she knelt there, a fierce soldier raised his ax high overhead and brought it down for her. She knew she could not react it in time and she braced herself—when suddenly Leo lunged forward and sunk his fangs into the man's stomach.

Kyra sensed motion out of the corner of her eye and she turned to see another soldier raise his halberd and bring it down for the back of her neck. Unable to react in time, she braced herself for the blow, expecting to die.

There came a clang, and she looked up to see the blade hovering right before her head—stopped by a sword. Her father stood over her, wielding the sword, saving her from the deadly blow. He spun his sword around, twisting the halberd out of the way, then stabbed the soldier in the heart.

The move, though, left her father defenseless, and Kyra watched, horrified, as another soldier stepped forward and stabbed her father in the arm; he cried out and went stumbling back as the soldier bore down on him.

As Kyra knelt there, an unfamiliar feeling began to overcome her; it was a warmth, beginning in her solar plexus and radiating from there. It was a foreign sensation, yet one she embraced immediately as she felt it giving her infinite strength, spreading through her body, one limb at a time, coursing through her veins. More than strength, it gave her focus; as she looked around, it was as if time slowed. In a single glance, she took in all the enemy soldiers, saw all their vulnerabilities, saw how to kill each and every one.

Kyra did not understand what was happening to her—and she did not care. She embraced the new power that took over her and allowed herself to succumb to its sweet rage and do with her as it would.

Kyra stood, feeling invincible, feeling as if everyone else moved in slow motion around her. She raised her staff and pounced into the crowd.

What happened next was a flash, a blinding blur that she could barely process and barely remember. She felt the power overtake her arms, felt it instruct her who to strike, where to move, and she found herself attacking enemy soldiers in a blur as she cut through the crowd. She smashed one soldier in the side of the head, then reached back and jabbed one in the throat; then leapt high and with two hands brought her staff straight down on two soldiers' heads. She twisted and spun her staff end over end as she cut through the mob like a whirlwind, felling soldiers left and right, leaving a trail in her wake. No one could catch her—and no one could stop her.

The clang of her metal staff hitting armor echoed in the air, all happening impossibly fast. For the first time in her life, she felt at one with the universe; she felt as if she were no longer trying to control—but allowing herself to be controlled. She felt as if she were outside of herself. She did not understand this new power, and it terrified and exhilarated her at the same time.

Within moments she had cleared all the Lord's Men off the bridge. She found herself standing on the far side and jabbing one last soldier between the eyes.

Kyra stood there, breathing hard, and suddenly time became fast again. She looked around and saw the damage she had done, and she was more shocked than anyone else.

The dozen or so soldiers who remained of the Lord's Men, on the far side of the bridge, looked back at her, panic in their eyes, and turned and ran, slipping in the snow.

There came a shout, and Kyra's father led the charge as his men pursued them. They hacked them down, left and right, until there were no survivors left.

A horn sounded. The battle was over.

All her father's men, all the villagers, stood there, stunned, realizing they had achieved the impossible. Yet, oddly, there wasn't the jubilant outcry that normally would follow such a victory; there came no cheering and embracing of men, no shouts of joy. Instead, the air was strangely silent, the mood somber; they had lost many good brothers on this day, their bodies scattered before them, and perhaps that caused the men to pause.

But it was more than that, Kyra knew. That wasn't what caused the silence. What caused it, she knew, was her.

Every eye on the battlefield turned and looked at her. Even Leo looked up at her, fear in his eyes, as if he no longer knew her.

Kyra stood there, still breathing hard, her cheeks still flush, and felt them all staring. They looked at her with awe—but also with suspicion. They looked at her as if she were a stranger in their midst. All of them, she knew, were asking themselves the same question. It was a question which she herself wanted answered, and one that terrified her more than anything:

Who was she?

CHAPTER TWENTY-ONE

Alec drifted in and out of sleep as he stood in the cart, sandwiched between the mass of boys, dreaming fast, troubled dreams. He saw himself being squeezed to death in a coffin filled with boys, the lid being slammed on him.

He woke with a start, breathing hard, realizing he was standing in the cart. More stops had been made and more boys were crammed in as the cart jolted along its way, all day long for a second day, up and down hills, weaving in and out of the wood. Alec had been on his feet ever since the confrontation, feeling safer to stand, and his back was killing him. But he longer cared. He found it easier to doze off while standing, especially with Marco beside him. The boys who had attacked him had retreated to the far side of the carriage, but at this point, he did not trust anybody.

The jolting of the cart had sunk into Alec's consciousness, and he forgot what it was like to stand on steady ground. He thought of Ashton and took solace in the fact that at least his brother wasn't standing here right now. It gave him a sense of purpose, and gave him the courage to go on.

As the shadows grew longer, no end in sight to their journey, Alec began to lose hope, to feel as if they would never reach The Flames.

More time passed, and after he dozed off several times, he felt a nudge in his ribs. He opened his eyes to see it was Marco, gesturing with his head.

Alec felt a wave of excitement rippling through the crowd of boys, and this time he sensed something was different. All the boys perked up as they began to turn and look through the iron bars. Alec turned and tried to look out, disoriented, but he could not see through the thick crowd of bodies.

"You've got to see this," Marco said, looking out.

Marco shifted out of the way so Alec could peek through. As he did, Alec saw a sight which he would never forget:

The Flames.

160

Alec had heard about The Flames his entire life, but he had never imagined they could exist. It was one of those things so hard to imagine that, try as he did, he just could not picture how it could be possible. How could flames really reach the sky? How could they burn forever?

But now, as he laid eyes upon them for the first time, he realized it was all true. It took his breath away. There, on the horizon, sat The Flames, rising, as legend had it, to the clouds, so thick he could not see where they ended. He could hear the crackling of it, feel the heat of it, even from here. It was awe-inspiring and terrifying at once.

Up and down The Flames, Alec saw stationed hundreds of soldiers, boys and men, standing guard, spread out every hundred feet or so. On the horizon, at the end of the road, he saw a black, stone tower, around which sat several outbuildings. It was a hub of activity.

"Looks like our new home," Marco observed.

Alec saw the rows of squalid barracks, packed with boys covered in soot. He felt a pit in his stomach, realizing this was a sorry glimpse of his future, of the hell his life would become.

*

Alec braced himself as he was yanked off the cart by Pandesian handlers and went tumbling down, with a mass of boys, into the hard ground below. Boys landed on top of him, and as he struggled to breathe, it shocked him how hard the ground was—and that it was covered in snow. He wasn't used to this northeastern weather, and he realized immediately that his Midland clothes, too thin, would be useless here. Back in Soli, though it was but a few days' ride south, the ground was soft, covered in green moss, lush; it never snowed there and the air smelled of flowers. Here it was cold and hard, lifeless—and the air smelled only of fire.

As Alec disentangled himself from the mass of bodies, he had barely gained his feet when he was shoved in the back. He stumbled forward and turned to see a handler behind him, herding all the boys like cattle toward the barracks.

Behind him Alec watched as several dozen boys emerged from his cart; more than one, he was surprised to see, fell out limply, dead. He marveled that he'd survived the journey, crammed in as he'd been.

He ached in every bone in his body, his joints stiff, and as he marched, he had never felt more weary. He felt as though he hadn't slept in months, and as he felt as if he'd arrived at the end of the world.

Crackling filled the air and Alec looked up and saw, perhaps a hundred yards away, The Flames. They walked toward them, and they loomed larger and larger. They were awe-inspiring in person, up close, and he appreciated their heat, growing warmer with each step he took. He feared, though, how hot it would become when he got up close, as the others on patrol who stood hardly twenty yards away. He noticed they wore unusual protective armor. Even so, some lay there, limp, having clearly collapsed.

"See those flames, boy?" came a sinister voice.

Alec turned to see the boy he'd confronted in the carriage coming up beside him, his friend beside him, sneering.

"When I take your face to them no one's gonna recognize you—not even your mama. I'll burn your hands off until they're nothing but stumps. Appreciate what you got before you lose it."

He laughed, a dark, mean noise, sounding like a cough.

Alec stared back with defiance, Marco now beside him.

"You couldn't beat me in the carriage," Alec replied, "and you won't beat me now."

The boy snickered.

"This ain't no carriage, boy," he said. "You'll be sleeping with me tonight. Those barracks are all of ours. One night, one roof. It's you and me. And I've got all the time in the world. It might be tonight or it might be tomorrow—but one of these nights, when you least expect it, you'll be sleeping and we'll get you. You'll wake up to find your face in those flames. Sleep tight," he concluded with a laugh.

"If you're so tough," Marco said, beside him, "what are you waiting for? Here we are. Try it."

Alec saw the boy hesitate as he glanced back at the Pandesian handlers.

"When the time is right," he replied.

With that, they slinked away into the crowd.

"Don't worry," Marco said. "You'll sleep when I wake, and I'll do the same for you. If that scum come near us, they'll wish they hadn't."

Alec nodded in agreement, grateful, as he looked out at the barracks and wondered. A few feet from the packed entrance, Alec could already smell the body odor emanating from the building. He recoiled as he was shoved inside.

Alec tried to adjust to the dark barracks, lit only by the weak light coming through a few windows, high up. He looked down at the dirt floor and realized immediately that the carriage, as bad as it was, was better than this. He saw rows of suspicious, hostile faces, only the whites of their eyes visible, judging him up. They started to hoot and holler, clearly trying to intimidate them, the newbies, and to stake out their territory, and the barracks became filled with loud voices.

"Fresh meat!" called one.

"Fodder for The Flames!" cried another.

Alec felt a deepening sense of apprehension as they were all shoved deeper and deeper into the one big room. He finally stopped, Marco beside him, before an open patch of straw on the ground—only to be immediately shoved from behind.

"That's my spot, boy."

Alec turned to see an older recruit glaring at him, holding a dagger.

"Unless you want me to cut your throat," he warned.

Marco stepped forward.

"Keep your hay," he said. "It stinks anyway."

The two of them turned and continued deeper into the barracks, until, in a far corner, Alec found a small patch of hay deep in the shadows. He saw no one nearby, and he and Marco sat, a few feet away from each other, their backs against the wall.

Alec immediately breathed a sigh of relief; it felt so good to rest his aching legs, to not be in motion. He felt secure with his back to the wall, in a corner, where he could not get easily ambushed, and having a view of the room. He saw hundreds of recruits milling about, all in some state of argument, and dozens more pouring in by the second. He also saw several being dragged out by their ankles, dead. This place was a vision of hell.

"Don't worry, it gets worse," said a voice beside him.

Alec turned to see a recruit lying in the shadows a few feet away, a boy he hadn't noticed before, on his back, hands behind his head, looking up at the ceiling. He chewed on a piece of straw, and he had a deep, jaded voice.

"Hunger will probably kill you," the boy added darkly. "It kills about half the boys that come through here. Disease kills most others. If that doesn't get you, another boy will. Maybe you'll fight over a piece of bread—or maybe for no reason at all. Maybe he won't like the way you walk, or the way you look. Maybe you'll remind him of someone. Or maybe it'll just be pure hate for no reason. There's a lot of that going around here."

He sighed.

"And if all that doesn't get you," he added, "those flames will. Maybe not on your first patrol, or your second. But trolls break through when you least expect it, usually on fire, always looking to kill something. They've got nothing to lose and they come out of nowhere. I saw one the other night, sank its teeth in a boy's throat before the others could do anything."

Alec exchanged a look with Marco, each wondering what kind of life they'd signed up for.

"Nope," the boy added, "I haven't seen any boy survive more than one moon of duty."

"*You're* still here," Marco observed.

The boy grinned, chewing on his straw, still looking up.

"That's because I learned how to survive," he replied.

"How long have you been here?" Alec asked.

"Two moons," he replied. "The longest of all of them."

Alec gasped, shocked. Two moons, and the oldest survivor. This really was a factory of death. He started to wonder if he had made a mistake in coming here; maybe he should have just fought the Pandesians when they'd arrived in Solis and died a quick, clean death back at home. He found his thoughts turning to escape; after all, his brother had been spared—what did he have to gain by staying here now?

Alec found himself searching the walls, checking the windows and doors, counting the guards, wondering if there was a way.

"That's good," the boy said, still staring at the ceiling, yet somehow observing him. "Think of escape. Think of anything but this place. That's how you survive."

Alec flushed, embarrassed the boy read his mind, and amazed he could do it without even looking directly at him.

"But don't really try it," the boy said. "I can't tell you how many of us die each night trying. Better to be killed than to die that way."

"Die what way?" Marco asked. "Do they torture you?"

The boy shook his head.

"Worse," he replied. "They let you go."

Alec stared back, confused.

"What do you mean?" he asked.

"They chose this spot well," he explained. "Those woods are filled with death. Boars, beasts, trolls—everything you can imagine. No boy ever survives."

The boy grinned, and looked at them for the first time.

"Welcome, my friends," he said, smiling wide, "to The Flames."

CHAPTER TWENTY-TWO

Kyra walked through the winding streets of Volis, snow crunching beneath her boots, in a daze after her first battle. It had all happened so quickly, had been more vicious, more intense than she could have imagined. Men died—good men—men she had known all her life, in horrible and painful ways. Fathers and brothers and husbands now lay dead in the snow, their corpses piled outside of the fort's gates, the ground too hard to bury them.

She closed her eyes and tried to shake out the images.

It had been a great victory, and yet it had also humbled her, made her see how real battle was, how fragile life could be. It had shown her how easily men could die—and how easily she could take a man's life—both of which she found equally disturbing.

Being a great warrior was what she had always wanted; yet she could see now that it came with a heavy price. Valor was what she strived for, yet there was nothing easy, she was realizing, about valor. Unlike the spoils of war, it was not something she could hold in her grasp, not something she could hang on her wall. And yet it was what men strived for. Where was this thing called valor? Now that the battle was over, where had it gone?

More than anything, the day's events forced Kyra to wonder about herself, her mysterious power, which came from nowhere and seemed to disappear just as quickly. She tried to summon it again, but could not. What was it? Where did it come from? Kyra did not like what she could not understand, what she could not control. She would rather be less powerful and understand where her talents came from.

As Kyra walked the streets, she was puzzled by her townsfolk's reaction. After the battle, she had expected them to be panicked, to board up their homes or prepare to evacuate the fort. After all, many of the Lord's Men had died, and surely they would also soon see the wrath of Pandesia. A great and terrible army would be coming for them all; it might be the next day, or the day after that, or the week after that—but surely it was coming. They were all the walking dead here. How could they be unafraid?

Yet as she mingled with her people, Kyra detected no fear. On the contrary, she saw a jubilant people, energized, rejuvenated; she saw a people that had been set free. They bustled in every direction, clapping each other on the back, celebrating—and preparing. They sharpened weapons, strengthened gates, piled rocks high, stored food, and hurried about with a great sense of purpose. The Volisians, following her father's example, had an iron will. They were a people not easily deterred, and in fact, it seemed as if they looked forward to the next confrontation, whatever the cost and however grim the odds.

Kyra also noticed something else as she walked amongst her people, something which made her uncomfortable: the new way they looked at her. Clearly word had spread of what she had done, and she could feel the whispers behind her back. They looked at her as if she were not of them, these people she had known and loved her entire life. It made her feel as if she were a stranger here, and made her wonder where her true home was. Most of all, it made her wonder about her father's secret.

Kyra walked over to the thick wall of the ramparts and climbed the stone steps, Leo right behind her, ascending to the upper levels. She passed all her father's men, standing guard every twenty feet or so, and she could see they, too, all viewed her differently now, a new respect in their eyes. That look made it all worth it for her.

Kyra turned a corner and in the distance, standing above the arched gates, looking out over the countryside, she saw the man she had come for: her father. He stood there, hands on his hips, several of his men around him, gazing out into the rising snow. He blinked into the wind, unfazed by it—or by his fresh wounds from battle.

He turned at her approach and gestured to his men. They all walked off, leaving them alone.

Leo rushed forward and licked his hand, and her father stroked his head.

Kyra stood there, facing her father alone, and she did not know what to say. He looked back at her, expressionless, and she could not tell if he was angry with her, proud of her, or both. He was a complicated man in even the most simple of times—and these were not simple times. His face was hard, like the mountains beyond them, and as white as the snow that fell, and he looked like the ancient stone from which Volis had been quarried. She did not know if he was of this place, or if this place was of him.

He turned and looked back out at the countryside, and she stood beside him, looking out, too. They shared the silence, punctuated only by the wind, as she waited for him to speak.

"I used to think that our safety, our secure life here, was more important than freedom," he finally began, his voice a low rumble. "Today, I realized I was wrong. You have taught me what I have forgotten: that freedom, that honor, is worth more than all."

He smiled as he looked over at her, and she was relieved to see warmth in his eyes.

"You have given me a great gift," he said. "You have reminded me what honor means."

She smiled, touched by his words, relieved he was not upset with her, feeling the rift in their relationship repaired.

"It is hard to see men die," he continued, reflective, turning back to the countryside. "Even for me."

A long silence followed, and Kyra wondered if he would bring up what had happened; she sensed that he wanted to. She wanted to bring it up herself but was unsure how.

"I am different, Father, aren't I?" she finally asked, her voice soft, afraid to ask the question.

He continued to stare out at the horizon, inscrutable, until finally he nodded slightly.

"It has something to do with my mother, doesn't it?" she pressed. "Who was she? Am I even your daughter?"

He turned and looked at her, sadness in his eyes, mixed with a nostalgic look she did not fully understand.

"These are all questions for another time," he said. "When you are ready."

"I am ready *now*," she insisted.

He shook his head.

"There are many things you must learn first, Kyra. Many secrets I have had to withhold from you," he said, his voice heavy with remorse. "It pained me to do so, but it was to protect you. The time is near for you to know everything, to know who you truly are."

She stood there, her heart pounding, desperate to know, yet afraid at the same time.

"I thought I could raise you," he sighed. "They warned me this day would come, but I did not believe it. Not until today, not until I saw your skill. Your talents…they are beyond me."

She furrowed her brow, confused.

"I don't understand, Father," she said. "What are you saying?"

His face hardened with resolve.

"It is time for you to leave us," he said, his voice filled with determination, taking on the tone he used when his mind was set. "You must leave Volis at once and seek out your uncle, your mother's brother. Akis. In the Tower of Ur."

"The Tower of Ur?" she repeated, shocked. "Is my uncle a Watcher, then?"

Her father shook his head.

"He is much more. It is he who must train you—and is he, and only he, who can reveal the secret of who you are."

While learning the secret thrilled her, she was overwhelmed by the idea of leaving Volis.

"I don't want to go," she said. "I want to be here, with you. Especially now, of all times."

He sighed.

"Unfortunately, what you and I want no longer matters," he said. "This is no longer about you and me. This is about Escalon—*all* of Escalon. The destiny of our lands lies in your hand. Don't you see, Kyra?" he said, turning to her. "It is *you*. You are the one who will lead our people out of the darkness."

She blinked, shocked, hardly believing his words.

"How?" she asked. "How is that possible?"

But he merely fell silent, refusing to say anymore.

"I can't leave your side, Father," she pleaded. "I *won't*. Not now."

He studied the countryside, sadness in his eyes.

"Within a fortnight, all you see here will be destroyed. There is no hope for us. You must escape when you can. You are our only hope—your dying here, with us, will help no one."

Kyra felt pained by his words. She could not bring herself to leave while her people died.

"They will come back, won't they?" she asked.

It was more of a statement than a question.

"They will," he replied. "They will cover Volis like a plague of locusts. All you have known and loved will soon be no more."

She felt a pit in her stomach at his response, and yet she knew it was the truth, and was grateful at least for that.

"And what of the capital?" Kyra asked. "What of the old King? Could you not go to Andros and resurrect the old army and make a stand?"

He shook his head.

"The King surrendered once," he said, wistfully. "The time to fight has passed. Andros is run by politicians now, not soldiers, and none are to be trusted."

"But surely they would stand up for Escalon, if not for Volis," she insisted.

"Volis is but one stronghold," he said, "one they can afford to turn their backs on. Our victory today, as great as it was, was too small for them to risk rallying all of Escalon."

They both fell into silence as they studied the horizon, Kyra pondering his words.

"Are you scared?" she asked.

"A good leader must always know fear," he replied. "Fear sharpens our senses, and helps us to prepare. It is not death I fear, though—it is only not dying well."

They stood there, studying the skies, as she realized the truth in his words. A long, comfortable silence fell over them.

Finally, he turned to her.

"Where is your dragon now?" he asked, then suddenly turned and walked off, as he sometimes did.

Kyra, alone, stood there and studied the horizon; strangely enough, she had been wondering the same thing. The skies were empty, thick with rolling clouds, and she kept hoping, in the back of her mind, to hear a screech, to see its wings dip down from the clouds.

But there was nothing. Nothing but emptiness and silence, and her father's lingering question:

Where is your dragon now?

CHAPTER TWENTY-THREE

Alec felt himself rudely awakened by a kick in the ribs and he opened his eyes, exhausted, disoriented, trying to get his bearings. He pulled hay from his mouth, saw he was lying face-first on the ground, and he remembered: the barracks. He had been up most of the night, watching his and Marco's back as the night was filled the sounds of boys fighting, creeping in and out of the shadows, calling out to each other threateningly. He had watched more than one boy get dragged out, feet first, dead—but not before boys pounced on his corpse and raided it for anything they could salvage.

Alec was kicked again, and this time, alert, he rolled over, ready for anything. He looked up, blinking in the blackness, and was surprised to see not another boy but rather two Pandesian soldiers. They were kicking boys all up and down the line, grabbing them, yanking them to their feet. Alec felt rough hands beneath his arms, felt himself yanked up, too, then pushed and prodded out of the barracks.

"What's happening? What's going on?" he mumbled, still unsure if he was awake.

"Time for duty," the soldier snapped back. "You're not here for pleasure, boy."

Alec had wondered when he would be sent to patrol The Flames, but it had never occurred to him it would be in the middle of the night, and so soon after such a long ride. He stumbled forward, drunk with exhaustion, wondering how he could survive this. They had given them nothing to eat since he had arrived, and he still felt weak from the long journey.

Before him a boy collapsed, perhaps from hunger, or from exhaustion, it didn't matter—the soldiers pounced on him, kicking him viciously until he stopped moving altogether. They left him on the frozen ground, dead, and continued marching.

Realizing he did not want to end up like that boy, Alec strengthened his resolve and forced himself wide awake. Marco came up beside him.

"Sleep much?" Marco asked with a wry smile.

Alec shook his head gloomily.

"Don't worry," Marco said. "We'll sleep when we're dead—and we'll be dead soon enough."

They turned a bend and Alec was momentarily blinded by The Flames, hardly fifty yards away, their heat tremendous even from here.

"If trolls come through, kill them," an Empire soldier called out. "Otherwise, don't kill yourselves. At least not until morning. We want this place well-guarded."

Alec was given a final shove, and he and the group of boys were left near The Flames, while the soldiers turned and marched off. He wondered why they trusted them to stand guard, not to run—but then he turned and saw the watchtowers everywhere, manned with soldiers with crossbows, fingers on the trigger, all waiting eagerly for a boy to make a run for it.

Alec stood there, with no armor and no weapons, and wondered how they could expect him to be an effective guard. He looked over and saw some of the other boys had swords.

"Where did you get that?" Alec called out to a boy nearby.

"When a boy dies, get it from him," he called back. "If someone else doesn't beat you to it."

Marco frowned.

"How do they expect us to stand guard with no weapons?" he asked.

One of the other boys, face black with soot, snickered.

"Newbies don't get weapons," he said. "They expect you to die anyway. If you're still here after a few nights, you'll find a way to get one."

Alec stared at The Flames, crackling so intensely, the heat warming his face, and he tried not to think about what lay on the other side, waiting to burst through.

"What do we do in the meantime?" he asked. "If a troll breaks through?"

One boy laughed.

"Kill them with your bare hands!" he called out. "You might survive—but then again, you might not. He'll be on fire, and will probably burn you with him."

172

The other boys turned their backs and dispersed, each spreading out for their own stations, and Alec, weaponless, turned and looked at The Flames with a despairing feeling.

"We have been set up to die," he said to Marco.

Marco, about twenty feet away from him, staring at The Flames, looked disillusioned.

"Keeping the Flames was once a noble calling," he said, his voice glum. "Before Pandesia invaded. The Keepers were once honored, well-armed and well-equipped. It was why I volunteered. But now…it seems to be something else entirely. The Pandesians don't want the trolls coming through—but they don't use their own men. They want us to guard it—and they leave us to die here."

"Perhaps we should let them through then," Alec said, "and let them kill them all."

"We could," Marco said. "But they'd raid Escalon and kill our families, too."

They fell silent, the two of them standing there, staring into The Flames. Alec did not know how much time had passed while he stared, wondering. He could not help but feel as if he were staring into his own death. What was his family doing right now? he wondered. Were they thinking of him? Did they even care?

Alec found himself getting lost in depressing thoughts and knew he had to change his mood. He forced himself to look away, to glance back over his shoulder and to study the dark woodline. The woods were pitch black, foreboding, the soldiers in the watchtowers not even bothering to watch them. Instead, they kept their eyes fixed on the recruits, on The Flames.

"They are afraid to stand guard themselves," Alec observed, looking up at the soldiers. "Yet they don't want us to leave. Cowardly."

Barely had Alec uttered the words when he suddenly felt a tremendous pain in his back, sending him stumbling forward. Before he knew what was happening, he felt a club being jammed into his ribs and found himself landing face-first on the ground.

He heard a sinister voice in his ear, one he recognized:

"I told you I'd find you, boy."

Before he could react Alec felt rough hands grab him from behind and drag him forward, toward The Flames. There were two of them—the boy from the carriage and his friend—and Alec tried to resist, but it was useless. Their grip was too tight and they carried him closer and closer, until his face felt the intense heat of The Flames.

Alec heard struggling and he looked over and was surprised to see Marco wrapped up in chains, two other boys grabbing him from behind, holding him in place. They had planned this well. They really wanted them dead.

Alec struggled, but he could not gain leverage. They dragged him closer and closer to The Flames, hardly ten feet away, the heat of it so intense he could already feel the pain, feel as if his face were going to melt. He knew that with but a few more feet, he would be disfigured for life—if not dead.

Alec bucked, but they had him in such a tight grip, he could not break free.

"NO!" he shrieked.

"Time for payback," hissed the voice in his ear.

There suddenly came a horrific shriek, and Alec was shocked to realize it was not his own. The grip loosened on his arms and as it did he immediately pulled back from The Flames. At the same moment, he saw a burst of light and he watched, transfixed, as a creature burst forth from The Flames, on fire, and suddenly landed on the boy beside him, pinning him to the ground.

The troll, still on fire, rolled with the boy on the ground, sinking its fangs into his throat. The boy shrieked as he died instantly.

The troll turned and looked about, in a frenzy, and its eyes, large and red, met Alec's. Alec was terrified. Still aflame, it breathed through its mouth, its long fangs covered in blood, and looked ravenous for a kill, like a wild beast.

Alec stood there, frozen with fear, unable to move even if he wanted to.

The other boy ran, and the troll, detecting motion, turned and, to Alec's relief, lunged for him instead. In one bound it tackled him to the ground, still on fire, and sank its fangs into the back of his neck. The boy cried out as it killed him.

Marco shook off the stunned boys, grabbed their chain and swung it around, smashing one in the face and the other between the legs, dropping them both.

Bells started to toll in the watchtowers and chaos ensued. Boys came running from up and down The Flames to fight the troll. They jabbed at it with spears, but most, inexperienced, were afraid to get too close. The troll reached out, grabbed a spear and pulled a boy close, hugging him tight and, as the boy shrieked, setting him aflame.

"Now's our time," hissed an urgent voice.

Alec turned to see Marco running up beside him.

"They're all distracted. This may be our only chance."

Marco looked out and Alec followed his glance: he looked to the woods. He meant to escape.

Black and ominous, the woodline was foreboding. Alec knew that even greater dangers likely lurked in there, but he knew Marco was right: this was their chance. And nothing but death awaited them here.

Alec nodded and without another word they broke into a sprint together, running farther and farther from The Flames, toward the woods.

Alec's heart slammed in his chest as he expected at any moment to be shot in the back by a crossbow, and he ran for his very life. But as he glanced back over his shoulder, he saw everyone surrounding the troll, distracted.

A moment later, they entered the woods, engulfed in blackness, entering, he knew, a world of dangers greater than he could ever imagine. He would probably die here, he knew. But at least, finally, he was free.

CHAPTER TWENTY-FOUR

Kyra stood outside the gates of Volis, studying the wintry landscape as the snow fell, the sky streaked with scarlet as if the sun were struggling to break through, and she leaned forward on the emerging wall, breathing hard as she plopped down yet another stone. Kyra had joined the others in gathering these huge stones from the river to erect yet another wall around the perimeter of Volis. As the mason beside her smeared the plaster, she plopped down one stone after the next. Now, arms trembling, she needed a break.

Kyra was joined by hundreds of her people, lined up all along the wall, all building it higher, deeper, adding rings to the embankments. Others, beyond the wall, worked with shovels, digging fresh ditches, while others still dug graves for the dead. Kyra knew that all of this was futile, that it would not hold back the great Pandesian army when it came, that no matter what they did, they would all die in this place. They all knew it. But they built it anyway. It gave them something to do, some sense of having control while staring death in the face.

As Kyra took a break, she leaned against the wall, looked out at the landscape, and wondered. All was so still now, the snow muffling all sound, as if the world contained nothing but peace. But she knew differently; she knew the Pandesians were out there somewhere, preparing. She knew they would return, in a deafening rumble, and destroy all that she held precious. What she saw before her was an illusion: it was the calm before the storm. It was hard to understand how the world could be so still, so perfect, one moment—and so filled with destruction and chaos the next.

Kyra glanced back over her shoulder and saw her people winding down their work for the day, laying down trowels and shovels as night began to fall and filtering back toward their homes. Smoke rose from chimneys, candles were lit in windows, and Volis looked so cozy, so protected, as if it could not be touched by the world. She marveled at the illusion.

As she stood there, she could not help but hear her father's words, ringing in her ears, his request that she leave at once. She thought of her uncle, whom she had never met, of the journey it would require, across Escalon, through Whitewood, all the way to the Tower of Ur. She thought of her mother, of the secret being withheld from her. She thought of her uncle training her to become more powerful—and it all thrilled her.

And yet as she turned and looked at her people, she knew she just could not abandon them in their time of strife, even if it meant saving her life. It was just not who she was.

Suddenly, a low, soft horn sounded, one signaling the end of the work day.

"Night falls," said the mason, standing beside her, laying down his trowel. "There is little we can do in the dark. Our people return for the meal. Come now," he said, as rows of people turned and headed back across the bridge, through the gates.

"I will come in a moment," she said, not yet ready, wanting more time to enjoy the peace, the silence. She was always happiest alone, outdoors.

Leo whined and licked his lips.

"Take Leo with you—he's hungry."

Leo must have understood because he already leapt off after the mason while she was still speaking, and the mason laughed and returned with him for the fort.

Kyra stood outside the fort, closing her eyes against the noise and becoming lost in her thoughts. Finally, the sound of the hammers had stopped. Finally, she had true peace.

She looked out and studied the horizon, the darkening woodline, the rolling gray clouds covering up the scarlet, and she wondered. When were they coming? What size force would they bring? What would their army look like?

As she looked out, she was surprised to detect motion in the distance. Something caught her eye and as she watched, she saw a lone rider materialize, emerging from the wood and taking the main road for their fort. Kyra reached back and gripped her bow unconsciously, bracing herself, wondering if he were a scout, if he were heralding an army.

But as he neared, she loosened her grip and relaxed as she recognized him: it was one of her father's men. Maltren. He galloped, and as he did, led a riderless horse beside him by the reins. It was a most curious sight.

Maltren came to an abrupt stop before her and looked down at her with urgency, appearing scared; she could not understand what was happening.

"What is it?" she asked, alarmed. "Is Pandesia coming?"

He sat there, breathing hard, and shook his head.

"It is your brother," he said. "Aidan."

Kyra's heart plummeted at the mention of her brother's name, the person she loved most in the world. She was immediately on edge.

"What is it?" she demanded. "What's happened to him?"

Maltren caught his breath.

"He's been badly injured," he said. "He needs help."

Kyra's heart started pounding. Aidan? Injured? Her mind spun with awful scenarios—but mostly, confusion.

"How?" she demanded. "What was he doing in the wood? I thought he was in the fort, preparing for the feast?"

Maltren shook his head.

"He went out with your brothers," he said. "Hunting. He took a bad fall from his horse—his legs are broken."

Kyra felt a flash of determination rush through her. Filled with adrenaline, not even stopping to think it all through carefully, she rushed forward and mounted the spare horse.

If she had taken just a moment to turn around, to check the fort, she would have found Aidan, safely inside. But fueled by urgency, she did not stop to question Maltren.

"Lead me to him," she said.

The two of them, an unlikely duo, charged off together, away from Volis and, as night fell, toward the blackening wood.

*

Kyra and Maltren galloped down the road, over the rolling hills, toward the wood, she breathing hard as she dug her heels into her horse, anxious to save Aidan. A million nightmares swarmed through her head. How could Aidan have broken his legs? What were her

178

brothers doing hunting out here, close to nightfall, when all of her father's people had been forbidden to leave the fort? None of it made any sense.

They reached the edge of the wood, and as Kyra prepared to enter it, she was puzzled to see Maltren suddenly bring his horse to a stop before it. She stopped abruptly beside him and watched as he dismounted. She dismounted, too, both horses breathing hard, and followed him, baffled, as he stopped at the forest's edge.

"Why are you stopping?" she asked, breathing hard. "I thought Aidan was in the wood?"

Kyra looked all around, and as she did, she suddenly had a feeling that something was terribly wrong—when suddenly, out of the woods, she was horrified to see, there stepped the Lord Governor himself, flanked by two dozen men. She heard snow crunching behind her, and she wheeled to see a dozen more men encircle her, all aiming bows at her, one grabbing the reins to her horse. Her blood ran cold as she realized she had walked into a trap.

She looked at Maltren in fury, realizing he had betrayed her.

"Why?" she asked, disgusted at the sight of him. "You are my father's man. Why would you do this?"

The Lord Governor walked over to Maltren and placed a large sack of gold in his hand, while Maltren looked away guiltily.

"For enough gold," the Lord Governor turned and said to her, a haughty smile on his face, "you will find that men will do anything you wish. Maltren here will be rich forever, richer than your father ever was, and he will be spared from your fort's looming death."

Kyra scowled at Maltren, hardly fathoming this.

"You are a traitor," she said.

He scowled back at her.

"I am our savior," he replied. "They would have killed all of our people, thanks to you. Thanks to me, Volis will be spared. I made a deal. You can thank me for their lives." He smiled, satisfied. "And, to think, all I had to do was hand over you."

Kyra suddenly felt rough hands grab her from behind, felt herself hoisted in the air. She bucked and writhed, but she could not shake them as she felt her wrist and ankles bound, felt herself thrown into the back of a carriage.

179

A moment later, iron bars slammed on her and her cart jostled away, bumping over the countryside. She knew that, wherever they were taking her, no one would ever see or hear from her again. And as they entered the wood, blocking out all view of the falling night, she knew that her life, as she knew it, was over.

CHAPTER TWENTY-FIVE

The giant lay at Vesuvius's feet, bound by a thousand ropes, held down by a hundred trolls, and as Vesuvius stood over it, so close to its fangs, he studied it in awe. The beast craned its neck, snarling, trying to reach out and kill him—but it could not budge.

Vesuvius grinned, delighted. He took pride in having power over helpless things, and more than anything, he loved watching trapped things suffer.

Seeing this giant here, back in his cave, in his own territory, gave him a thrill. Being able to stand so close to it made him feel all powerful, made him feel as if there were nothing in the world he could not conquer. Finally, after all these years, his dream had been realized. Finally, he would be able to achieve his lifelong goal, to create the tunnel that would lead his people under The Flames and into the West.

Vesuvius sneered down at the creature.

"You see, you are not as strong as I," he said, standing over it. "*No one* is as strong as I."

The beast roared, an awful sound, and struggled in vain. As it did, all the trolls holding it swayed left and right, the ropes shifting, but not giving. Vesuvius knew their time was short. If they were going to do this, the time was now.

Vesuvius turned and surveyed the cave: thousands of workers stopped their labor to watch the giant. At the far end sat the unfinished tunnel, and Vesuvius knew this would be the tricky part. He would have to put the giant to work. Somehow, he would have to goad it to enter the tunnel and smash through the rock. But how?

Vesuvius stood there, racking his brain, until an idea came to him.

He turned to the giant and drew his sword, aglow against the flames of the cave.

"I will cut your ropes," Vesuvius said to the beast, "because I do not fear you. You will be free, and you shall follow my command. You will smash through the rock of that tunnel, and you shall not stop until you have burrowed beneath The Flames of Escalon."

The giant let out a roar of defiance.

Vesuvius turned and surveyed his army of trolls, awaiting his command.

"When my sword lowers," he called out, his voice booming, "you shall cut all of its ropes at once. You shall then prod it with your weapons until it reaches the tunnel."

His trolls looked back nervously, all clearly terrified at the idea of freeing it. Vesuvius feared it, too, though he would never show it. And yet he knew there was no other way—this moment would have to come.

Vesuvius wasted no time. He stepped forward decisively, raised his sword, and slashed the first of the thick ropes binding the giant's neck.

Immediately, hundreds of his soldiers stepped forward, raised their swords high and slashed the ropes, and the sound of ropes snapping filled the air.

Vesuvius quickly retreated, backing off, but not too conspicuously, not wanting his men to see his fear. He slithered back behind his ranks of men, into the shadows of the rock, out of reach of the beast after it gained its feet. He would wait to see what happened first.

A horrific roar filled the canyon as the giant rose to its feet, enraged, and without wasting a second, swiped down with its claws in each direction. It scooped up four trolls in each hand, raised them high overhead and threw them. The trolls went flying end over end through the air, across the cave, until they smashed into the far wall and collapsed, sliding limply down, dead.

The giant bunched its hands into fists, raised them high and suddenly smashed the ground, using them like hammers, aiming for the trolls who scurried about. Trolls fled for their lives, but not in time. He crushed them like ants, the cave shaking with each smash.

As trolls tried to run between its legs, the giant raised its feet and stomped, flattening others.

Enraged, it killed trolls in every direction. No one seemed able to escape its wrath.

Vesuvius watched with a mounting dread. He signaled to his commander, and immediately, a horn sounded.

On cue, hundreds of his soldiers marched forward from the shadows, long pikes and whips in hand, all preparing to poke and prod the beast. They encircled it, rushing forward from all directions, doing their best to prod it towards the tunnel.

But Vesuvius was horrified to watch his plan collapse before his eyes. The beast leaned back and kicked a dozen soldiers away at once; it then swung its forearm around and swatted fifty more soldiers, smashing them into a wall along with their pikes. It stomped others, holding whips, killing so many so quickly that none could get near it. They were useless against this creature, even with their numbers and with all their weapons. Vesuvius' army was dissolving before his eyes.

Vesuvius thought quickly. He could not kill the beast—he needed it alive, needed to harness its strength. Yet he needed it to obey him. But how? How could he goad it into the tunnel?

Suddenly, he had an idea: if he could not prod it in, then perhaps he could entice it.

He turned and grabbed the troll beside him.

"You," he commanded. "Run for the tunnel. Make sure the giant sees you."

The solder stared back, wide-eyed with fear.

"But, my Lord and King, what if it follows me?"

Vesuvius grinned.

"That is exactly the point."

The soldier stood there, panic-stricken, too scared to obey—and Vesuvius stabbed him in the heart. He then stepped up to the next soldier and held the dagger to his throat.

"You can die here now," he said, "by the edge of my blade—or you can run for that tunnel and have a chance to live. You choose."

Vesuvius pushed the blade tighter against his throat, and the troll, realizing he meant it, turned and darted off.

Vesuvius watched as he ran across the cave, zigzagging his way amidst all the chaos, between all the dying soldiers, through the beast's legs, and ran for the entrance to the tunnel.

The giant spotted him, and he swatted down and missed him. In a rage, and attracted to the one soldier running away from him, the giant, as Vesuvius had hoped, immediately followed. It ran through the cave, each step shaking the earth, the walls.

The troll ran for his life and finally entered the massive tunnel. Though wide and tall, the tunnel was shallow, ending after a mere fifty yards despite years of work, and as the troll ran inside, he soon reached the dead end, a wall of rock.

The giant, enraged, charged in after it, never even slowing. As it reached the troll it swiped for him with its massive fists and claws. The troll ducked and the giant instead smashed into rock. The ground shook, a great rumble followed, and Vesuvius watched in awe as the wall crumbled, as an avalanche of rocks came pouring out in a massive cloud of dust.

Vesuvius' heart quickened. That was it. It was exactly what he had always dreamt, exactly what he needed, what he had envisioned from the day he set out to find this beast. It swiped again, and smashed out another chunk of rock, taking out a good fifty feet in a single swipe— more than Vesuvius's slaves had been able to do in an entire year of digging.

Vesuvius was overjoyed, realizing it could work.

But then the giant found the troll, grabbed it, lifted it into the air, and bit off its head.

"CLOSE THE TUNNEL!" Vesuvius commanded, rushing forward and directing his soldiers.

Hundreds of trolls, waiting on standby, rushed forward and began pushing the slab of Altusian rock that Vesuvius had positioned before the entrance to the tunnel, a rock so thick that no beast, not even this creature, could break it. The sound of stone scraping stone filled the air as Vesuvius watched the tunnel slowly seal up.

The giant, seeing the entrance being closed, turned and charged for it.

But the entrance sealed a moment before the giant reached it. The entire cave as it slammed into it—but luckily the stone held.

Vesuvius smiled; the giant was trapped. He was right where he wanted him.

"Send the next one in!" Vesuvius ordered.

A human slave was kicked forward, lashed by his captors, again and again, toward a tiny opening in the stone slab. The human, realizing what was about to happen, refused to go, kicking and struggling; but they beat him savagely, until finally they were able to run him through the opening, giving him one last shove through.

From inside there came the muffled shouts of the slave, clearly running for his life, trying to get away from the giant. Vesuvius stood there and listened with glee as he heard the sound of the enraged giant, trapped, swatting and smashing at rock, digging his tunnel for him.

One swipe at a time, his tunnel was being dug—each swipe, he knew, bringing him closer to The Flames, to Escalon. He would turn the humans into a nation of slaves.

Finally, victory would be his.

CHAPTER TWENTY-SIX

Kyra opened her eyes to blackness, lying on a cold stone floor, her head splitting, her body aching, and wondered where she was. Shivering from the cold, her throat parched, feeling as if she hadn't eaten in days, she reached out and felt the cobblestone floor beneath her fingers, and she tried to remember.

Images flooded her mind, and she was unsure at first if they were memories or nightmares. She recalled being captured by the Lord's Men, thrown into a cart, a metal gate slamming on her. She remembered a long, bumpy ride, remembered resisting as the gate opened, struggling to break free and being clubbed on the head. After that, all had, mercifully, been blackness.

Kyra reached up and felt the lump on the back of her head and she knew it had not been a dream. It had all been real. The reality sunk in like a stone: she had been captured by the Lord's Men, carted off, and imprisoned.

Kyra was furious at Maltren for his betrayal, furious at herself for being so stupid as to have believed him. She was also scared, pondering what would come next. Here she lay, alone, in the Governor's custody, and only terrible things could be coming for her. She felt sure that her father and her people had no idea where she was. Perhaps her father would assume she had heeded him and ventured to the Tower of Ur. Maltren would surely lie and report back that he had seen her fleeing Volis for good.

As Kyra scrambled in the dark, she instinctively reached for her bow, her staff—but they had all been stripped. She looked up and saw a dim glow coming through the cell bars, and she sat up and saw torches lining the stone walls of a dungeon, beneath which stood several soldiers, at attention. There sat a large iron door in the center of it, and it was silent down here, the only sound that of a dripping coming from somewhere in the ceiling, and of rats scurrying in some dark corner.

Kyra sat up against the wall, hugging her knees to her chest, trying to get warm. She closed her eyes and breathed deep, forcing herself to imagine herself someplace else, anywhere. As she did, she saw Theos' intense yellow eyes staring back at her. She could hear the dragon's voice in her mind's eye.

Strength is not defined in times of peace. It is defined in hardship. Embrace your hardship, do not shy from it. Only then can you overcome it.

Kyra opened her eyes, shocked at the vision, looking around and expecting to see Theos in front of her.

"Did you see him?" a girl's voice suddenly cut through the darkness, making Kyra jump.

Kyra wheeled, stunned to hear the voice of another person here in this cell with her, coming from somewhere in the shadows—and even more stunned to hear it was a girl's voice. She sounded about her age, and as a figure emerged from the shadows, Kyra saw she was right: there sat a pretty girl, perhaps fifteen, with brown hair and eyes, long tangled hair, face covered in dirt, clothes in tatters. She looked terrified as she stared back at Kyra.

"Who are you?" Kyra asked.

"Have you seen him?" the girl repeated, urgently.

"Seen who?"

"His son," she replied.

"His son?" Kyra asked, confused.

The girl turned and looked outside the cell, terror-stricken, and Kyra wondered what horrors she had seen.

"I haven't seen anyone," Kyra said.

"Oh God, please don't let them kill me," the girl pleaded. "Please. I hate this place!"

The girl began to weep uncontrollably, curled up on the stone floor, and Kyra, her heart breaking for her, got up, went over and draped an arm around her shoulder, trying to soothe her.

"Shhh," Kyra said, trying to calm her. Kyra had never seen anyone in such a broken state; this girl looked positively terrified about whoever it was she was talking about. It gave Kyra a sinking feeling for what was to come.

"Tell me," Kyra said. "Who are you talking about? Who hurt you? The Governor? Who are you? What are you doing here?"

She saw the bruises on the girl's face, the scars on her shoulders, and she tried not to think of what they had done to this poor girl. She waited patiently for her to stop weeping.

"My name is Dierdre," she said. "I've been here…I don't know. I thought it was a moon cycle, but I have lost track of time. They took me from my family, ever since the new law. I tried to resist, and they took me here."

Dierdre stared into space as if reliving it all again.

"Every day there await new tortures for me," she continued. "First it was the son, then the father. They pass me off like a doll and now…I am… nothing."

She stared back at Kyra with an intensity that scared her.

"I just want to die now," Dierdre pleaded. "Please, just help me die."

Kyra looked back, horrified.

"Don't say that," Kyra said.

"I tried to take a knife the other day to kill myself—but it slipped from my hands and they captured me again. Please. I'll give you anything. Kill me."

Kyra shook her head, aghast.

"Listen to me," Kyra said, feeling a new inner strength rise up within her, a new determination as she saw Dierdre's plight. It was the strength of her father, the strength of generations of warriors, coursing through her. And more than that: it was the strength of the dragon. A strength she did not know she had until this day.

She grabbed Dierdre's shoulders and looked her in the eye, wanting to get through to her.

"You are *not* going to die," Kyra said firmly. "And they are *not* going to hurt you. Do you understand me? You are going to live. I will make sure of it."

Dierdre seemed to calm, drawing strength from Kyra's strength.

"Whatever they have done to you," Kyra continued, "that is in the past now. Soon you are going to be free—*we* are going to be free. You are going to start life over again. We will be friends and I will protect you. Do you trust me?"

Dierdre stared back, clearly shocked. Finally, she nodded, calm.

"But how?" Dierdre asked. "You don't understand. There is no escape from here. You don't understand what they're like—"

They both flinched as the iron door slammed open. Kyra watched as the Lord Governor strutted in, trailed by a half dozen men, and joined by a man who was his spitting image, with that same bulbous nose and smug look, perhaps in his thirties. He must have been his son. He had his father's same sneering, stupid face, his same look of arrogance.

They all crossed the dungeon and neared the cell bars, and his men approached with torches, lighting up the cell. Kyra looked around in the bright light and was horrified to see her accommodations for the first time, to see the bloodstains all over the floor. She did not want to think of who else had been here—or of what had happened to them.

"Bring her here," the Governor ordered his men.

The cell door opened, his men marched in and Kyra found herself hoisted to her feet, arms yanked behind her back, unable to break free as much as she tried. They brought her close to the Lord Governor and he looked her up and down like an insect.

"Did I not warn you?" he said softly, his voice low and dark.

Kyra frowned.

"Pandesian law allows you to take unwed girls as wives, not prisoners," Kyra said, defiant. "You violate your own law to imprison me."

The Lord Governor exchanged a look with the others, and they all broke into laughter.

"Do not worry," he said, glowering at her, "I will make you my wife. Many times over. And my son's, too—and anyone else's whom I wish. And when we're done with you, if we haven't killed you yet, then I'll let you live out your days down here."

He grinned an evil grin, clearly enjoying this.

"As for your father and your people," he continued, "I've had a change of heart: we are going to kill every last one of them. They will be a memory soon enough. Not even that, I'm afraid: I will see to it that Volis is erased from the history books. As we speak, an entire division of the Pandesian army approaches to avenge my men and destroy your fort."

Kyra felt a great indignation bubbling up within her. She tried desperately to summon her power, whatever it was that had helped her on the bridge, but to her dismay, it would not come. She writhed and bucked, but could not break free.

"You have a strong spirit," he said. "That is good. I shall enjoy breaking that spirit. I shall enjoy it very much."

He turned his back on her, as if to leave, when suddenly, without warning, he wheeled and backhanded her with all his might.

It was a move she did not expect, and Kyra felt the mighty blow smash her jaw and send her reeling down to the floor, beside Dierdre.

Kyra, stung, jaw aching, lay there and looked up, watching them all go. As they all left her cell, locking it behind them, the Lord Governor stopped, face against the bars, and looked down at her.

"I will wait for tomorrow to torture you," he said, grinning. "I find that my victims suffer the most when they are given a full night to think about the hardship to come."

He let out an awful laugh, delighted with himself, then turned with his men and left the dungeon, the massive iron door slamming behind them like a coffin on her heart.

CHAPTER TWENTY-SEVEN

Merk hiked through Whitewood at sunset, his legs aching, his stomach growling, trying to keep the faith that the Tower of Ur was out there on the horizon, that eventually he would reach it. He tried to focus on what his new life would be like once he arrived, how he would become a Watcher and start again.

But he couldn't focus. Ever since he had met that girl, heard her story, it had been gnawing away at him. He wanted to push her from his mind, but try as he did, he could not. He was so sure he had been turning away from a life of violence. If he went back for her and helped kill those men, when would the killing ever end? Would there not be another job, another cause, right behind that one?

Merk hiked and hiked, poking the ground with his staff, leaves crunching beneath his feet, furious. Why had he had to run into her? It was a huge wood—why couldn't they have missed each other? Why did life always have to throw things in his way? Things beyond his understanding?

Merk hated hard decisions, and he hated hesitation; his entire life he had always been so sure of everything, and he had regarded that as one of his strong points. He had always known what he was. But now, he was not so sure. Now, he found himself wavering.

He cursed the gods for having him run into that girl. Why couldn't people take care of themselves, anyway? Why did they always need him? If she and her family were unable to defend themselves, then why did they deserve to live anyhow? If he saved them, wouldn't some other predator, sooner or later, kill them?

No. He could not save them. That would be enabling them. People had to learn to defend themselves.

And yet perhaps, he pondered, there was a reason she had been put before his eyes. Maybe he was being tested.

Merk looked up at the skies, the sunset a thin strip on the horizon, barely visible through Whitewood, and he wondered at his new faith.

Tested.

It was a powerful word, a powerful idea, and one he did not like. He did not like what he did not understand, what he could not control, and being tested was precisely that. As he hiked and hiked, stabbing the leaves with his staff, Merk felt his carefully constructed world collapsing all around him. Before, his life had been easy; now, it life felt like an uncomfortable state of questioning. Being sure of things in life, he realized, was easy; questioning things was what was hard. He had stepped out of a world of black and white and into a world filled with shades of gray, and the uncertainty unsettled him. He did not understand who he was becoming, and that bothered him most of all.

Merk crested a hill, leaves crunching, breathing hard but not from exertion. As he reached the top, he stopped and looked out, and for the first time since embarking on this journey, he felt a ray of hope. He almost could not believe what he was seeing.

There it sat, on the horizon, glowing against the sunset. Not a legend, not a myth, but a real place: the Tower of Ur.

Nestled in a small clearing in the midst of a vast and dark wood, it rose up, an ancient stone tower, circular, perhaps fifty yards in diameter, and rising to the treeline. It was the oldest thing he had ever seen, older, even, than the castles in which he had served. It had a mysterious, impenetrable aura to it. He could sense it was a mystical place. A place of power.

Merk breathed a deep sigh of exhaustion and relief. He had made it. Seeing it here was like a dream. Finally, he would have a place to be in the world, a place to call home. He would have a chance to start life over, a chance to repent. He would become a Watcher.

He knew he should be ecstatic, should double his pace and set off on the final leg of the journey before nightfall. And yet, try as he did, for some reason he could not take the first step. He stood there, frozen, something gnawing away at him.

Merk turned around, able to see the horizon in every direction, and in the far distance, against the setting sun, he saw black smoke rising. It was like a punch in the gut. He knew where it was coming from: that girl. Her family. The murderers were setting fire to everything.

As he followed the trail of smoke he they had not reached her farm yet. They were still on the outskirts of her fields. Soon enough, they would reach it. But for now, for these last precious minutes, she was safe.

Merk cracked his neck, as he was prone to do when torn by an inner conflict. He stood there, shifting in place, filled with a great sense of unease, unable to go forward. He turned and looked back at the Tower of Ur, the destination of his dreams, and he knew he should forge ahead. He had arrived, and he wanted to relax, to celebrate.

But for the first time in his life, a desire welled up within him. It was a desire to act selflessly, a desire to act purely for justice's sake. For no fee and no reward. Merk hated the feeling.

Merk leaned back and shouted, at war with himself, with the world. Why? Why now, of all times?

And then, despite every ounce of common sense he had, he found himself turning away from the Tower, towards the farm. First it was a walk, then a jog—then a sprint.

As he ran, something deep within him was being set free. The Tower could wait. It was time for Merk to do right in the world. It was time for these murderers to meet their match.

CHAPTER TWENTY-EIGHT

Kyra sat against the cold stone wall, her eyes bloodshot as she watched the first rays of dawn seep through the iron bars, cover the room in a pale light. She had been awake all night, as the Lord Governor had predicted, turning over in her mind the horrific punishment to come. She pondered what they had done to Dierdre, and tried not to think of the ways these cruel men would try to break her.

Kyra turned over in her mind a thousand schemes to resist, to escape. The warrior spirit in her refused to break—she would rather die first. Yet, as she mulled all possible ways of defiance, of escape, she kept returning to a feeling of hopelessness and despair. This place was more well-guarded than any place she had ever been. She was in the midst of the Lord Governor's fort, a Pandesian stronghold, a massive military complex holding thousands of soldiers. She was far from Volis, and even if somehow she managed to escape, she knew she would never make it back before they hunted her down and killed her. Assuming Volis still stood for her to return to. Worse, her father had no idea where she was, and he never would. She was utterly alone in the universe.

"No sleep?" came a soft voice, shattering her reverie.

Kyra looked over to see Dierdre sitting against the far wall, her face illuminated with the first light of dawn, she looking too pale, dark circles under her eyes. She appeared utterly dejected, and she stared back at Kyra with haunted eyes.

"I didn't sleep either," Dierdre continued. "I was thinking all night of what they will do to you—the same they've done to me. But for some reason it hurts me worse to think of them doing it to you than me. I'm already broken; there's nothing left of my life. But you're still perfect."

Kyra felt a deepening sense of dread as she contemplated her words. She could not imagine the horrors her newfound friend had gone through, and seeing her this way just made her more determined to fight back.

"There must be another way," Kyra said.

Dierdre shook her head.

"There is nothing here but a miserable existence of life. And then death."

There came the sudden sound of a door slamming across the dungeon hall, and Kyra stood, prepared to face whatever came at her, prepared to fight to the death if need be. Dierdre suddenly jumped to her feet and ran over to her, grabbing her elbow.

"Promise me one thing," Dierdre insisted.

Kyra saw the desperation in her eyes, and she nodded back.

"Before they take you," she said, "kill me. Strangle me if you have to. Do not let me live like this anymore. Please. I *beg* you."

As Kyra stared back, she felt a sense of resolve bubbling up within her. She shook off her self-pity, all of her doubts. She knew, in that moment, that she had to live. If not for herself, then for Dierdre. No matter how bleak life seemed, she knew she could not give up.

The soldiers approached, their boots echoing, their keys clanging, and Kyra, knowing there remained little time, turned and grabbed Dierdre's shoulders with a firm grip as she looked her in the eye.

"Listen to me," Kyra implored. "You are going to live. Do you understand me? Not only are you going to live, but you are going to escape with me. You are going to start your life over—and it is going to be a beautiful life. We will wreak vengeance on all the scum that did this to you—together. Do you hear me?"

Dierdre stared back, wavering.

"I need you to be strong," Kyra insisted, speaking also to herself, she realized. "Living is not for the weak. Dying, giving up, is for the weak—living is for the strong. Do you want to be weak and die? Or do you wish to be strong and live?"

Kyra kept staring at her intensely as light flooded the cell from the torches and soldiers came marching in—and finally, she thought she could see something shift in Dierdre's eyes. It was like a tiny glimmer of hope, and it was followed by a tiny nod of affirmation.

There came a clanging of keys, the cell door opening and she turned to see the soldiers approach. Rough, callused hands grab her wrists, and Kyra was yanked out of the cell, as the cell door slammed behind her. She let herself go slack. She had to conserve her energy. Now was not the time to fight back. She had to catch them off guard, to find the perfect moment. Even a powerful enemy, she knew, always had one moment of vulnerability.

Two soldiers held her in place, and through the iron door there appeared a man whom Kyra dimly recognized: the governor's son.

Kyra blinked, confused.

"My father sent me to get you," he said as he approached, "but I am going to have you first. He won't be pleased when he finds out, of course—but then again, what's he to do when it is too late?"

The son's face contorted in a cool, evil smile.

Kyra felt a cold dread as she stared back at this sick man, who licked his lips and examined her as if she were an object.

"You see," he said, taking a step forward, beginning to take off his fur coat, his breath visible in the cold cell, "my father need not know all the goings-on of this fort. Sometimes I like to have first dibs on whatever passes through—and you, my dear, are a fine specimen. I'm going to have fun with you. Then I will torture you. I will keep you alive, though, so that I have something left to bring to him."

He grinned, getting so close she could smell his foul breath.

"You and I, my dear, are going to become very familiar."

The son nodded to his two guards, and she was surprised as they released their grip and backed off, each retreating to a side of the room to give him space.

She stood there, hands free, and furtively glanced across the room, summing up her odds. There were the two guards, each armed with a long sword, and the son himself, far taller and broader than she. She would be unable to overpower them all, even if armed, which she was not.

She noticed in the far corner, leaning against the wall, her weapons—her bow and staff, her quiver of arrows—and her heart beat faster. What she wouldn't give to have them now.

"Ahh," the son said, smiling. "You look for your weapons. You still think you can survive this. I see the defiance in you. Don't worry, I will break that soon enough."

Unexpectedly, the son reached back and backhanded her so hard it took her breath away, her entire face stinging with pain. Kyra stumbled back, landing on her knees, blood dripping from her mouth, the pain rudely awaking her, ringing in her ear, her skull. She knelt there, on her hands and knees, trying to catch her breath, realizing this was a preview of what was to come.

"Do you know how we tame our horses, my dear?" asked the son, as he stood over her and smiled down cruelly. A guard threw him Kyra's staff and the son caught it and without missing a beat raised it high and brought it down on Kyra's exposed back.

Kyra shrieked, the pain unbearable, and collapsed face-first on the stone, feeling as if he had broken every bone in her body. She could barely breathe and she knew that if she did not do something soon, she would be crippled for life.

"Don't!" cried Dierdre, pleading from behind the bars. "Don't harm her! Take me instead!"

But the son ignored her.

"It begins with the staff," he said to Kyra. "Wild horses resist, but if you break them, again and again, beat them mercilessly, day after day, one day they will submit. They will be yours. There is nothing better than inflicting pain on another creature, is there?"

Kyra sensed motion, and out of the corner of her eye she watched him raise the staff again with a sadistic look, preparing for an even mightier blow.

Kyra's senses became heightened, and her world slowed. That feeling she'd had back on the bridge came rushing back, a familiar warmth, one that began in her solar plexus and radiated through her body. She felt it filling her with energy, with more strength and speed than she could ever dream.

Images flashed before her eyes. She saw herself training with her father's men, recalled her endless sparring, her learning how to feel pain and not be stunned, how to fight several attackers at once. Anvin had drilled her relentlessly for hours, day after day, until she had perfected her technique, until it had finally became a part of her. She had insisted on the men teaching her everything, however hard the lesson, and now it all came rushing back to her. She had trained for a time exactly like this.

As she lay there, the shock of the pain behind her, the warmth taking over her body, Kyra looked up at the son and felt her instincts taking over. She would die—but not here, not today—and not by this man's hand.

An early lesson came rushing back: *The low ground can give you an advantage. The taller a man is, the more vulnerable he is. The knees are an easy target if you find yourself on the ground. Sweep them. They will fall.*

As the staff came down for her, Kyra suddenly laid her palms flat on the stone, propped herself up enough to gain leverage, and swung her leg around quickly and decisively, aiming for the back of the son's knees. With all of her might, she felt the satisfying feeling of kicking the soft spot behind them.

His knees buckled and he was airborne, landing flat on his back on the stone with a thump, the staff falling from his hands and rolling across the floor. She could hardly believe it had worked. As he fell, he landed on his skull and it was such a loud crack, she was sure she had killed him.

But he must have been invincible, for he immediately began to sit up, glaring at her with the venom of a demon, preparing to pounce.

Kyra did not wait. She gained her feet and lunged for the staff, lying on the floor several feet away, knowing that if she could just grab her weapon, she could have a fair chance against all these men. As she ran for it, though, the son jumped up and reached out to grab her leg, to try to hold her back.

Kyra reacted, her nimbleness taking over, and leapt like a cat over him, missing his grip, and landed on the stone in a roll behind him, grabbing her staff as she did.

She stood there, holding her staff cautiously before her, so grateful to have her weapon back, the staff fitting perfectly in her hands. The two guards approached with swords drawn and, encircled, she looked quickly about in every direction, like a wounded animal backed into a corner. She was lucky, she realized, that it had all happened so quickly, buying her time before the guards could join.

The son stood, wiped blood off his lip with the back of his hand, and scowled back at her.

"That was the biggest mistake of your life," he said. "Now not only will I torture you—"

Kyra had had enough of him, and she was not going to wait for him to strike first. Before he could finish speaking, she lunged forward, raised her staff and jabbed quickly, like a snake striking, right between his eyes. It was a perfect strike, and he cried out as she broke his nose, the crack echoing.

He dropped to his knees, whimpering, cradling his nose.

The two guards came at her, swords swinging for her head. Kyra turned her staff and blocked one blade, sparks flying as it clanged in the room, then immediately spun and blocked the other, right before it hit her. Back and forth she went, blocking one blow after the next, the two coming at her so fast she barely had time to react.

One of the guards swung too hard and Kyra found an opening: she raised her staff and brought it straight down on his exposed wrist, smashing it and loosening his grip on his sword. As it landed on the floor with a clang, Kyra jabbed sideways, into the other guard's throat, stunning him, then she swung around and smashed the first guard in the temple, felling him.

Kyra took no chances: as one guard, on his back, tried to rise, she leapt high into the air and brought her staff down on his solar plexus—then as he sat straight up, she kicked him in the face, knocking him out for good. And as the other guard rolled, clutching his throat, beginning to get up again, Kyra jabbed down and struck him on the back of his head, knocking him out.

Kyra suddenly felt rough arms squeezing her in a hug from behind and realized the son was back; he was trying to squeeze the life out of her, to make her drop her staff.

"Nice try," he whispered in her ear, his mouth so close she could feel his hot breath on her neck.

Kyra, a flash of energy coursing through her, found a new strength within her, just enough to reach forward with her arms, lock her elbows, and burst free from the man's hug. She then grabbed her staff and swung behind her, upwards, with two hands, driving it between the son's legs.

He moaned, releasing his grip as he fell to his knees, and she turned and stood over him, he finally helpless as he looked up at her with shocked eyes filled with pain.

"Say hello to your father for me," she said, raising back her staff and with all her might striking him in the head.

This time, he collapsed, unconscious, on the stone.

Kyra, still breathing hard, still enraged, surveyed her handiwork: three men, formidable men, lay unmoving on the floor. She, a defenseless girl, had done it.

"Kyra!" cried a voice.

She turned and remembered Dierdre, and without wasting another second ran across the room. Grabbing the keys from the guard's waist, she unlocked the cell, and as she did, Dierdre ran into her arms, hugging her.

Kyra pulled her back and looked her in the eyes, wanting to know if she was mentally prepared to escape.

"It's time," Kyra said firmly. "Are you ready?"

Dierdre stood there, shell-shocked, staring at the carnage in the room.

"You beat him," Dierdre said, staring at the bodies in disbelief. "I can't believe it. You beat him."

Kyra watched something shift in Dierdre's eyes. All the fear drifted away, and Kyra saw a strong woman emerging from deep inside, a woman she had not recognized before. Seeing her attackers unconscious did something to her, infused her with a new strength.

Dierdre walked to one of the swords lying on the floor, picked it up, and walked back over to the son, still lying prone, unconscious. She stared down, and her face molded into a sneer.

"This is for everything you did to me," she said.

She raised the sword with trembling hands, and Kyra could see a great battle going on within herself as she hesitated.

"Dierdre," Kyra said softly.

Dierdre looked at her, a wild grief in her stare.

"If you do it," Kyra said softly, "you will be just like him."

Dierdre stood there, arms trembling, going through an emotional storm, and finally, she lowered the sword, dropping it on the stone. It clanged at her feet.

She spit in the son's face, then leaned back and with her boot kicked him a mighty blow across the face. Dierdre, Kyra was beginning to see, was a much stronger person than she'd thought.

She looked back at Kyra with shining eyes, life restored in them, as if her old self were coming back.

"Let's go," Dierdre said, her voice filled with strength.

*

Kyra and Dierdre burst out of the dungeon into the early light of dawn, finding themselves smack in the middle of Argos, the Pandesian stronghold and the Lord Governor's military complex. Kyra blinked in the light, feeling so good to see daylight again, despite its being cold out here, and as she got her bearings she saw they were in the center of a rambling complex of stone keeps, all of it encased by a high stone wall and a massive gate. The Lord's Men were still slowly waking up, beginning to take positions all around the barracks; there must have been thousands of them. It was a professional army, and this place was more a city than a town.

The soldiers took positions along the walls, looking out toward the horizon; none looked inward. Clearly none were expecting two girls to escape from within their midst, and that gave them an advantage. It was still dark enough, too, to help obscure them, and as Kyra looked ahead, to the well-guarded entrance at the far end of the courtyard, she knew that if they had any chance of escape, it was now.

But it was a long courtyard to cross on foot, and she knew they might not make it—and even if they did, once they ran through it, they would be caught.

"There!" Dierdre said, pointing.

Kyra looked and saw, on the other side of the courtyard, a horse, tied up, a soldier standing beside it, holding its reins, his back to them.

Dierdre turned to her.

"We'll need a horse," she said. "It's the only way."

Kyra nodded, surprised they were thinking the same way, and that Dierdre was so perceptive. Dierdre, whom Kyra had at first thought would be a liability, she was coming to see was actually smart, quick, and decisive.

"Can you do it?" Dierdre asked, looking at the soldier.

Kyra tightened her grip on her staff and nodded.

As one, they ran out from the shadows and silently across the courtyard, Kyra's heart slamming in her chest as she focused on the soldier, his back to her, getting closer with each step—and praying they weren't discovered in the meantime.

Kyra ran so fast she could barely breathe, willing herself not to slip in the snow, no longer feeling the cold as adrenaline pumped through her veins.

Finally she reached the soldier, and at the last second, he heard them and spun.

But Kyra was already in motion, raising her staff and jabbing him in the solar plexus. As he grunted and dropped to his knees, she swung it around and brought it down on the back of his head—knocking him face-first into the snow, unconscious.

Kyra mounted the horse while Dierdre untied it and jumped up behind her—and they both kicked and took off.

Kyra felt the cold wind through her hair as the horse charged across the snowy courtyard, heading for the gate at the far end, perhaps a hundred yards away. As they went, sleepy soldiers began to take notice, and to turn their way.

"Come on!" Kyra yelled to the horse, urging it faster, seeing the exit looming closer and closer.

A massive stone arch lay straight ahead, its portcullis raised, leading to a bridge, and beyond that, Kyra's heart quickened to see, open land. Freedom.

She kicked the horse with all her might as she saw the soldiers at the exit taking notice.

"STOP THEM!" yelled a soldier from behind.

Several soldiers scurried to large iron cranks and, to Kyra's dread, began to turn the cranks that lowered the portcullis. Kyra knew that if it closed before they reached it, their lives would be over. They were but twenty yards away and riding faster than she'd ever had—and yet the portcullis, thirty feet high, was lowering slowly, one foot at a time.

"Get as low as you can!" she shrieked to Dierdre, Kyra bending all the way over until her face was on the horse's mane.

Kyra raced, heart pounding in her ears, as they charge through the arch, the portcullis lowering, so low that she had to duck. It was so close, she did not know if they would make it.

Then, just as she was sure they would die, their horse burst through, the portcullis slamming down right behind them with a great boom. A moment later they were across the bridge and, to Kyra's immense relief, out under open sky.

Horns sounded behind them, and a moment later, Kyra flinched as she heard an arrow whiz by her head.

She glanced back and saw the Lord's Men taking positions up and down the ramparts, firing at them. She zigzagged on the horse, realizing they were still within range, urging it faster.

They were making progress, perhaps a fifty yards out, far enough so most arrows fell short—when suddenly, to her horror, she watched an arrow land in their horse's side. It immediately reared—throwing them both off.

Kyra's world turned to chaos. She hit the ground hard, winded, as the horse rolled right next to her, luckily missing them by an inch.

Kyra knelt on her hands and knees, dazed, her head ringing, and looked over and saw Dierdre beside her. She glanced back and saw, in the distance, the portcullis being raised. Hundreds of soldiers were lined up, waiting, and as the portcullis opened, they tore out the gates. It was a full-scale army, on its way to kill them. She was confused as to how they could have assembled so quickly, but then she realized: they were already assembling, at dawn, to attack Volis.

Kyra, on foot, looked over at their dead horse, at the vast open plains before them, and she knew, finally, their time had come.

CHAPTER TWENTY-NINE

Aidan marched for his father's chamber impatiently, Leo at his side, with a deepening premonition that something was wrong. He had been searching for his sister Kyra all over the fort, Leo at his side, checking all her usual haunts—the armory, the blacksmith's, Fighter's Gate—and yet she was nowhere to be found. He and Kyra had always had a close connection, ever since he was born, and he always knew when something was off with her—now, he felt warning signs inside. She had been absent from the feast, and he knew she would have not missed it.

Most concerning of all, Leo was not with her—which never, *ever* happened. Aidan had grilled Leo, but the wolf, clearly trying to tell him something, could not communicate. He only stuck to Aidan's side, and would not leave it.

Aidan had spent the feast with a knot in his stomach, checking the door constantly for any sign of Kyra. He had tried to mention it to his father during the meal, but Duncan had been surrounded by too many men, all of them too focused on discussing the battle to come, and none taking him seriously.

At first light Aidan, awake all night, jumped up and ran to his window, checking the breaking dawn for any sign of her. There was none. He burst out of his chamber, down the corridor, past all his father's men and into Kyra's room and he did not even knock as he put a shoulder to it, running inside, looking for her.

But his heart had fallen to find her bed empty, still made from the day before. He knew then, for certain, something was wrong.

Aidan ran all the way down the corridors to his father's chambers, and now he stood before the giant door and looked back at the two guards before it.

"Open the door!" Aidan ordered urgently.

The guards exchanged an unsure look.

"It was a long night, boy," one guard said. "Your father won't take kindly to being awakened."

"Today could bring battle," said the other. "He needs to be rested."

"I will not say it again," Aidan insisted.

They looked at him, skeptical, and Aidan, unable to wait, rushed forward and slammed the knocker.

"Whoa, boy!" one of them said.

Then realizing his determination, the other guard said, "All right—but it's your head if anything happens. And the wolf stays here."

Leo snarled, but the guard reluctantly pushed open the door just enough for Aidan to step inside, closing it behind him.

Aidan rushed to his father's bed to find him sleeping in his furs, snoring, a half-dressed serving girl lying beside him. He grabbed his father's shoulder and shoved him, again and again.

Finally, his father opened his eyes with a fierce look, staring back as if he were going to whack him. But Aidan would not be deterred.

"Father, you must wake up now!" Aidan urged. "Kyra is missing!"

His father's look morphed into one of confusion, and he stared back, eyes bloodshot, as if in a drunken haze.

"Missing?" he said, his voice deep, gravelly, rumbling in his chest. "What do you mean?"

"She did not return to her chamber last night. Something has happened to her—I'm certain of it. Alert your men at once!"

His father sat up, this time looking more alert, rubbing his face and trying to shake off the sleep.

"I am sure your sister is fine," he said. "She's always fine. She survived an encounter with a dragon—do you think a small snowstorm blew her away? She's just somewhere you cannot find her—she likes to go off by herself. Now go on. Be on your way before you end up with a good spanking."

But Aidan stood there, determined, red-faced.

"If you won't find her, I'll find her myself," he yelled and turned and ran from the chamber, hoping that somehow he had gotten through to him.

*

Aidan stood outside the gates of Volis, Leo beside him, standing proudly on the bridge and watching dawn spread across the countryside. He checked the horizon for any signs of Kyra, hoping perhaps she'd return from firing arrows, but he found none. His foreboding worsened. He had spent the last hour waking everyone from his brothers to the butcher, asking who had seen her last. Finally, one of his father's men had reported that he had seen her riding off toward the Wood of Thorns with Maltren.

Aidan had combed the fort for Maltren and had been told he was out for his morning hunt. And now he stood here, watching for Maltren to return, eager to confront him and find out what happened to his sister.

Aidan stood there, shin deep in snow, shivering but ignoring it, hands on his hips, waiting, watching, until finally, he squinted as he saw a figure appearing on the horizon, charging forward in the snow, galloping, wearing the armor of his father's men, the dragon's crest shining on his breastplate. His heart lifted to see it was Maltren.

Maltren galloped toward the fort, a deer draped over the back of his horse, and as he neared, Aidan saw his disapproval. He looked down at Aidan and came to a reluctant stop before him.

"Out of the way, boy!" Maltren called out. "You're blocking the bridge."

But Aidan stood his ground, confronting him.

"Where is my sister?" Aidan demanded.

Maltren stared back, and Aidan saw a moment of hesitation cross his face.

"How should I know?" he barked back. "I am a warrior—I don't keep track of the frolicking of girls."

But Aidan held his ground.

"I was told she was with you last. Where is she?" he repeated more firmly.

Aidan was impressed by the authority in his own voice, reminding him of his own father, though he was still too young and lacked the deepness of tone he so badly craved.

He must have gotten through to Maltren, because he slowly dismounted, anger and impatience flashing in his eyes, and walked toward Aidan in a threatening matter, armor rattling as he went. As he neared, Leo snarled, so viciously that Maltren stopped, a few feet away, looking from the wolf to Aidan.

He sneered down at Aidan, stinking of sweat, and even though he tried not to show it, Aidan had to admit he was afraid. He thanked God he had Leo at his side.

"Do you know what the punishment is for defying one of your father's men?" Maltren asked, his voice sinister.

"He is *my* father," Aidan insisted. "And Kyra is his daughter, too. Now where is she?"

Inside, Aidan was trembling—but he was not about to back down—not with Kyra in danger.

Maltren looked about, over his shoulder, apparently checking to see if anyone were watching. Satisfied that no one was, he leaned in close, smiled, and said:

"I sold her to the Lord's Men—and for a handsome price. She was a traitor and a troublemaker—just like you."

Aidan's eyes widened in shock, furious at his betrayal.

"As for you," Maltren said, reaching in and grabbing Aidan's shirt, pulling him close. Aidan's heart jumped as he saw him slip his hand on a dagger in his belt. "Do you know how many boys die in this moat each year? It's a very unfortunate thing. This bridge is too slippery, and those banks too steep. No one will ever suspect this was anything but another accident."

Aidan tried to wiggle his way free, but Maltren's grip was too tight. He felt flushed with panic, as he knew he was about to die.

Suddenly, Leo snarled and leapt for Maltren, sinking his fangs into his ankle. Maltren let go of Aidan and raised his dagger to stab the wolf.

"NO!" Aidan shouted.

There came the sound of a horn, followed by horses bursting through the gate, galloping across the bridge, and Maltren stopped, dagger in mid-air. Aidan turned and his heart lifted with relief to see his father and two brothers approaching, joined by a dozen men, their bows already drawn and pointed for Maltren chest.

Aidan broke free and Maltren stood there, looking afraid for the first time, holding his dagger in his hand, caught red-handed. Aidan snapped his fingers, and Leo reluctantly backed off.

Duncan dismounted and stepped forward with his men, and as they did, Aidan turned to them.

"You see, Father! I told you! Kyra is missing. And Maltren has betrayed her—he has sold her to the Lord Governor!"

Duncan stepped forward and a tense silence overcame them as his men surrounded Maltren. He looked nervously over his shoulder to his horse, as if contemplating escape, but the men came forward and grabbed its reins.

Maltren looked back at Duncan, clearly nervous.

"You were going to lay your hands on my boy, were you?" his father asked, looking Maltren in the eye, his tone hard and cold.

Maltren gulped and said nothing.

Duncan slowly raised his sword and held the point to Maltren's throat, death in his eyes.

"You will lead us to my daughter," he said, "and it will be the last thing you do before I kill you."

CHAPTER THIRTY

Kyra and Dierdre ran for their lives across the snowy plains, gasping for breath, as they slipped and slid on the ice. They sprinted through the icy morning, steam rising from their mouths, the cold burning Kyra's lungs, her hands numb as she gripped her staff. The rumble of a thousand horses filled the air, and she looked back and wished she hadn't: on the horizon charged the Lord's Men, thousands of them bearing down. She knew there was no point in running. With no shelter on the horizon, nothing but open plains before them, they were finished.

Yet still they ran, driven on by some instinct to survive.

Kyra slipped, falling face first in the snow, winded, and she immediately felt a hand under her arm, pulling her up; she looked over to see Dierdre yanking her back to her feet.

"You can't stop now!" Dierdre said. "You didn't leave me—and I won't leave you. Let's go!"

Kyra was surprised by the authority and confidence in Dierdre's voice, as if she had been reborn since she had left prison, her voice filled with hope, despite their circumstances.

Kyra broke back into a run, both of them heaving, as they finally began to crest a hill. She tried not to think of what would happen when this army caught up with them, when they reached Volis and slaughtered her people. And yet, Kyra had been trained not to give up—however bleak.

They crested the hill and as they did, Kyra stopped in her tracks, stunned at the sight before her. From up here she had a view of the countryside, a huge plateau stretching before her, and her heart leapt with ecstasy as she saw, riding toward them, her father, leading a hundred men. She could not believe it: he had come for her. All of these men had come all this way, had risked their lives in a suicide mission, just for her.

Kyra burst into tears, overwhelmed with love and gratitude for her people. They had not forgotten her.

Kyra ran for them, and as she neared, she saw Maltren's severed head tied to his horse, and realized at once what had happened: they had discovered his treachery and had come for her. Her father seemed equally surprised to see her, running out here in the open; he had probably expected to free her from the fort, she realized.

They all stopped as they met in the middle, her father dismounting, rushing to her and meeting her in a strong embrace. As she felt his strong arms around her she was overwhelmed with relief, felt that everything would be well in the world, despite their overwhelming odds. She had never felt so proud of her father as she did in that moment.

Her father's expression suddenly changed, his face growing serious as he looked over her shoulder, and she knew he had seen it: the vast army of the Lord's Men, cresting the hill.

He gestured to a waiting horse, and another vacant one for Dierdre.

"Your horse is waiting for you," he said, pointing to a beautiful white stallion. "You will fight with us now."

With no time left for words, Kyra immediately mounted her horse as her father did his, and she fell in line with all his men, all of them facing the horizon. Before her, on the horizon, she saw the Lord's Men, spread out before them, thousands of men against their mere hundred. Yet her father's men sat proudly, and not one backed away.

"MEN!" her father yelled, his voice strong, booming. "WE FIGHT FOR ETERNITY!"

They let out a huge battle cry, sounded their horns, and as one, they all charged forward, rushing to meet the enemy.

Kyra knew this was suicide. Behind the thousand Lord's Men lay another thousand, and another thousand behind them. Her father knew that; all his men knew that. But no one hesitated. For they were not fighting for their land, but for something even more precious: their very existence. Their right to live as free men. Freedom meant more to these men than life, and while they could all be killed, they would all, at least, die by choice, die as free men.

As Kyra rode beside her father, beside Anvin, Vidar and Arthfael, she was exhilarated, overcome with a rush of adrenaline. In her haze, she felt her life pass before her eyes. She saw all the people she had known and loved, the places she had been, the life she had led, knowing it was all about to end. As the two armies neared, she saw the Lord Governor's ugly face, leading the way, and she felt a fresh sense of anger at Pandesia. Her veins burned for vengeance.

Kyra closed her eyes and made one last wish.

If I am truly prophesied to become a great warrior, let the time be now. If I truly have a special power, show me. Let it come out now. Allow me to crush my enemies. Just this one time, on this one day. Allow justice to be done.

Kyra opened her eyes, and she suddenly heard a horrific screech cut through the air. It raised the hair on the back of her neck, and she searched the skies and saw something that took her breath away.

Theos.

The immense dragon flew, swooping down right for her, staring at her with his large, glowing yellow eyes, the eyes she had seen in her dreams, and in her waking moments. They were the eyes she could not shake from her mind, the eyes that she had always known she would one day see again.

His wing healed, Theos lowered his claws and dove down, right for her head, as if to kill her.

Kyra watched as all of her father's men looked up, mouths agape with fear, crouching, preparing to die. But she herself felt unafraid. She felt the strength within the dragon, and she knew this time that she and the dragon were one.

Kyra watched in awe as Theos came right for her, his wings so wide they blocked the sun, and screeched a mighty screech, enough to terrify the men. He came so close, then rose back up at the last second, his claws nearly grazing their heads.

Kyra turned and watched Theos fly straight up, then turn around and circle back. This time he flew behind her men, rushing forward as if to fight with them, right for the Lord's Men.

It opened its great jaws and flew over them until finally it led the way, out in front of her father's men, racing single-handedly to meet the Lord's Men in battle first.

Kyra watched, awestruck, as the dragon approach and the Lord Governor's face morphed from arrogance to fear; indeed, she saw the terror in all their faces, all of them, finally, afraid, all realizing what was to come. Vengeance.

Theos opened its mouth overhead and with a great hissing and crackling noise breathed fire, a stream of flame lighting up the snowy morning. The shrieks of men filled the air, as a great conflagration spread through the army's ranks, killing row after row of men.

The dragon continued, flying again, circling, breathing fire, killing every enemy in sight until finally, there was no one left. Nothing but endless piles of ash where men and horses once stood.

Kyra watched it unfold with a surreal feeling. It was like watching her destiny unfold before her. At that moment she knew that she was different, she was special. The dragon had come just for her.

There was no turning back now: the Lord's Men were dead. Pandesia had been attacked, and Escalon had struck the first blow.

The dragon landed before them, in the fields of ash, as she and all of the men stopped, staring back, in awe. But Theos looked only at Kyra, with his glowing yellow eyes, transfixed on hers. He raised his wings, stretching forever, and shrieked, and awful shriek of rage that seemed to fill the entire universe.

The dragon knew.

It was time for the Great War to begin.

Rise of the Valiant
(Kings and Sorcerers—Book #2)

"An action packed fantasy sure to please fans of Morgan Rice's previous novels, along with fans of works such as *The Inheritance Cycle* by Christopher Paolini…. Fans of Young Adult Fiction will devour this latest work by Rice and beg for more."
--*The Wanderer, A Literary Journal* (regarding *Rise of the Dragons*)

The #1 Bestselling series!

RISE OF THE VALIANT is book #2 in Morgan Rice's bestselling epic fantasy series KINGS AND SORCERERS!

In the wake of the dragon's attack, Kyra is sent on an urgent quest: to cross Escalon and seek out her uncle in the mysterious Tower of Ur. The time has come for her to learn about who she is, who her mother is, and to train and develop her special powers. It will be a quest fraught with peril for a girl alone, Escalon filled with dangers from savage beasts and men alike—one that will require all of her strength to survive.

Her father, Duncan, must lead his men south, to the great water city of Esephus, to attempt to free his fellow countrymen from the iron grip of Pandesia. If he succeeds, he will have to journey to the treacherous Lake of Ire and then onto the icy peaks of Kos, where there live the toughest warriors of Escalon, men he will need to recruit if he has any chance of taking the capital.

Alec escapes with Marco from The Flames to find himself on the run through the Wood of Thorns, chased by exotic beasts. It is a harrowing journey through the night as he quests for his hometown, hoping to be reunited with his family. When he arrives, he is shocked by what he discovers.

Merk, despite his better judgment, turns back to help the girl, and finds himself, for the first time in his life, entangled in a stranger's affairs. He will not forego his pilgrimage to the Tower of Ur, though, and he finds himself anguished as he realizes the tower is not what he expects.

Vesuvius spurs his giant as he leads the Trolls on their mission underground, attempting to bypass The Flames, while the dragon, Theos, has his own special mission on Escalon.

With its strong atmosphere and complex characters, RISE OF THE VALIANT is a sweeping saga of knights and warriors, of kings and lords, of honor and valor, of magic, destiny, monsters and dragons. It is a story of love and broken hearts, of deception, ambition and betrayal. It is fantasy at its finest, inviting us into a world that will live with us forever, one that will appeal to all ages and genders. Book #3 in KINGS AND SORCERERS is also now available!

Books by Morgan Rice

KINGS AND SORCERERS
RISE OF THE DRAGONS

THE SORCERER'S RING
A QUEST OF HEROES
A MARCH OF KINGS
A FATE OF DRAGONS
A CRY OF HONOR
A VOW OF GLORY
A CHARGE OF VALOR
A RITE OF SWORDS
A GRANT OF ARMS
A SKY OF SPELLS
A SEA OF SHIELDS
A REIGN OF STEEL
A LAND OF FIRE
A RULE OF QUEENS
AN OATH OF BROTHERS
A DREAM OF MORTALS

THE SURVIVAL TRILOGY
ARENA ONE (Book #1)
ARENA TWO (Book #2)

the Vampire Journals
turned (book #1)
loved (book #2)
betrayed (book #3)
destined (book #4)
desired (book #5)
betrothed (book #6)
vowed (book #7)
found (book #8)
resurrected (book #9)
craved (book #10)
fated (book #11)

About Morgan Rice

Morgan Rice is the #1 bestselling and USA Today bestselling author of the epic fantasy series THE SORCERER'S RING, comprising seventeen books; of the #1 bestselling series THE VAMPIRE JOURNALS, comprising eleven books (and counting); of the #1 bestselling series THE SURVIVAL TRILOGY, a post-apocalyptic thriller comprising two books (and counting); and of the new epic fantasy series KINGS AND SORCERERS. Morgan's books are available in audio and print editions, and translations are available in over 25 languages.

Morgan loves to hear from you, so please feel free to visit www.morganricebooks.com to join the email list, receive a free book, receive free giveaways, download the free app, get the latest exclusive news, connect on Facebook and Twitter, and stay in touch!

Made in the USA
Monee, IL
07 July 2022

99211763R10125